Escaping Nobility

GG SHALTON

Other Books by GG Shalton

Amelia's Deception
A Previous Time

Chapter 1

Boston, MA
Early 1800's

THE CITY BUSTLED WITH ACTIVITY as people pushed and elbowed their way through the crowds in their rush to get to their destinations. Jasper Townsend kicked his horse into a canter, urging the animal through the traffic. Horses and carriages filled the streets, making the journey even longer. At least this gave him time to practice the words again. He repeated them like a cadence to achieve perfection. Today would be life-changing. Thoughts of Julia raced through Jasper's mind—he had been courting the beautiful Lady Julia Ramsey for weeks and planned to make an offer for her hand. He had never officially met her father, the Seventh Earl of Savory, as he had been traveling abroad on business these last several weeks. Rumor had it that the earl had arrived in Boston a few nights ago, and Jasper intended to have a private audience with him today to let his intentions be known. Julia had many suitors. His careful forethought had dictated the arrangement be secured today.

The familiar turn onto the cobblestone drive appeared

longer than at his prior visits. Jasper hesitated with nervous anticipation before handing his reins to the groom. Straightening his jacket, he pulled his gloves tighter on his hands while thinking about his upcoming conversation with the earl. The Earl of Savory was a prominent businessman known throughout Boston for his stern business practices. Friends had warned Jasper that he was a man not to trifle with. Jasper's family was considered respectable but not rich. English nobility such as the earl could be proud and respected titles, and Jasper would have to convince the earl that he was worthy and could provide a good living for his daughter. Hopefully, the earl would agree to the match, and her dowry could help subsidize their income. Jasper swallowed his nerves and followed the winding staircase up to the front door. He greeted the butler, requesting a private audience with his lordship. After a few moments, the butler escorted him to the earl's study.

The earl's large stature filled the room with his commanding presence, and the stoic look on his face did not welcome company. He ran his fingers through his thinning gray hair and sighed out loud in seemingly irritation.

"What is the nature of your business, Mr. Townsend? I am a busy man. The butler said it has something to do with my daughter?"

Jasper paused for a moment and contemplated turning around and going home. Shaking the thoughts from his head, he took in a deep breath and looked the earl in the eye with all the confidence he could muster.

"I request permission to marry your daughter, my lord."

The earl appeared stunned at Jasper's request as he studied him for a few seconds.

The silence was deafening.

Jasper nervousness betrayed his composure as he wiped his forehead with his handkerchief. Unable to breathe, he reached for his cravat, pulling it down before it choked the life out of him. Beads of sweat trickled down his neck as his heart beat faster. Thoughts of Julia plagued him, after all, he belonged with her, and she *had* to be his wife. They had spent a lot of time together attending various balls and other functions. Despite that she was the most sought-after girl in Boston, she had his heart completely.

"Marriage?" cried the Earl of Savory. "Impossible!" The earl's sharp words were mixed with shock and annoyance at the prospect of such a question. He stood up from his desk, his forehead creased with anger. Smoothing the edge of his jacket, he took in a breath before responding more calmly, "She is already engaged."

Jasper could feel the blood draining slowly from his face as he pondered the thought of Julia with someone other than him. The hope he'd had in his heart slowly vanished, and he sat in the closest chair before his legs buckled.

The earl walked from behind his desk, sitting on the edge of the settee, and in a matter-of-fact tone said, "Her engagement was arranged several years ago with the Duke of Shallot. She is moving to London within a fortnight and will not be returning to America."

Jasper's breathing became labored. Taking quick breaths to soothe himself, he was unsure that he had heard the earl correctly. Somehow, through the shock, he managed to answer, "This can't be. We have spoken about our future together."

Standing up from the settee, the earl walked to the study

door and summoned a footman for assistance. Turning to Jasper, he said sharply, "This conversation is over, and to continue it would be preposterous. My daughter will not be marrying you. I wish you to leave at once. My footman will show you out. Good day, sir."

Jasper stood on shaky legs, taking his leave, carefully avoiding the earl's stern gaze. Before the door closed, he heard the earl say to a maid, "Summon my daughter immediately to my study."

Julia left her room with a knot in her stomach. She knew being summoned to her father's study was never good news. The earl's relationship with his only daughter had been strained most of her life. He had allowed her to live in America for the last ten years at the request of her mother's father, who had needed help running a lucrative tool manufacturing business. Her grandfather had asked the earl to help him look after his business interests in New York and Boston. The earl agreed to help because it added to his vast fortune. Although the earl had traveled back to London on occasion, his family had not accompanied him and had stayed in America.

Julia descended the grand staircase, walking quickly over the marble floors, her footsteps echoing through the foyer. She stopped short of her father's study to gather her thoughts. Making a quick mental list, she could think of no possible reason why her father needed to speak to her. There were no pending offenses or mischiefs that came to her mind. Although, last week she had upset Mrs. Morgan by not attending her musicale and instead went to the park with Mary without telling her mother. Lady Savory had been cross but did not punish her. Surely, her mother would have given her some words of wisdom or warning? Julia straightened her shoulders and tried to reassure herself that it may be a pleasant reason her father needed to speak to her though doubtful.

She forced herself to take a step forward, inhaling the wood odor of the room. The familiar scent brought back memories of her childhood. She inched her way into the doorway, peeking into the classical study. Her father's enormous mahogany desk occupied the corner of the room. Julia remembered hiding under it when she was a child. Her father's study remained off limits to children, but when he traveled, it had made a great hiding spot for her games. She smiled at the memory, wavering before announcing herself.

Her father was sitting behind the desk, looking through some papers. He barely looked up from the desk as Julia entered. Her mother was sitting in a chair in front of her father's desk, and she did not make eye contact with her as she walked farther into the room.

"Please sit down," her father demanded. Her breathing slowed as she approached the empty chair.

The earl's eyes rose from the paperwork with a self-imposed scowl. "Julia, we had a visitor, a suitor named Mr. Townsend who was unaware of your pending engagement—you can imagine my surprise when he made an offer for your hand."

Julia felt her stomach contents coming up in her throat. Catching her breath, she tried to comprehend what her father had just told her. Jasper? He was a dandy in the worst way—fun to dance with but not the marriage type.

Although she knew he'd briefly mentioned a future together, she had been completely unaware he would make an offer. Bewildered about how to feel about his proposal, she knew this was not why her father was angry. The heaviness of his words clung to her chest. She was not ready to marry.

"My engagement?" she questioned clutching her stomach. "You can't be serious, Father." Julia's palms moistened with sweat. She had heard about the arranged marriage but never thought her parents would go through with it. After all, they had left England several years ago and did not go back for visits. How could two people marry that did not know each other and make a relationship work based on a business deal made by their fathers? *How unromantic and positively old-fashioned!* All she knew was that her intended was at least ten years older than her. Stories of dukes in England were dreadful. Julia had heard they married for bloodlines or huge dowries and most of them kept mistresses. They had no interest in their wives' welfares other than making heirs. Dukes were known to be pompous and look down at others even in their peerage. They were the leaders of propriety and probably quite boring. She would have preferred being a spinster than marrying a duke through an arranged marriage.

"Father, I have been in America for over ten years," she cried. The earl was a rough man, but Julia tried to appeal to his fatherly side. "I don't think an arranged marriage is binding due to an agreement made so many years ago."

Julia waited for any kind of acknowledgment from her father, but he only narrowed his eyes at her, his mouth slowly forming a scowl.

Her mother still refused to make eye contact.

Julia panicked. She needed to plead her cause before it was too late. "I don't understand, Father. You are a wealthy man here in America and abroad. Why would you need this business deal?" Julia begged her father, sobbing loudly, "I want to marry for love, and there are many good families here in Boston and even in New York. I don't want to move back to London."

Julia's father held up his hand for her to stop talking. Julia faltered turning to her mother. "Mother! Please help me."

Her mother sighed, turning to her husband. "Charles, please take care of your daughter." The earl stood up and hit his fist on the desk demanding silence. The loud noise vibrated through the room.

"We have coddled and spoiled you too long, Julia. You have an obligation to your family. You will marry the Duke of Shallot sooner rather than later. I will make arrangements to leave in a fortnight."

Julia felt faint—she stayed seated in her chair looking at the floor. Tears pooled in her eyes, falling upon her cheeks. She choked out a whisper, "I will not marry him."

The room was silent. After a few seconds, she composed herself, standing from her chair. She looked at her father. "I would rather live poor without connections or family than agree to an arranged marriage."

Lord Savory turned red with fury. He lifted a clenched fist, causing Julia to step back. Her father had never raised a hand to her before, and she cowered beneath him. Julia's mother stood up, inserting herself between father and daughter. "Julia, go to your room until I find you. I wish to speak to your father alone."

Julia left quickly and ran to her bedroom, choking back tears. Several servants tried to comfort her, but she refused until Mary saw her. Mary was more than a servant—she was Julia's best friend. Propriety would not allow that friendship to remain open, so they hid it from the family. Mary quickly came to Julia's room and held her as she cried.

"Charles." Lady Savory said in an exasperated tone.

The earl lifted his brow, pointing toward the study door. "She will do as I say. That is final."

Lady Savory touched his arm. "She will refuse to marry him if we don't make an agreement with her."

The earl snorted at the suggestion. "I don't make deals with my daughter. She will do what I say because I tell her to."

Lady Savory shook her head. "Charles, she needs to feel she is a part of this decision. Tell her we will not announce the engagement until after the season. She's never experienced a London season before, and we want her to have this time, so she can become more familiar with the workings of the *ton*. She probably doesn't know that the *ton* is considered London's high society."

The earl walked to the table and poured a glass of brandy. He took a drink, enjoying the stinging warmth of the liquid running through him. He poured another glass, turning to sit on the settee.

Lady Savory sat beside him. "Just make her think she has a choice. We can guarantee compliance until she understands the importance of this union. It's not only an obligation, but a privilege to marry a duke. She was not brought up in London and does not understand the significance of such a match."

The earl was quiet. He didn't want to admit his wife made sense. The last thing he needed was an undutiful daughter to manage for the next six months. Reluctantly, he agreed to her proposal. "You are responsible for her actions and must assure she complies with the marriage. She will be ruined if she refuses the arrangement. I will hold you personally responsible."

Lady Savory nodded her head in agreement.

Chapter 2

London, England
Two months later

JULIA KEPT QUIET ON THEIR way to her aunt's town house in Mayfair—a skill she'd mastered when her parents were cross with her. After fits of crying, her mother had assured her that they would let her have a few months to get to know the duke before announcing their engagement. Julia resented the terms of the agreement but knew she had to comply. To refuse would only cause disorder within the family, and she wished to buy some time for a different plan in her life. If she could find a way to support herself, she could marry for love.

As they entered the city, Julia took in her surroundings. Merchants hustled down the sidewalks, selling goods as crowds filled the streets. People walked in droves, entering and exiting shops, smiling and laughing and seeming to enjoy life. She took in a deep breath to capture smells of food cooking while eyeing the smoke filtering through areas of the city. It reminded her of Boston, except the air seemed thicker. London boasted a combination of new buildings and older crumbling structures. The history alone outdated

America by centuries. Looking at the city, she wondered how many of her ancestors had walked along those same sidewalks. All walks of life from servants to gentlemen were going about their daily business.

The buildings went on for blocks with traffic jammed on every corner. The streets were filled with carriages, carts, and animals. Luxury townhomes came into view, and Julia's father said they were getting close. Their carriage slowed its pace as they passed around the corner of the affluent and prestigious Mayfair district. Julia's family had chosen to stay with her mother's sister due to not having a residence in London. Most of the earl's land was in Savory, and across the river was the duke's land in Shallot. The late Duke of Shallot had made a business deal with the earl to combine the lands and river access, and Julia's marriage to the duke would seal the deal.

The entrance to the family's town house was lined with footmen, and Julia nodded a greeting to them as she exited the carriage. The flagstone stairs led up the curved walkway to the wrought iron banisters connected to the arched front doors. The statue near the front entrance displayed a sculpted swan, and Julia admired the beauty of it. The entrance to the foyer was overflowing with marble that partially covered the walls. Julia's uncle was a viscount, and he followed her aunt to greet them. Julia noticed her cousins, Sara and Ryan, behind them.

"Oh, Julia! I have been so excited to finally see you again!" Sara was Julia's age with red curly hair. Her pointed chin and green eyes were an exact image of Julia's grandmother's. The resemblance was astonishing.

"Thank you, Cousin Sara. I have been excited as well."

The footmen saw to their bags and showed them into the drawing room for some tea.

"I would imagine you are exhausted after your journey?" the viscount asked the earl, slapping him on the back. The earl asked for some brandy, and the viscount invited him to his study, so they could speak privately.

The women remained in the drawing room as Julia's cousin Ryan made his exit. The boy was not quite old enough to join the men and chose to take his leave. Julia watched him run through the foyer and back up the stairs, thinking fondly of the carefree days of youth.

Sara interrupted her thoughts. "Julia, I am so excited for you to finally meet your betrothed." She smiled before biting into a tea biscuit. Julia blushed at her statement, taking a sip of tea.

Julia's aunt Vivian replied, "You have grown into an exquisite beauty, Julia. We are eager for your coming out with Sara."

Sara nodded her head in agreement with her mother. "We have dined with the duke on a few occasions—he is quite the catch. You're so lucky! Mother said the engagement was not to be announced yet, so I have not told anyone."

Julia twisted in her chair, looking at her mother for some reference to their agreement. None came.

Her cousin's incessant chatter continued, "We have been looking forward to you making the formal announcement because many debutantes have their claws out for his attention." She snorted. "The mothers of the *ton* will not be happy that the most eligible bachelor in London is off the market."

Julia's good manners could only take so much. *Nothing*

had been decided about her marital status! She kept waiting for her mother to explain the circumstances of her waiting period. After all, Aunt Vivian was family and should not be kept in the dark regarding her intentions. Julia looked back and forth between the two women, waiting for the explanation to come from her mother. A few more agonizing moments crept by as they awkwardly drank their tea. Realizing her mother had no intention of telling them she was not announcing any marital plans, she decided to take matters into her own hands.

Clearing her throat, she looked at her cousin. "Actually, I am not announcing my engagement. I have yet to decide if I will go through with the arranged marriage. My father has agreed that I can wait until after the season to make my decision."

One could have heard a pin drop. Complete silence hung in the room.

"I don't understand," her aunt blurted out. "This sounds a bit unorthodox."

Julia's mother took a sip of tea, raising her eyebrows at her sister. A look of exasperation passed between them.

Julia wrung her hands in her lap. She didn't like having to explain her wishes to put off the engagement. Julia's family had grown up in England—they didn't see anything wrong with business arrangements for a marriage. The "season" in London also made Julia uncomfortable. Her friends from Boston had explained it as a marriage mart where people shopped for mates within London society. Not that it mattered what her wishes were—she knew her family would disapprove of any explanation she would offer.

After more silence hung in the air, she finally answered

her, "I don't remember the duke at all. My hope for marriage is based on mutual affection, even love. I won't marry for titles or land."

Her mother moaned as she took another drink. Sara opened her mouth, but no words came out. Julia's heart beat faster at her aunt's disapproving stare. She didn't want to insult her family's graciousness. But honestly, how could a duke want to marry someone he did not know either? He must have been mad to agree to a marriage of convenience. Was it only for making an heir? She would not allow that to happen to her. Her parents had a marriage of convenience—she refused to live a life without love. She shivered at the thought.

Julia's confession was interrupted by the maid who brought in more refreshments. "Thank you, Teresa." Julia's aunt pointed toward the table dismissing the maid. Turning back to Lady Savory, she whispered. "Does he know?"

Lady Savory peeked at Julia. "Not yet. We have requested a private audience with His Grace this afternoon. It will be only Charles and I attending."

Lord and Lady Savory pulled up in front of a luxurious town house. The iron gates opened to a huge porch with Greek sculptures. "This is impressive," whispered Lady Savory. "I knew their estate in Shallot was grand, but the London town house is extraordinary."

The earl grunted and gave a half smile. "He is a duke, Cheryl. What did you expect?"

A footman greeted them at the door, and the earl gave

him a calling card. "One moment, my lord." The footman left, and a butler appeared.

He motioned with his arm. "Right this way, my lord. His Grace is in his study with his mother."

The study doors opened, and the duke stood up to greet the couple. "So good to see you again, Lord Savory. My father always spoke so highly of you." The duke bowed, offering them a seat. His fashionable clothes were topped off with a dark-blue coat filled out by his broad shoulders. His large stature compared evenly with the earl's frame.

"Thank you, Your Grace. We are happy to see you." The earl pulled the chair out for his wife, taking the seat beside her.

"Lady Savory, I am happy for your safe journey. I have looked forward to your visit all week," said the dowager duchess. Lady Savory curtsied. The dowager duchess had a very regal appearance—her gold gown and diamond necklace reflected her expensive taste. She had been widowed for the last few years yet held up well for her age. Her anticipation of the match was evident.

"I am hoping you received my letter, Your Grace?" The earl shifted uncomfortably in his chair, hoping that the conversation would stay pleasant.

"I did and must admit I was a little surprised by the request. I would agree we should spend some time together to see if we suit, but I had imagined the request to wait to make an announcement would have come from me."

The dowager duchess huffed, raising her brow. "My son is a duke for goodness' sake." She shook her head. "He is highly respected with many admirers. Not exactly wanting for the attention of women." She smiled at her son, then turned toward the couple. "We felt this union would be advantageous and respected by *your* daughter. Does she not realize the opportunity that she has been given? As you know, the marriage contract did have exceptions, and either of them could decline the marriage, voiding the contract."

Lady Savory shifted uncomfortably in her chair. The earl spoke, trying to pacify the duchess, "I understand your concern and assure you that she does respect the arrangement. She is still young and was not brought up in London. She is frightened at the prospect of marrying someone she does not remember."

The duke finally spoke after a long silence. "I will agree to wait until after the season to give you my decision on the marriage contract. But it will be my decision and not Lady Julia's."

The earl remained silent as Lady Savory murmured a reply, "Thank you, Your Grace. I believe you will find our daughter most charming. I look forward to a wedding soon."

The duke grinned. "Very well, then. I will see you at our ball tomorrow night. I look forward to meeting Lady Julia again. The last time I saw her, she was a child."

"Good day, Your Grace." The Earl and Lady Savory took their leave.

Chapter 3

JULIA MANAGED TO GET THROUGH the next day by avoiding her family. All their conversations revolved around the duke. She couldn't imagine liking him, let alone marrying him. There had to be a way to persuade them to cancel the engagement. Or at least allow her to marry someone else of her choosing. Her maid, Mary, was already working on her friendships with the other servants, so Julia would know the inside gossip of the *ton*. Her intended had created quite a name for himself per the papers. He was linked to a few ladies in certain circles, but no one knew of any scandalous behavior.

Julia needed privacy to gather her thoughts. Deciding to spend a few hours in the gardens alone, she left the house without telling anyone. Stepping out onto the terrace, the cool air felt good on her cheeks. The sun's warm rays made the wind more bearable as she ventured deeper into the gardens. Shivering slightly, she squeezed her shawl tighter against her body. She'd enjoyed taking walks when she lived in Boston. Her curious nature found exploring a favorite pastime.

The stone pathways created a welcoming maze—a beloved game she had played as a child—as she took care of which stones to step on. The paths were worn and many stones broken, with chips that produced vivid colors sparkling in the sunlight. Julia's amusement escalated as she chose different trails to take as the maze tempted her through the grounds.

She noticed from afar a small house near the trees. As she approached the structure, streams of sunlight beaconed through the windows, showing overgrown vines spreading over parts of the glass. A smile slid across her mouth after she realized that it must be a greenhouse. Taking off her gloves, she ran her fingers over the vines while glancing through the dirty windows that obstructed her view of the flowers inside. Frustration filled her as she came upon the door and twisted the handle... only to find it locked.

Giving up on the greenhouse, she walked around the corner of the house, noticing a bench a few feet away surrounded by bushes. Feeling tired, she walked to the bench, taking a seat. Resting her eyes and enjoying the wind blowing against her, she felt so relaxed that she could have almost fallen asleep. Her thoughts turned to the prospect of meeting her intended. The faint memories took her back to the day years ago when her mother and father had taken her to a huge estate where children were playing outdoors. There had been small boats that a boy dragged through the water with sticks. Her parents warned her to stay out of the mud if she insisted on watching the boy play. One of the older boys was watching his little brother from the docks before he was called inside by his mother. Julia's parents asked her to accompany him. He was tall with sandy-blond hair, if Julia remembered correctly. They were asked to sit in huge wingback chairs as their parents spoke of a "contract." The older boy stole a few glances at her and then offered her a tart. He told her he was going to Oxford the following year for his studies. Julia smiled to be polite but preferred to be outside playing with the boats. She gave him not another thought, and it wasn't until her parents left the house that her mother mentioned she would marry that young man someday. Julia remembered thinking that was such a long time away and the day may never come.

She heard footsteps behind her and was startled by a voice asking her for assistance. She quickly turned around to see a friendly-looking man with a garden tool. Julia stood up. "Oh, hello. I was admiring the gardens."

He nodded his head. "Me name is Ralph, and it is a pleasure to meet ye."

Julia covered a smile to hide her surprise as he spoke with an Irish accent. His graying hair and round belly reminded Julia of her favorite baker back home. She would have given all her pin money for a taste of the cinnamon buns from Boston—her mouth was watering imagining the taste of the warm, creamy frosting. Realizing he was waiting for her to answer, she made herself stop woolgathering and gave her attention back to Ralph.

"My name is Miss Ramsey or Lady Julia, if you prefer." Julia grinned as he bowed. Thinking about the propriety of speaking to a man she didn't know, she pushed the thoughts aside, assuming he worked for her uncle, probably a servant. She would have to ask her mother later.

"Me lady, would ye like a tour?" He pointed to the greenhouse. Julia looked around the gardens and did not see anyone. No harm in seeing the inside.

She nodded. "Yes, Mr. Ralph. Indeed, I would."

Following him inside, a delectable smell invaded her senses all at once. It was a cross between lavender and rosemary. If only she could bottle it and smell it whenever she wished! Julia was mesmerized by Ralph's knowledge of the plants, finding herself more relaxed as he jested about the rose bushes. He offered her a chance to watch him plant some small bushes he was growing inside. He kept them inside until they bloomed enough to add to the bushes outside. Julia enjoyed her tour but knew the hour was growing later and she needed to get ready for the ball.

"Thank you, Ralph, for a delightful visit. I never met anyone who knows as much as you do about flowers." Julia smiled at him, watching him blush at her compliment.

"Me pleasure, milady." He tipped his hat and gave her a parting gift of a yellow rose. Julia smiled as she skipped up the path to the house.

Looking up from her feet, she stopped dead in her tracks, losing her smile. Her mother was waiting for her with a glare on her face. "Julia! Where is your bonnet? Skipping through the gardens is not ladylike. You are eighteen now and must stop this horseplay!"

Julia rolled her eyes and kissed her mother on the cheek as she ran up the stairs to her room. Her mother called after her, complaining more about her behavior. Ignoring her mother's criticisms, she closed the door to her chamber, blocking out her mother's voice. She collapsed on her bed. Mary entered shortly afterward to join her. Julia told Mary about Ralph, and they giggled over Julia's impersonation of his Irish accent. Mary prepared a bath for her while helping her choose which gown to wear.

"Lady Julia, you will take the London ballroom by

storm!" Mary gave her a huge smile as she finished putting the jewelry on her. She fixed her hair in a beautiful updo with tendrils of curls cascading down to her shoulders.

Pressing her hand against her stomach, she ached to cancel her night out. "Oh, Mary. The thought of a London ballroom makes me uneasy. What if everyone knows that I am supposed to marry the duke and asks me why I have delayed the marriage? Will they think I am daft and laugh at me?"

Mary smiled reassuringly. "Don't fret. I know you will do great! I remember my mother used to say that London ballrooms were the same as any other assembly hall—they just wear fancier dresses."

Julia smiled. "I wish I could have met your mother."

Mary turned away, swishing her hand. "Me too. It seems like yesterday she took me to America to start a new life. My brother stayed with my grandfather after my Papa died, but my mother's sister told her how great America was. I can't believe that I am back in London again."

Julia looked around her room. "Sometimes I think it's all a dream and I will wake up soon."

Mary took her hand. "My lady, you have no idea how special you are. Once people know you, they will love you."

"That's just it, Mary. I must guard my heart—I can't be so trusting of people. The people here are different than in America. Titles and bloodlines are important. They laugh at the idea of love."

"I think you will conquer the *ton*," Mary smirked at her friend.

"I wish you could go with me and see the London ballroom."

Mary hugged Julia and straightened out her dress,

so she could make her appearance below. The viscount had ordered two carriages, so each family could be more comfortable on the way to the ball.

Julia's mouth fell open as they approached the duke's residence. She stared in awe at the size of the home and the many manicured gardens. The grounds exhibited tailored flower beds, sculpted shrubs, and streaming fountains. Julia smiled at the grandeur of the atmosphere. Fancy carriages filled the entrance with beautiful ladies in ball gowns who were being escorted up the steps into a foyer. Julia's unsettled stomach reminded her that she had not eaten all day.

The footman helped her down from the carriage. Her heart beat faster the more steps she took toward the front doors. She could not put off the inevitable any longer. It was time to face him—her future husband, as absurd as that sounded. Practicing on her curtsy and saying, "Your Grace," all afternoon made her exhausted. She hoped to make an elegant introduction, then leave as soon as possible. As much as she had prepared the last few weeks on dancing and the titles of the *ton*, she didn't feel prepared for her first ball in London.

Julia waited in the receiving line after being introduced as part of her family. She was given a dance card and stood beside her father as he was speaking to an acquaintance. They waited for their turn to be received by the duke and his extended family. Julia studied him as he welcomed other guests. He was tall, very mature, and handsome—she had not expected that. Closer observation revealed that he might not be *quite* as old as she had imagined. His well-tailored suit was filled out by his broad shoulders, and he wore a warm smile on his face. Her heart suddenly pounded harder as she approached the family. The dowager duchess offered a guarded smile as her parents approached. The duke briefly met her eyes, furrowing his brow with a mix of surprise and admiration. He quickly recovered his expression and welcomed her father and mother. After exchanging pleasantries, they all looked down at Julia. His brother, Lord Jacob, grinned while lightly poking his brother. The duke did not acknowledge his brother, giving Julia his full attention. Her father introduced her, and she curtsied to the duke.

He smiled at her with his eyes and mouth. "It is pleasure to finally meet you again, Lady Julia." His gaze made her knees weak.

"Thank you, Your Grace." She curtsied again, taking a step back, but felt her hand touched. She looked behind her. The duke smiled as he held it.

"Would you do me the honor of a dance later?"

Julia tensed at the touch of his hand. She took a sharp breath, recovering from her shock. It was a familiarity that was not recognized as proper in some circles. However, no one made mention of it.

"Of course, Your Grace." Julia blushed because the family stared at them. The duke clutched her dance card, signing his name to the waltz and the supper dance. He smiled at Julia as her family escorted her into the ballroom.

Watching Julia walk away, Lord Jacob grinned. "Indeed, my brother. You didn't even have to gamble to hit the jackpot."

The duke laughed at his little brother. "I had no idea how beautiful she was."

"She is, my brother, and the *ton* is not going to know what hit them." They stared after her until the next guest drew their attention away.

Julia made her way through the crowds with her parents. They had separated from her cousin and were headed toward the refreshment table for a cold drink. The ballroom temperature was soaring due to the number of people in attendance. She heard whispers of how everyone wanted to attend the duke's balls as the most influential people were in attendance.

Julia's eyes tried to take in the festivities—she twisted around to admire the many decorations. She eyed young debutantes with their fans spread out, fanning themselves as they flirted with young lords. Julia giggled, remembering her first ball in Boston. She did not think of herself as a flirt, although some accused her of such affections. She thought it was difficult to be witty with the older men of the Boston society. She preferred the boys her age—their honesty was refreshing. Her first ballroom dance had been at her neighbor's coming-out party—it was a country dance with Eli Baird. He was a childhood friend, an Irish boy whose father had made a fortune in Boston. His request saved her from the dreadful wallflower label. They became the best of friends, and he ended up married to her next-door neighbor.

Those balls had been nothing compared to London's. She strained to watch the dancing through a break in the crowds. She wanted to dance. Her mother had hired the best dance instructor in Boston for Julia's first ball. Even with all the lessons, she had tripped through her first waltz. Her mother thought that dance was scandalous but agreed Julia could participate since other ladies were permitted too. She grinned to herself as she remembered how much her mother had fretted over Julia's ball gowns and making sure she looked perfect.

Her thoughts were interrupted by her cousin, who reappeared at her side. "Julia, there you are! Is this not wonderful? Look at all the people and the decorations. I heard there is even a royal guest here tonight. Royalty! Can you believe it?"

Julia smiled at her cousin's excitement. She looked around at the crowd and saw her father motioning for her. She held on to her cousin's arm, walking toward him. He was standing with some associates who were waiting for an introduction. "This is my daughter, Lady Julia, and my niece, Miss Reynolds."

The men smiled. "Nice to meet you both. I am Lord Martin, and this is my son, Lord Jason."

"Lady Julia, is your dance card full?"

"It is not, my lord." Julia smiled at Lord Jason and held out her card. He quickly signed it, then turned to Sara and signed hers. He exchanged pleasantries and made his exit. Julia looked up to see her aunt and uncle approaching. Her uncle looked at her father.

"Charles, my associate asked if you could introduce Julia to Prince Randolph? It seems he has noticed her and asked for an introduction. Apparently, he is visiting his cousin the Prince Regent. His entourage is in the corner."

The request astounded Julia, and her nerves would not settle. She had never met royalty before. Her stomach leaped into her throat at the thought of an introduction. What would she call him? Your Highness? That sounded like a fairy-tale novel. But she didn't have a lot of time to think about it because her father took her hand, escorting her toward the corner of the ballroom. Her mother followed close behind along with her cousin and uncle.

Julia noticed a tall man with well-tailored clothes approach her uncle. "Thank you, John. The prince will be most pleased." He motioned toward a man who was tall and dark. He wore his long hair pulled back in a band. With his hair pulled back away from his face, she could see his chiseled jawline. He smiled as Julia approached, passing the military guards to reach him. The tall man introduced her father and uncle first, and the prince tore his gaze from her to briefly make the introduction, then he turned his attention back to her.

"It's a pleasure to meet you, my lady." His husky voice gave Julia goose bumps. "May I have a dance this evening?"

Julia could not find her voice and caught herself leaning toward her father. She was nervous to dance with him. Her father glanced down at her with a look in his eye urging her to respond to the prince. "Of course, Your Highness." She did her best curtsy while handing him her dance card. He signed it, smiling as he handed it back to her. He bent down and asked with a raspy voice close to her ear, "Are you thirsty?"

She did not want any lemonade but agreed to accompany him to the table. He leaned toward the earl and whispered in his ear before offering Julia his arm, waving off his guards.

Julia observed many people staring at them as they passed. Prince Randolph looked oblivious to the attention. "Lady Julia, may I compliment you on your beauty?" His throaty compliment may have been lost in translation. She gathered he liked the way she looked.

She blushed avoiding eye contact. "Thank you, Your Highness." He grinned down at her, causing her heart flutter, and guided her to the table of refreshments, picking up two glasses of champagne.

He put his free hand on the small of her back—a possessive gesture that gave her chills. She attempted to steady her breathing. He escorted her to a magnificent terrace that overlooked the gardens. "I hope you don't mind stepping outside? The ballroom is very hot."

He had an accent, but she couldn't quite put her finger on it. She knew he was a cousin to the Prince Regent and was visiting from out of the country.

"Not at all," she smiled shyly.

The prince stopped at the end of the terrace, and they stood together looking out over the darkening sky. "I heard you came from America. How do you find London?"

Julia found it hard to look straight at him. His features were so handsome, and that grin could have made her lose herself. "Yes, Your Highness. Perhaps my accent gives me away?" Julia looked away, unable to meet his stare. "We came from Boston, and I must confess that I have not seen much of London yet. This is my first ball, and I am trying to remember all the rules and titles."

"Rules?" he questioned, letting out a laugh.

Julia's face felt warm because she was not sure how to answer him. "I know that must make me sound like a ninny. The rules of society are different in London. We are more relaxed in America, and I am trying not to "ruin" myself, as my mother would say." She said it with a serious face before bursting out in laughter—quickly putting her hand over her mouth. "Forgive me. I wasn't supposed to laugh out loud like that—it sounds so improper."

"I understand." The prince continued smiling down at her. "I am finding myself in the same predicament as I am not from London and have to remember the rules as well." He nodded at her, moving a step closer. "Perhaps we can work together so we are improper."

Julia gasped at his remark.

The prince's eyes widened. "I mean proper. Please forgive me—my English was backward." His face turned bright red, and Julia could not help but laugh. She covered her mouth as they both started laughing together.

"Julia?" her cousin interrupted them as she came closer. "Forgive me, but your parents are asking for you. It's almost time for the waltz."

Julia smiled at the prince and gave a curtsy. "I must go. Thank you for the drink."

"I will find you later for our dance."

Julia nodded, putting her arm through her cousin's as they walked back inside. Neither of them spoke because it was hard to hear over all the people talking, dancing, and drinking.

"Lady Julia, I have been looking for you. The dance should have begun a while ago." Julia looked up to see the duke offering her his arm. "I will tell them to begin the music now that I have found you." His tone was sharp as he motioned to a footman, who nodded for the music to start.

He slid his arms around her waist. "We're lucky the orchestra waited to begin. We will need to work on your promptness." Looking away from her, he lifted her hand and stepped to the music.

Julia bit back a retort and tried to change the subject. "I have met the most interesting people, Your Grace." She smiled up at him as he moved her across the dance floor.

"One must be careful whom one associates with." He lifted the corner of his mouth.

Ignoring his comment, she allowed him to guide her as they danced. Relaxing a little more, she was curious to know more about him. "Have you been dancing, Your Grace?" Julia waited for an answer, but he seemed preoccupied with the musicians. "Your Grace?"

"Indeed." He looked down at her, seemingly bothered by her questions. *How proud he was acting!* Julia took a minute to analyze him, making a mental list of his attributes or lack thereof. He was very proper and could even have been described as stuffy. His lack of eye contact with her while they were dancing was rude. He seemed preoccupied with spectators instead of her. She didn't like his behavior and decided to finish the dance without further conversation. Purposely avoiding eye contact.

After a few more turns, the duke looked down at her as he readjusted his hands on her waist. He was still a little annoyed at her tardiness for the dance but chose to forget it. Instead, he decided to change the subject. "I believe you have missed a few steps, my lady. We could arrange dance lessons, if you would like?" He meant it as a jest, but it came out awkwardly.

Julia snorted and mumbled loud enough for him to hear, "Perhaps if I had a better partner, then I would dance better."

He creased his brow at her offensive comment. Jest or not, that was rude. Choosing not to engage in her childish remarks, he had to remember her age and lack of manners could be a result of her time in America. He would have to keep a close eye on her to make sure that she could fill the role of his duchess.

After swinging around the dance floor a few more turns, the music came to an end. The duke bowed and held out his arm to escort her back to her parents.

Julia looked at his arm and purposefully did not take it. Firmly holding her hands to her sides, she curtsied, "Thank you for the dance, Your Grace." She turned away and walked off the floor, leaving him alone looking after her. Manners dictated that she be escorted back to her parents by him. Her rude gesture would be noted by society.

The duke's jaw flexed as he tried to rein in his anger. He smoothed the edges of his new jacket and left the dance floor alone. He made his way through the crowd toward the refreshment table. His brother approached him, laughing at the anger on his face. "Nice dance, Your Grace," he said in a sarcastic jest. "She gave you the cut!"

The duke was frustrated at the lack of engagement with his future bride and her indifference toward him. He'd never had to work hard to court any girl in his life. They fell over him on most occasions—he could have had his choice of women of the *ton*. After all, he was a duke, and the rumors in London had him as quite the catch.

The prince spotted Julia immediately, and he could not take his eyes off her while she danced with the duke. He quickly approached her for their dance. "My lady, I believe this dance is mine."

Julia gave him her arm, smiling as they reached the dance floor. The music began, and they were dancing a popular country dance. Their hands would meet on occasion, but the constant movement made it hard to carry on a deeper conversation. Although they switched partners a few times, he kept his gaze on her. When the dance was finally over, Julia's parents were there to meet with her, and she curtsied to the prince, thanking him for the dance.

Her parents looked concerned, and he overheard them speaking to her in hushed tones. "Julia, the duke was supposed to escort you off the dance floor. You are acting inappropriately! Now, come to the ladies drawing room to freshen up before the supper dance."

The prince watched her leave, trying to think of a way to see her again without all the crowds.

"How was your first London ball?" her mother asked while she was yawning. The carriage ride back to her family's home was taking too long. Julia just wanted to get out of the binding clothes and take her shoes off. Her mother smiled. "I saw you sit by the duke at supper, and I thought you might be enjoying yourself."

Julia thought back to the supper with the duke. He had sat by her at the table, and they'd engaged in polite conversation. Almost too polite. Their conversation had been brief but consisted of the weather, music preference, and the opera. Julia found him boring! She couldn't understand him at all. His vocabulary was so proper, and he'd looked uninterested in anything *she* had to say. She'd quickly agreed with whatever he was saying so she wouldn't have to speak. Her parents had no idea the pressure they were putting on her.

Her mother's voice interrupted her thoughts. "Julia, the duke and dowager duchess have invited us to their estate in a few weeks for a house party. It's a little unusual to have one in the middle of the season, but she said it was only for a week. She thought it would be good for our families to spend some time together. They will, of course, include some other select families but not too big she assured me."

"Sounds wonderful, Mother." Julia gave her the best smile she could stomach. She was getting good at telling people what they wanted to hear. It saved a lot of headaches as she came up with her plan to leave London. In truth, she would have preferred cleaning the stables every day to spending a week with the duke.

The carriage finally stopped, and she jumped out, running up the stairs. "Julia, slow down. It's not ladylike to run up the stairs!" Her mother bellowed after her, but Julia did not stop. She nearly ran into the butler at the door. "Forgive me." She plowed past him, taking the stairs two at a time.

Mary was waiting for her on her bed. She sat up as

soon as she saw Julia. "Don't keep me waiting—tell me everything!"

Julia tried to catch her breath. "Oh, Mary! I met the most wonderful man at the ball tonight. He is foreign and related to the Prince Regent. He asked me to dance, and he had such an adorable accent."

"Who is he, my lady? And where was the duke?" Mary looked at her friend with a confused expression.

Julia danced around her room. "I was told he is a prince as well, and his name is Randolph. He is very handsome! Those eyes would melt you into a puddle." Julia lay on her bed after Mary untied her dress.

She rolled her eyes. "The duke is just like we imagined him to be. He is boring, very proper, and arrogant."

Mary sat beside her on the bed. "Can you imagine becoming a princess? I thought the duchess was high class, but a princess? Your parents surely would consent to that!"

"Oh Mary, let's not get ahead of ourselves. I don't know when I will see him again." Julia couldn't help but smile. She would have to find him.

"London is not that big, my lady. I will see what I can find out about him from the other servants. I met a very handsome footman named Kashan who has a cousin that works at the palace."

"Thank you, Mary. I knew I could count on you." Mary smiled at Julia as they giggled for the next hour.

Chapter 4

THE NEXT DAY, IT WAS raining in London, causing the roads to be messy. The duke noticed the gray clouds forming above the city and a mist in the air causing a chill. He decided to pay a call to Lady Julia. A nice ride through the park when the rain stopped would no doubt impress her. If the rain continued, he could probably take her to the museum or a bookstore. As his future intended, it was important for them to be seen together.

He properly waited for calling hours before pulling up to her family's town house. Giving his calling card to the butler, he waited to be escorted to the drawing room. A few moments later, Julia's mother appeared to greet the duke. "Your Grace, how wonderful for you to call upon us. Can I offer you some tea?"

He followed her into the drawing room, refusing the refreshments. "Good afternoon, Lady Savory. I actually came to call upon Lady Julia, if she is in residence?"

"I am sorry, Your Grace. She is out shopping with her cousin. She should be home within the hour, if you would like to wait?"

The duke slowly looked around the room, frowning upon the many flower arrangements adorning the room.

He hesitated for a brief second as he came up with a lie in response. "I apologize, but I have other appointments today. I will call upon her another day."

The duke bowed, bidding her a good day as he took his leave. He approached his carriage outside, feeling quite foolish. He did not wish to wait upon the minx. The cards he'd spied on the receiving table showed the names of many lords who were no doubt showering her with flowers.

He thought back to the conversation with her father. To think that he had the same reservations that she had when his mother told him she was coming from America. The hold on the engagement had originally been his idea before he'd received the letter from the earl. The correspondence had surprised him as most women would have been drooling at such a marriage contract. Why did she not see that?

He took the reins and rode down the road. Thinking about her again, he realized she was consuming his thoughts and he had only just met her. He realized that he was attracted to her. She was beautiful, but it was more than just her beauty. It was true that she did not have the same grace as some of the other ladies in society, but she was enchanting. Her smile lit up her whole face, and she was not afraid to laugh out loud—a trait most debutantes refused to display. He had heard her infectious laugh on a few occasions last night. She was the talk of the ball but seemed oblivious to the attention. He relinquished his hesitation and admitted that she had captured his attention last night and he needed to get a hold of himself.

"Julia, wait for me!" her cousin yelled after her. Julia pretended not to hear Sara, annoyed that she walked too slowly, stopping to look at everything. Her growling stomach reminded her that she had missed breakfast and seeing the bakery a block over had sent her on an urgent quest. The smells of sweetness were making her mouth water. She wanted to see if they had some cinnamon bread and couldn't get to the shop fast enough. Suppressing a smile, she thought of the look on her mother's face if she had known that she had practically run down the sidewalk without an escort.

Just as Julia was about to pull open the door, a strange hand gripped the door handle first. Startled, she looked up, almost losing her balance.

"Your Highness?" Julia smiled timidly. "How nice to see you again."

Prince Randolph held the door for her, offering his arm. "The pleasure is all mine, my lady." He winked at her. "I thought I saw you running and tried to catch up with you."

Julia laid her gloved hand across his arm. "I am sure you are mistaken. I never run in public down sidewalks. It would not be proper." She laughed sarcastically as he smiled down at her.

"Can I join you for a bite to eat?" The prince questioned as his eyes roamed over her.

Feeling a little exposed, she tried steadying her breathing. "I would enjoy that, Your Majesty. I was craving cinnamon bread and hoped they had some in London."

Julia couldn't help but savor the smells in the bakery. Her cousin and their maids finally caught up with her and joined them in the store. Mary looked up at the prince, peeking between Julia and Randolph. "You remember my cousin Miss Reynolds, and these are our chaperones. Our footmen are waiting for us at the carriage."

The prince bowed and introduced his companion, but Julia barely paid attention to the introduction. She was concentrating on what she would say next. Feeling nervous and awkward around him, she tried hard to appear nonchalant. Prince Randolph ordered cinnamon bread with tea for all of them, and they took some seats in the corner. She could see his military guards outside the shop and wondered if they were always with him. Thanking him for the bread, she took a bite, savoring the creamy sweet glaze on the tip of her tongue.

"Did you ladies have a good day of shopping?" The prince grinned at them.

Julia took an exaggerated sigh. "It was exhausting, and I am quite ready to retire from it. I know most women like to shop, but there have to be limits." Oh, no! She was babbling again, unsure of what to say.

"Yes, I agree, Julia," Sara injected. Julia was relieved that Sara had rescued her.

"I think you may need some amusement." Prince Randolph touched his chin, tapping his finger on his jaw. His chiseled jaw that Julia could not stop staring at. She forced her eyes to look at Sara instead.

"What kind of amusement?" Sara questioned as she took a bite of her bread.

The prince lifted the corner of his mouth in a smile. "I want to invite you both to the house that I am staying at near the palace grounds for a picnic tomorrow. It's used for guests of the king. You can bring your chaperones, and we have an extensive garden that includes room to fly a kite and perhaps do some fishing in the pond. My sister will be in attendance as well."

"We must ask our fathers. We can send a messenger when they answer." Sara explained, looking at Julia. "Perhaps if we tell him we are having tea with your sister, they will be more obliging."

"Oh, the rules of society?" The prince questioned, sounding amused. "It seems Lady Julia loves learning about those."

Julia smiled at him, realizing he was teasing her. She reminded her cousin that she was not from London but was still navigating the waters.

Chapter 5

"HOW DID YOU GET THEIR permission so fast with so little questions?" Sara quizzed Julia, questioning her honesty. The ladies rode in the viscount's carriage to Prince Randolph's residence. Mary was riding with the new footman, Kashan, outside of the carriage.

"I just told them the truth and had to talk fast," Julia smirked triumphally. "The truth is that we are having tea with Princess Mallory as she was introduced to us at the ball."

"You didn't mention the prince?" Sara frowned with concern.

"Not exactly," Julia sighed. "If they ask us about it, then we will tell them that we had some casual words with him at tea."

Sara appeared wary of Julia but did not voice her opinions. She did not like to tell her parents falsehoods. After all, society could question Julia's behavior if she was to be engaged to the duke in a few short months. Her infatuation with the prince was fun but could be dangerous to her reputation, not to mention Sara's if society blamed her for any scandalous behavior. Julia didn't even seem to care that the duke had come by for a visit and she hadn't been there to receive him. She was even oblivious to the upcoming house party at the duke's estate. Only a selected few were invited while many craved for his attention. Sara realized that her cousin didn't understand how lucky she was to have the duke's attention.

Julia giggled. "I am just so excited. I can hardly keep still."

Sara gave a guarded smile, watching Julia pinching her cheeks to bring color to her face while smoothing her dress trying to look perfect. Her gloves were sticking to her hands from the excessive sweat from her nerves.

Looking out the carriage window, she thought about Julia. They had grown up on different sides of the world, and she had only just begun to get to know her cousin. There was a lot about her that she did not understand. Julia had the makings of a duchess, but she seemed to resent London society. She only wanted to comply to her own rules, looking down upon those who did abide by society's expectations. Sara wanted a friendship with Julia but needed to guard her own reputation as well.

"We are here!" Julia cried letting out a squeal.

Sara was so deep in her musings that she had not noticed their approach to the house. Although it was officially a guesthouse of the king, it was more of a mansion. The wrought iron gates opened, and two footmen opened the carriage door. A pretty girl in a silk gown the color of roses approached them. She had long, black curls framing unique green eyes. She was tall and slender with a birthmark on her right cheek. Sara found her most intriguing as she approached them.

She smiled at the girls as they stepped toward her. "So nice to meet you. I am Princess Mallory."

"Of course, Princess." Julia replied. "We thank you for having us for tea today."

"Please, girls, call me Mallory."

"Please call me Julia and this is my cousin, Sara." The girls smiled, watching Mary appear with the footmen.

"My brother is waiting for us in the garden. Let me show you the way." Mallory led the girls down a stone path behind the residence. Along the way were many old statues and a beautiful fountain. Julia noticed the prince coming toward them when they rounded the corner.

"Ladies, so good to see you. You look lovely today." Prince Randolph greeted them with a bow. "I have kites set up on the lawn, and there are fishing poles by the pond. Tea will be served in about an hour."

Julia curtsied. "Thank you, Your Highness. We are most happy to be here."

The group walked over the manicured lawn and chose kites. The prince offered to share one with Julia, so he could teach her how to fly it. Sara chose a purple one, and one of the prince's friends offered to show her how to glide it. The prince stood behind Julia and wrapped his hands around her shoulders as they tried to hold on to the kite together.

They finally got it up in the air and ran across the lawn with the string. Julia and Randolph were laughing as they watched a bird fly by, afraid of the kite. The kite finally collapsed as it lost wind and scraped across the ground again. "Oh, that was fun," Julia said, out of breath. She walked to some blankets that were set up for them under a tree and sat down.

Prince Randolph put out his hand. "Not so fast, Lady Julia. I want to show you something in the west garden. Will you accompany me on a walk? Your chaperone can follow behind us."

Julia took his hand, and he placed it in the crook of his arm. Staring at his eyes for a moment, he held her hand a little longer than was proper—but she enjoyed the close contact. After a pause, he led her toward the gardens. She could smell his cologne as she tried to listen to him speak about some of the history of the home. They soon approached a maze leading to the west garden, and the prince asked Mary to wait outside on a bench as they would be back in a few minutes. Julia's heart was beating fast. Mary agreed and gave her a nod.

The prince escorted her through the lush foliage-covered grounds, passing flowers that she had never seen before. Taking in all the colors, she smiled as he pointed out a statue near the fountains. It was beautiful—Julia studied the woman sitting on a pool of water. Her long hair wrapped around her, displaying her beautiful features. The artist had captured her looking down with long eyelashes carved into the stone. Julia ran her hand down the statue's arm. "It's beautiful."

He gazed at her, seemingly trying to read her thoughts. "I wanted to show you because she reminded me of you."

Julia blushed, feeling her whole face burning hot. "I think you are most kind and a bad liar." She chuckled, embarrassed by his flattery and quickly looking away to hide her discomfort.

He touched her chin, turning her face to look at him. "It's true, Lady Julia. Only I don't think it can do you justice." Feeling his fingers caress her lips made her tremble slightly. Almost seeing the desire in his face, she closed her eyes as he gently brushed his lips against hers. Letting out her breath, she relished her first real kiss. He held her tighter in his arms, pulling her closer. If he hadn't been holding her waist so tight, she would have swooned.

He gently backed away. "I hope you don't mind that I kissed you. I am finding you most irresistible."

Julia bit her bottom lip. "I enjoyed it, Your Highness."

"That is another thing—can you call me Randolph when we are alone?"

The thought of using first names excited her. "If you will call me Julia."

"Very well, Julia." He motioned for her to sit down, taking her hand into his, and gave her a questioning look. "What I am trying hard to figure out about you is your lack of an attachment. I would have thought you would have already been spoken for the minute you turned a marriageable age."

Julia looked down. She didn't know if she should tell Randolph the truth or not. But deciding it was better coming from her instead of London gossip, she answered, "Actually, my parents have arranged a marriage for me here in London." Feeling sick, she did not want to look at him. "But I have not agreed to their arrangement, and they have given me the season to decide."

Julia concentrated on the fountains—there was a long

pause before she spoke again. "I don't wish to marry for business or obligations. I want a love match." She finally looked up at him.

The prince looked down at her, staring at her hair and moving a runaway tendril behind her ear. "I understand, Julia." He looked away from her. "I have an arrangement as well."

Julia had not expected his response though it was normal within royal families. Randolph continued, "My marriage was arranged when I was five summers to align my country with another. I have no choice in marriage where I come from. The marriage contract is an obligation and privilege to support my country." Randolph looked at the gardens as he spoke.

Julia sighed, looking down at her hands. "I understand obligations, but marriage means more to me than that." She did not understand how something so intimate could involve so many other people.

Randolph turned to her, "Come, Julia. Let's not put a damper on our fun today. Let's not talk about obligations or our uncertain futures. I have a rowboat near the pond, and I would like to take you on a boat ride."

Julia laughed. "I agree. Let's have fun." She walked with the prince out of the maze, and they found Mary waiting for them on the bench. Mary glanced at Julia quickly, hiding a smirk on her face as she walked behind the couple.

The prince escorted her to the edge of the lake and helped her into the boat. He teased her by rocking the boat until she giggled. He rowed her slowly across the lake, telling her about the history of the house he was residing in. She loved the sound of his voice, mesmerized by his accent. His English was good, but his pronunciation was strained. Julia closed her eyes to enjoy the breeze coming off the lake.

"Have I put you to sleep?" She heard his deep voice with a bit of amusement in it.

Julia opened her eyes. "I apologize, Your Highness."

He laughed and rowed them to the shore, then helped Julia out of the boat. He suggested they sit under a tree and eat some food. Julia noticed Sara when they walked back up the hill. She had a look of concern but did not say anything to Julia. Julia sat by her on the blanket, and Sara handed her a tea biscuit. Julia was a little afraid to accept the treat given Sara's stern gaze. But she took it and hoped Sara would keep quiet.

Randolph approached them with his friend, and they all spoke of the lovely day. Sara kept mostly quiet, and Julia was nervous about her cousin's demeanor. She knew her parents would not approve of her closeness with the prince, and she hoped that Sara would not voice any concerns to her parents.

The prince kept close to Julia for the rest of the day, and she was sad when it ended. As she went to say goodbye to Mallory, the prince came up behind her to give her a single rose. It was beautiful. "You are most kind, Your Highness. Thank you." He smiled as he helped her into the carriage and watched their carriage pull away as she left the estate.

Chapter 6

JULIA'S MOTHER WAS WAITING FOR her when they arrived back at the town house. Tapping her foot, she huffed. "You're late." Julia hid the rose that Randolph had given her, following her mother into the drawing room.

Her mother faced her with her hands on her hips. "Julia, I had to give the duke your regrets again and assurances you would be here tomorrow. He wishes to take you on a carriage ride through Hyde Park."

"Mother, tomorrow is the Williams Ball—I don't want to look tired. I should decline the offer, so I can be well rested." She removed her cloak, handing it to Mary.

Lady Savory shook her head, on the verge of an outburst. "I won't hear of that, Julia. I already accepted his offer. It will be the third day that he has tried to see you. You promised me that you would be fair about your courtship."

Julia snorted. "Courtship? I hardly believe that I would call our brief acquaintance and two dances at a ball a courtship."

Lady Savory tightened her lips. "Enough, Julia. You will go on the ride tomorrow, and that is final." Julia's mother turned on her heel and left the drawing room.

Julia watched her leave. Exhausted, she ran up the stairs

a few minutes later, stomping to her room. How could her mother ruin such a perfect day? Julia thought about the duke and how he had suggested dance lessons. Would he try to be another father to her?

She didn't want to think about the duke, instead focusing her attention on the foreign prince. A smile crept upon her mouth, and unable to stop it, she spun around her room touching her lips. It was her first real kiss. So soft—she wanted to remember it forever. The prince was a gentleman, but what she liked most was that he knew how to laugh. He teased her yet was comforting. She thought about what it would be like to be his wife. Could they both ignore society's rules together? If they were together, it would not matter how they lived. Her stomach fluttered as she thought about seeing him at the ball again.

The family dinner was less formal than usual as the men had business in town. Julia and Lady Savory dined with Sara and her mother. The cook made roasted lamb with baby potatoes and minted peas. Their dinner conversation included talk of the *ton* and the new French dressmaker that was highly sought after in town. Apparently, she created the latest fashions that had the aristocrats monopolizing her time. Julia noticed that Sara hardly spoke a word to her. She wondered if she was upset about her interest in Prince Randolph.

The mothers must have noticed the lack of engagement, and they tried to get the girls to talk about their day. Julia's aunt inquired, "Did you enjoy your tea with Princess Mallory?"

Julia took a sip of water, being careful not to sound too enthusiastic about their outing. Sara glanced at Julia, then back to her mother. "It was pleasant. We enjoyed making a new friend." Julia let out a breath as Sara did not mention the prince.

Lady Savory smiled. "Yes, new royal friends are certainly good to have."

Julia looked up from her food, "Yes, royal friends have proven most interesting."

Sara choked, coughing into her napkin. Julia glanced at her, tilting her head in question. Sara's mother asked her if she was all right, and she simply nodded her head. Julia wondered if they suspected anything amiss about their visit.

The following evening, Julia reluctantly went downstairs after being informed the duke was waiting for her in the drawing room. She'd tried to feign a sickness that morning, but her mother would not hear of it. If she did not go on the carriage ride, then she would not go to the ball.

The duke stood as Julia entered the room. "Lady Julia, it is wonderful to see you again."

Julia smiled at him and curtsied. "Thank you, Your Grace. I am happy to accompany you on the ride today." Julia's mother smiled but gave her a warning look with her eyes.

The duke walked over to her, holding out his arm. "Your chariot awaits, my lady." Julia took his arm as they walked to the carriage. He assisted her onto a cushioned seat and took the seat beside her. It was an open carriage with his ducal seal on it. She was apprehensive to be seen together in the park, not wanting people to think they were a couple.

The duke spoke to her about some of the upcoming society events. After a few moments of speaking about rain, his conversation turned to his concern for his tenants and how the rain had affected some of their crops. The duke's efforts were all in vain as Julia kept quiet. He tried again at conversation, telling her about the illness of a distant aunt who had recovered. She didn't respond. Then he tried to make eye contact, but she kept her attention elsewhere. Changing topics, he talked about a new horse he may purchase, seeming to try and engage her in any conversation, and she finally took pity on him and nodded.

Julia could feel her eyelids growing heavy. She kept nodding and making an occasional sound with her voice. She always heard that a lady's place is to listen to her husband, but Julia was not for sure how much of this conversation she could handle. Forcing her mind to think of other thoughts, she drifted to her favorite subject—Randolph! She imagined him beside her, laughing at her jests. Her thoughts immediately went to their kiss, hoping he would do it again.

Her warmness was interrupted when something disturbed her thoughts. It was the duke—he was asking her something. She had not heard him. How could she respond?

"Forgive me, Your Grace. I must have been enjoying the scenery and missed your question," Julia lied.

"Quite understandable," he smiled. "I was asking you if you were cold. I have a blanket if you would like to use it."

"Oh, no, I am fine, Your Grace."

He looked around the park. "Very well. Perhaps we should stop and enjoy a stroll?"

Julia smiled again, accepting his offer. They walked

around Hyde Park, passing many lords and ladies. Most of them gave a greeting, and the duke acknowledged with a nod. They slowly moved to a more isolated part of the park, and he offered her a seat on a bench.

"Lady Julia, I want to ask you about your acclimation to London. I noticed that you have made some new friends. Your mother told me you had tea with Princess Mallory yesterday. I didn't realize that you were acquainted."

Julia gave him a blank stare, not sure how to answer. "I met her at your ball. She was very kind and asked me to tea because she is new to London society as well."

The duke brushed his jacket with his hands as Julia spoke. "I see," he said as he wiped the lint from his gloves. He breathed out a sigh, taking a seat on the other side of the bench. "I hope you don't mind me being forward, but I would like to discuss the letter that I received from your father regarding your request to hold off our engagement."

Julia felt uncomfortable as she twisted in her seat, feeling her heart beating faster. She looked at the duke. "My father said that you agreed."

He gazed at her for a few seconds before responding, "I did agree and believe we need to spend more time together to see if we are suited. However, I wanted to know about your reservations about the match. Are you hesitant because of marriage or because of me?"

Julia took in a breath, confused as to how to answer him. She was surprised he would ask her if she found something amiss with him. Julia bit her bottom lip. "Your Grace, I do not know you. It is not personal, but I must confess that I do not understand our arrangement. I barely remember that day at your house. I was only ten. My father never spoke of it with me again. My mother first mentioned it to me when I was sixteen but never again."

She fidgeted with her gloves. "When a young gentleman made an offer for me in Boston, my father told me that I had to leave Boston in a fortnight. I would uphold my obligation to our family. He gave me no choice." Julia looked back down. "My intentions are not to sound cold, but I don't want to marry a man that I don't love."

The duke stared at her, no emotion on his face.

She continued. "I am not sure if you would be happy with someone who questioned her ability to be a duchess."

After what felt like an eternity of silence, he narrowed his eyes thoughtfully. "Hmm. A love match? Not common in the *ton*. I didn't realize that was what you were looking for. I have heard of a few such love matches, but that usually happens after the marriage." Scooting a little closer, he gently spoke, "Julia, a marriage can be about mutual affection and friendship as well. It's not always about business but can be advantageous to all those involved."

Julia snorted. "All those involved? Whatever do you mean? Is not marriage between two people?"

He nodded his head. "Of course, but it's also about two families and the continuation of our heritage and traditions."

"What traditions would they be? I am not as naïve as you may think." Julia sat quietly for a few seconds. She was tired of this banter. Holding up her chin, she answered. "Would those *traditions* include having a mistress? Is it not common knowledge that titled men have indiscretions?"

The duke widened his eyes in shock, spurting out a cough. "Pardon me?"

Unfazed by his demeanor, Julia continued, "My parents

had an arranged marriage, and I don't think they ever liked each other. Even now." She paused. "I know our families could build an even bigger fortune if I agree to this match, but that is not what is important to me."

The duke stood up, walking across the cobblestone to the other side of the path. Seemingly distressed about their conversation, he straightened his cravat and came back to sit down beside her. "Lady Julia, it is most improper for you to speak of *indiscretions*. Please promise me that you will not talk in such a vulgar way again."

Julia snorted and looked away.

"However, to answer your *delicate* statement, I do not have a mistress nor plan to indulge in any indiscretion."

Julia did not like his condescending tone with her. He was treating her like a child. His chastising was enough to make her wish to leave. She turned away from him, focusing on the birds flying around the park.

The duke sighed, reaching for her gloved hands to hold them. "Lady Julia, please look at me."

She was uncomfortable, surprised by his touch.

He observed her face. "I know you are new to London and may not understand the ramifications of questionable behavior. Some actions or friendships may seem innocent, but they are judged harshly by society. If we are to continue with this arrangement until a decision is made regarding the status of our engagement, then I must ask you for a few considerations."

Julia raised her eyebrows inquisitively. "What kind of considerations?"

"I must first request that you act with the utmost propriety. You are not to entertain questionable behaviors or guests with such reputations. When you accompany me on outings, you will behave like a lady always."

She sat motionless, holding her tongue.

He turned to her and whispered in a gentle voice, "If you have any questions regarding any situation, you will ask me privately, so I can help you make the best decisions."

Julia resented his statement, and she pulled her hand away from him, unable to hide her frustration. Flaring her nostrils angrily, she replied, "How dare you question my behavior, Your Grace! I already have a father, and I don't need another one."

Seemingly baffled by her reply, he leaned back unable to speak.

She narrowed her eyes. "This is exactly why I don't wish to marry. You are not even my husband, and you are already trying to set rules for my behavior. I am not a child but a grown woman. Please understand that I know how to behave."

Standing up, she began to stomp off when the duke stood and tugged on her arm. "You misunderstand me. I only meant to help you. I know what a scandal can do to a young girl's reputation. I only want to save you from ruin." He let go of her arm and touched her face. "I did not mean to upset you. I think your very special, Lady Julia."

Julia didn't know how to respond. She was confused and felt the need to defend her actions. But further arguments would be futile. The only thing she knew for sure was that she did not wish to spend any more time with him. "May we go back now please, Your Grace? I am not feeling well, and I want to rest before the ball."

"Yes, of course." He seemed to hesitate, trying to find

the right words. When no other words came, he held out his arm, and they did not speak again on the way home.

Julia ran to her room after the duke left, falling upon her bed. The audacity of his behavior concerned her. She couldn't do anything right in his eyes. How could she marry such a man? She looked up at the ceiling, contemplating her life. Stretching her arms over her head, she felt a coarse object. She tilted her head, noticing a black leaf in her hand. It crumbled as she rubbed her thumb against it. Looking around, she found another leaf near her pillow. She went to touch it and spotted a stem. She pulled back the covers, "Oh!" Crying out, she covered her mouth. There lay a dead rose. Backing away from the bed, she pulled the bell for Mary to come up to her room.

When Mary arrived, she showed her the dead rose on her bed. Mary inspected it closely. "It was not there earlier when I made the bed." Mary threw the rose in the trash and changed the sheets on Julia's bed. It made Julia feel uncomfortable, but she felt there may be an explanation.

Julia shivered. "Perhaps my cousin Ryan is playing a jest."

Mary nodded her head and prepared Julia's bath, so she could get ready for the ball. She added some flower oil to the water to scent her skin. She wanted to look extra special tonight as Prince Randolph was to be in attendance.

After her bath, she picked out a lavender gown with lace trim to wear. Not wanting to look like every other debutante in the room, she chose to leave most of her hair down. Mary pinned up the sides, and her braids from the day created curls that cascaded down to her waist. She wore her mother's silver jewelry that had a lavender tint in one of the stones. Mary finished dressing her, and Julia spun around with her. The girls danced around the room and giggled in merriment. She told Mary not to worry about preparing her bed for later that night as the dress did not have laces in the back and she could tend to herself. She gave her the night off, so she could spend some time with Kashan.

Chapter 7

THE BALL WAS A CRUSH when Julia and her family arrived. Her father's business meeting had taken longer than expected, so they arrived after the dancing began. The guests were already moving to the music, and Julia was hoping to see Randolph.

She didn't have to wait very long as he came up behind her within a few moments of her arrival. "There you are, my beauty. I hope you did not give away my supper dance?" He gave her a charming grin.

Julia smiled, handing him her dance card.

"Looks like I will be seeing you soon." Reaching for her hand, he kissed her knuckles.

Her heart melted from his warm kiss on her hand. She stared after him until her cousin shook her from her thoughts. Sara tugged on her arm. "I need your help in the ladies drawing room." She covered her mouth, whispering in her ear, "My stocking keeps falling down."

Julia smirked and followed behind her. On their way to the drawing room, Julia spotted the duke looking around the dance floor. She turned suddenly, hiding behind a crowd of people. Not ready to see him again, she made haste toward the safety of the lady's drawing room. Her cousin finished quickly, too quickly for Julia's comfort, and she asked Sara to wait a few minutes for her to rest.

Sara wrinkled her nose. "Rest? We only just arrived, and I want to dance."

Julia sighed loudly, annoyed at Sara's persistence. Realizing that she could not hide in there forever, she smoothed her dress and walked arm in arm with her cousin into the ballroom.

A few minutes later, Julia heard a familiar voice, "Lady Julia?" Oh, drat! She had been caught by the duke. She recognized his voice and turned around to greet him. "Hello, Your Grace. So nice to see you again."

Julia's parents approached as she was speaking, and they all exchanged pleasantries with the duke. He whispered in her ear, "May I ask you for a dance later, Lady Julia?" His hot breath tickled her ear. Not knowing how to refuse, she handed him her dance card. Glancing at the card, he looked up and gave her a glare. "Prince Randolph seems to have stolen the supper dance?"

She brought her gloved hand to her chest in a feigned look of surprise. "Oh, I didn't realize that. He had asked to see my card, and I must not have noticed where he signed. I am sure there are other dances, Your Grace."

"Yes, indeed," scowled the duke. "I believe I will take the waltz, my lady." He bowed to her parents and turned to leave.

Julia looked down at her dance card after he left. "Indeed!" she said to herself. He had taken both waltzes! What would Randolph think?

A few dances later, the prince found her by the refreshment table. Her parents had just left her to speak with some acquaintances not far away. "Hello, my lady."

Julia was startled by his voice but smiled. "Hello, Your Highness."

He winked at her, laughing, "I saw you dancing with the duke earlier, and rumors were swirling."

"Do tell, Your Highness." Her long eyelashes swept her face in an attempt to appear nonchalant.

He nodded toward the duke. "Is he the one you are to marry?"

Julia lost her smile. "Is it that obvious?"

He lowered his voice. "I notice *everything* about you, Julia." His gaze rested on her eyes, and after a moment he shrugged his shoulders. "If the truth be told, he dances a lot better with that lady. They seem to suit each other."

"Pardon?" Julia felt a twinge of jealousy at his observations.

"I heard her name was Lady Janel—the one he is talking to now. The rumor is they will soon make an announcement." He did not smile, but Julia concluded he was trying to get a reaction out of her to gauge her attachment to the duke.

Julia looked over at them. They were smiling at each other as they spoke to a group of people. Lady Janel kept touching his arm in a possessive gesture. A little untoward in Julia's opinion. She tilted her head and studied her for a moment. Taking in her appearance, she would have guessed that some people may find her attractive if they liked that proper aristocratic type. But to Julia, she looked like every other debutant in the room. Not wanting to get caught staring at them, Julia looked away. What did she care if the duke was with another woman?

Randolph took a drink of his champagne, watching Julia. "She must not know he has an arrangement."

Julia snuck another look at Lady Janel's refined presence—she probably would have made an excellent duchess. Julia felt her stomach turn. "Matters not. I have not agreed to marry him."

He rubbed his lips together, suppressing a smile. "A formality."

She leaned closer to him and whispered, "Oh no, Your Highness. You have made an error in your observations. As I told you, I am not going to comply with the arrangements of my family. They just don't know it yet. I will choose my own match someday—just not today."

He stared at her with a serious face, studying her. Seemingly changing his mind of what he wanted to say, he took her hand and said, "I think the waltz is coming up."

Julia stared at him for a moment and then curtsied as she left. She braced herself for the waltz and kept the conversation limited with the duke. Propriety would not allow him to ask her too many questions in front of an audience, and he would feign having a wonderful time even if he didn't. Her parents would be pleased.

Later that evening, the prince found her for their supper dance, and she enjoyed moving to the music. Their earlier banter had ceased, and they enjoyed pleasantries until the music ended. Supper was served shortly afterward. The prince made her a plate and took it back to the table they shared with Sara and Lord Jason. He barely acknowledged the other couple, instead focusing his eyes on Julia. She took a bite of an éclair, squirting some cream onto her chin. Randolph grinned, touching her face and removing the smudge with his fingertips—all while the duke and her parents were watching the intimate exchange from another table in the room. Randolph, oblivious to the audience, showed her the cream on his hand, smiling.

Julia blushed. "Thank you."

She glanced at her mother and grimaced at the look of terror on her face. She quickly looked away, dreading the talk they would have later. They enjoyed the rest of the food but were soon interrupted by her parents saying they were ready to leave as her mother was not feeling well. Julia knew exactly what was wrong with her mother and quickly took her leave. She gave her regrets to the prince and exited the ballroom.

Her parents were quiet on the way home as Julia watched out the window. She thought back to the events of the night and felt such euphoria at the way he had touched her. The closeness she felt with him gave her chills up her spine. She didn't want to think about her future, only hoping to live in the moment.

She heard her father tapping his cane, ready to depart the carriage. She took the footman's hand to exit, being careful as she stepped down. Her anxiety rose as she walked up the stairs—her mother had asked for a private audience in the drawing room. Julia had no means of an escape as she followed her mother to the settee.

She sat down, but her mother remained standing. Lady Savory's face showed shades of red. Clearing her throat, she puckered her lips to chastise her daughter. "Julia, your behavior tonight was intolerable. You flaunted your relationship with the prince and ignored your betrothed."

Julia held her chin up. "He is not my betrothed! Besides,

Randolph and I are just friends. You are being impossible as usual." She rolled her eyes, standing up from the settee.

Her mother stared at her. "Randolph? Are you so familiar with him that you use his Christian name?"

Julia was shocked at her own admission. She must be more careful. "He asked me to since we are friends and only friends." Julia looked at her mother innocently. She knew it was improper to show such familiarity with a gentleman she hardly knew, but she would not admit that to her mother.

Lady Savory shook her head. "I don't like it, Julia, and I expect your behavior to change immediately. You will not embarrass this family or the duke."

"Forgive me if I am such an embarrassment, Mother," Julia said sarcastically. "I am aware of our arrangement. I don't need to be reminded of it every single day." She stomped out of the room, running up the stairs.

Julia slammed her door shut. She could not believe that her mother would be so forceful with her attention to the duke. She tried to unfasten her gown—with no luck—and pulled the bell for assistance.

Taking her pins out of her hair, she ran her fingers through it. She sat on her chair and removed her slippers. Glancing toward her bed, she jerked away suddenly, unable to decipher what she was seeing. Stepping closer with caution, she noticed black specks covering her pillows. Could they be bugs? Upon closer assessment, they were black rose petals. She covered her mouth, sickened at the mess.

Julia stood staring at the bed when Mary entered. "What's amiss, my lady? You look like you you're about to wretch." Julia pointed at the bed.

Mary turned to the bed, lifting her nose in disgust. "Eww! What is that all over your bed?"

Julia inspected closer, reaching out to touch them. They were wilted, displaying dark-black leaves. "They're dead rose petals."

Mary broke her gaze away from the bed, turning to Julia, "I think we need to speak to your mother."

Julia nodded but then changed her mind. She didn't want to see her mother. "Let's not get carried away, Mary. Let's see if someone is playing a jest first. By the way, I thought I gave you the night off?"

"My footman had to help his cousin. He said he was sick." Mary wrinkled her brow. "My lady, I don't think it's a jest. Lord Ryan has stayed at a friend's all afternoon. This is not funny."

Julia searched around her room as Mary collected the dead roses to dispose of them. "Perhaps it's not a jest, but maybe someone else is playing a game. I don't want my mother to worry. I need my freedom. We will just keep quiet for now unless something more happens." Mary reluctantly agreed as she left Julia's room.

Chapter 8

THE DUKE CAME TO VISIT early the next day and asked for Julia. Her mother left them in the drawing room with the door slightly open for propriety's sake. He was in a foul mood, and she gave him only a slight greeting.

He moved near her. "Lady Julia, I came to check on you due to your early departure last night. I had heard you were feeling ill?" He stretched out his words in a disbelieving tone.

Julia gave no indication that his mood bothered her. She took note that his clothes were a little disheveled and his hair looked unkept. He must have been running his fingers through it, messing up his normally neat appearance. Holding his arms behind him, his agitation was apparent as he shifted his feet.

She looked up at him, smiling. "I am feeling well, Your Grace. However, the early departure was due to my *mother's* illness. Not mine."

The duke paused at her statement. Stepping next to her, he leaned down to whisper near her ear and said, "I would like to speak to you privately and thought we could take a walk in the gardens?"

Julia took a step back from his closeness. "I am sure they are not as grand as your estate, but we can take a stroll as you wish."

Julia told her mother, and she agreed that they could go. Her mother asked Mary to accompany them from afar, so they would not be alone without a chaperone.

The duke escorted her down the pathway in silence. They walked past some benches, turning through a stone gate. The path took them past the garden shed and close to the pond with a rock garden beside it. The duke slowed his pace and asked her to have a seat on a big rock next to the flower bushes. They were out of sight from the house, and Julia could not see Mary from her position. The duke stood, pacing back and forth as he spoke. "Lady Julia, I noticed at the ball last night that you were on friendly terms with the visiting prince."

Julia's stomach dropped. She wasn't sure how to answer him. Thinking about her words carefully, she lifted her eyes slowly to meet his stare. "I am not sure what you mean, Your Grace."

The duke quickly answered her back with agitation in his voice. "There seems to be familiarity between the two of you."

Julia did not like where this conversation was going. "We are friends, Your Grace. There is nothing else."

The duke studied her face and took a minute to answer her. "You know he has an upcoming marriage in a few months?"

Julia did know, and it made her anxious. She tried to cover her discomfort and wanted to convince the duke that she was only his friend. "I am aware, Your Grace, and hope he has a most favorable wedding." She smiled at him, getting up from the rock to walk toward some bushes. She feigned watching a bird that was drinking from the pond.

The duke reached out and grabbed her hand. "Lady Julia, I wish you would stop calling me Your Grace and call me by my Christian name of Frank. It is short for Franklin."

Julia panicked. She did not want to lead him to believe that there was anything growing between them. She composed herself, holding firm with his request. "Don't you think that would be improper?"

The duke frowned, showing his irritation with her question. "Not if we are to be engaged soon."

Julia pulled her hand away and turned around. "I don't wish to share such familiarity." She sighed, looking back at him. "Perhaps after the official engagement, if it happens." She took a couple steps away from him, shrugging her shoulders.

The duke was silent. He stared at her wide-eyed with his jaw flexed. Julia did not know what else to say. "Are you cross with me, Your Grace?"

"I just don't understand you, Lady Julia. I am who your parents have chosen as your spouse, yet you show me no encouragement at all."

Julia bit her bottom lip, a little stunned by his admission. She tilted her head, questioning him. "I don't understand you either."

His brow furrowed.

She looked down and murmured, "Why would you want to marry me?"

He opened his mouth to speak and then closed it. Taking his time, he dragged his eyes across her face before answering, "There are many reasons why this marriage would benefit our families."

Julia let out a frustrated sigh. "Exactly! It would benefit our families, but you don't even know who I am."

Combing his fingers through his hair, he seemed to consider her outburst. "Of course, I know who you are, Lady Julia. But marriage is not always about romance."

"Romance? What do you know of romance? You send flowers, yet do not know the woman you send them to. Do you even know what my favorite flower is or my favorite color? Do you know any of my secrets? Those are things a fiancé should know about the woman he is going to marry."

She stood up, avoiding his confused expression. "You see me as a decoration to be added to your list of accomplishments. My father is an earl that owns land that is close to yours, making our match advantageous. I am young and healthy and can probably give you a few heirs so that you can do your duty and be done with me. You don't know me at all!" The tears were on the verge of falling, and one escaped, rolling down her cheek. She quickly wiped it away, swallowing hard.

The duke was dumbfounded by her blowup. He didn't know if he should choke her or kiss her. He had never met a woman who would dare talk this way to him. He thought maybe her upbringing in America had caused her manners to be more relaxed but realized that she had a mouth that did not know any limits—though it was a very kissable mouth.

He stood close behind her, whispering near her ear, "How could I know you when you refuse to get close to me?" He placed his hands on her shoulders. She shivered as he turned her toward him. "I have every intention of knowing your favorite flower, color, and at least one secret before I leave today."

He lifted her chin with his finger. "So, tell me, what is your favorite color?"

She sighed, her tears drying. "Very well, Your Grace. The answers to your questions are green, roses, and I want to wear pants." Julia backed away crossing her arms. She gave him her most satisfied look.

The duke studied her for a moment before releasing a laugh.

A smile slowly covered her face when she heard his laughter.

He shook his head. "Lady Julia, you are full of surprises." His body relaxed, finding a comfort around her without pretentiousness. Her infectious laugh lit up her whole face. Thinking of her wishes, he made a mental note to remember the roses. A dozen red would be nice. He suppressed a grin. "You must tell me about your desire to dress like a man." He enjoyed teasing her.

"I think pants look comfortable. It would make riding a horse so much easier. My mother caught me with a pair of my father's trousers a few years ago, and I was not allowed to leave the house for a week. She said it was not ladylike for women of my station to wear such clothing. She refused to let me even try a pair on."

"I would have loved to have seen that." He laughed again. They were interrupted by a footman who told them that the tea was ready, and her mother wished them to join her for refreshments. He escorted her back to the house to join her mother, and they exchanged pleasantries over tea. He told them he was looking forward to the house party coming up soon. After tea, he gave his regrets as he had to go out of town on business for a few days. He told Julia he would call upon her when he returned to town. Julia showed him to the door, and he kissed her hand. She smiled, watching him leave.

Chapter 9

A FEW DAYS LATER, A MESSENGER sent an invitation from Princess Mallory for a day of horseback riding and a picnic. The party was a few hours away in the countryside. Lady Savory was suspicious and reluctant to give her approval, but the earl was away on business and was not available for a consultation. Sara had been invited as well as Lord Jason, so Julia begged her mother for approval. They were finally given permission to go if two footmen accompanied them as guards. Mary was also assigned to be her chaperone, and she was excited to be near her new crush, Kashan.

They left early the next day to be there by lunchtime. Julia was anxious to see Randolph as she knew the invitation was from him and not his sister. Suppressing a grin, she thought about Mary's frustration with her earlier that morning. Julia had changed her dress four times and asked Mary to style her hair several different ways until she was satisfied. After all, she had to look perfect when she saw him again. Pressing her hand against her stomach, she tried to settle her nerves. All she could think about was the way he had touched her the last time they were together.

Touching her lips with her fingers, she imagined what it would feel like to kiss him again.

The ride was rough as they got closer to their destination. The dusty country roads were not as smooth as they were in London. Julia held on tight, hoping they would not throw a wheel. The roads became more open, and the fields of green were beautiful. Julia tried to participate in the conversation but found it difficult to concentrate as she was so focused on the time ticking by so slowly. Sara and Lord Jason kept themselves busy with a discussion about chess throughout most of the journey. The carriage finally arrived at the picnic a few hours later. Julia primped her hair and dabbed a dash of lavender perfume behind her ears.

When the carriage door opened, they breathed in the fresh country air with welcome. There were a few other carriages parked beside the beautiful cottage and the large stable. Julia wondered who lived there as they were escorted up to the entrance of the house. The grounds were immaculate, and there were more stables up on a hill near another small cottage. They walked up a pathway that overlooked the grounds, observing some movement to the side of the house. They peeked around, eyeing a crowd of people talking and laughing while playing badminton. Prince Randolph saw her approaching and met her party right away.

"Hello! We are so happy you could make it." He bowed to Lord Jason and kissed Sara's hand. He then turned his attention to Julia. "Lady Julia, you are lovely as always." Grinning, he kissed her hand as well. "I have a special surprise that I would like to show you later."

Julia curtsied and whispered, "I looked forward to it, Your Highness."

They went to greet Princess Mallory. The princess was very gracious and took them inside the cottage for some refreshments. Julia was amazed at all the tea biscuits, small tarts, and delicate vegetables on beautiful porcelain trays laid out on the large table. The princess went to the side table to retrieve a plate that was covered with a white cloth. She uncovered the plate, displaying a huge piece of cinnamon bread. Smiling like she was revealing a secret, she handed the plate to Julia. "My brother said this was your favorite and made me promise to have some made especially for you."

Julia felt her face grow warm at the personal gesture. "Thank you so much. That was so kind of him to remember." She took a piece of the bread and took a bite, enjoying the taste of the cream melting inside her mouth. Mallory placed the plate back on the table, her attention diverted as another guest took her arm and led her away. Glancing back, she saw Sara shaking her head in disapproval, whispering to Lord Jason. Julia avoided making eye contact with Sara. She did not want a lecture about her favor with Randolph. She decided to be careful with her affection for the prince in front of Sara, silently questioning if Sara would tell her parents.

They joined the group playing badminton—Randolph chose a seat beside Julia. The games were competitive, but Julia's attention was on him, sneaking peeks from the corner of her eye to not appear too obvious. His knee kept brushing against hers, causing her concentration to falter. She pretended not to notice but could not help grinning to herself. Feeling his warm breath on her cheek, he made excuses to talk to her. The smell of sandalwood in his aftershave lingered, and she enjoyed breathing it in every time he leaned closer. The games lasted another hour, until everyone was ready to go for a ride.

The prince followed closely beside Julia, offering his help with her mount. She accepted, and he placed his hands around her waist, lifting her up with ease as she adjusted herself on the sidesaddle. *How I hate these types of saddles!* Why couldn't she ride astride like the men? Pushing her aversions aside, she smiled with the grace of the lady that she was raised to be.

Prince Randolph picked out his horse, staying close to Julia as they rode behind the others in the group. "Tell me, Lady Julia… are you up for a challenge?"

"What kind of challenge?" she asked demurely, not realizing her own flirtation.

A low groan escaped his lips as he reached for his collar to loosen it. "A race, my lady. Whoever makes it to the white fence first has to give the winner their heart's desire."

The grin hardened on her face. "My heart's desire? Sounds too steep."

He winked good-naturedly. "Then don't lose!" Kicking his horse to a gallop, he pulled away from her.

Her eyes widened in surprise as she nudged her horse to run. They raced beside each other over the fields, leaving the group behind. Julia could see Randolph way ahead of her as she held on to the reins as tight as she could, knowing there was no way she could beat him on a sidesaddle. After a few moments, she saw him slow down as he waited for her by the white fence.

"You cheated with your head start," she protested, pulling the reins to stop beside him.

He grinned, relishing in his victory. "Perhaps. But maybe my heart's desire will be yours too."

She reached out to pet her horse, a little nervous to respond. He watched her for a long moment before turning to look up the hill at the other stables.

"Let's take the horses back to the groom. I would like to take you on a walk. I have a surprise for you. Would you accompany me?"

Julia narrowed her eyes. "I should be cross with you." After a second, she smiled again. "But I am not. I would love to, Your Highness. Let me fetch my maid."

Julia found Mary with her footman having lunch beside the carriage. She asked them both to chaperone her and the prince on their walk.

They walked up the hill to the stables. Julia could not imagine what could be inside as the other horses were kept in the larger stable below. They approached the door, and Randolph asked their chaperones for some privacy as he had a surprise for Julia inside. They both nodded, sitting at a nearby table. Julia felt a little uneasy being alone with him in the stable, but Mary gave her a reassuring smile, and she knew they were close by if she needed them.

Randolph led her inside. "Close your eyes." He reached over, covering her eyes with his hands. Unsure of his intentions, she moved her head back from his hands nervously. Randolph laid a finger over her mouth. "Trust me."

She closed her eyes.

"No peeking, Lady Julia." He chuckled covering her

eyes again. She could feel his chest brush against her back as he moved her across the room. "Okay, my lady. You can open your eyes."

Slowly opening her eyes, she focused on the surprise in front of her—beautifully carved wooden horses on a circle table. They were large enough to sit on and appeared exquisitely detailed. Pulling off her gloves, she rubbed her fingers over the etchings on each piece of wood. There were four horses with reins attached to their necks with real leather straps. The craftsmanship was impeccable.

Randolph stepped beside her, and she could feel him watching her for a reaction. "You can sit on the horses if you wish." She was hesitant but stepped up onto the table. He helped her onto the horse, holding her until she was stabilized on the mount.

He smiled as though he held a secret. "Hold on, my dear." Jumping off the table, he turned back once to make sure she was secure. Reaching over, he grabbed a large handle on the side and pushed the horses in a circle.

She started laughing. "Oh, Randolph, this is so much fun. What is this thing? I have never seen anything like it."

Randolph smiled, making the table go faster. After a few rounds, he stopped the spinning and helped her off the wooden horse. Julia's head felt dizzy, and she felt unstable on her feet. She lost her balance, but his arms wrapped around her waist, holding her stable. She steadied herself as he pulled her closer into his arms. Julia felt her heart beat faster from their closeness. Gently, he touched her face and whispered, "I like the feel of you in my arms."

Unable to move away, her eyes fixated on his mouth. He bent down to brush a soft kiss across her lips. He pressed in closer, holding her tighter. Julia opened her mouth slightly, feeling his tongue sliding inside. She was a little shocked by this type of kiss but remembered Mary telling her about such embraces. Opening her mouth wider, she accepted his kiss with more intensity. She felt her need growing deeper and finally broke away from him.

Breathlessly, Randolph put his forehead on top of hers. "Forgive me, Julia. I nearly lost myself."

Coming to her senses, she stepped away from him and straightened her dress, taking a quick look around the room to make sure they were alone. It would have ruined her if anyone had witnessed their embrace. She attempted to slow down her breathing. "Maybe we should leave now? Mary may have wondered what has happened to me."

Randolph wavered a moment. "I don't wish to leave yet. Come and sit down with me on the barrels."

Julia dithered but took his hand, following him over to the corner of the stable. He sat on one of the barrels, holding her hand. Julia turned to sit on the other, but he reached for her waist, pulling her onto his lap.

She tensed up, but he smiled at her. "Relax, my love. I only want to hold you." Randolph pleaded with his dark, tantalizing eyes, and her resolve failed as she sat on his lap. Laying her head on his shoulder, they sat in silence for a few moments. She closed her eyes, wanting to memorize his embrace so she would never forget.

Randolph reached into his pocket and pulled out a chain with a locket. Julia moved her head up and was shocked when he handed it to her. Flattered by his gesture, she opened the locket to look inside. The engraving read "No Rules" with a heart.

Julia busted out laughing. "It's perfect. I love it." He unlatched it and put it around her neck.

Kissing him on the cheek, she felt such happiness. "Thank you for the gift." Randolph pulled her tightly against him kissing her head.

She put her cheek on his chest. He placed his chin on top of her head, wrapping his arms around her to hold her close. She was lost in her thoughts, looking at the carved horses. They sat there in silence as she rubbed the necklace around her neck. Finally, she whispered, "Tell me about your country and your family."

He ran his fingers gently down her back. "What is it that you want to know?"

"I want to know everything."

He squeezed her tight. "My curious little butterfly. I am afraid if I told you too much about me, that you would find out that I am not that special and lose interest."

"Not possible. Now stop avoiding my question. Tell me about your family."

"Very well, you know that I can deny you nothing. I am the third son of the King. I have two older brothers and two younger sisters. My country is a lot smaller than England, and our 'rules' as you say, are a lot more relaxed. I was in the military for ten years and have finished serving my time. I came to England for a holiday before my royal duties begin. My father plans for me to head the agriculture council in my country."

"What were you like as a child?"

"I was always into mischief. My oldest brother had a lot of responsibilities as he was the heir. He always did everything my parents told him to. My second brother was a little braver, but he was the spare heir and had responsibilities. That left me more freedom to get into trouble the most."

"You did not have responsibilities?" Julia questioned him.

"Quite the opposite. I had responsibilities and still do. My responsibilities are just different and give me more leeway than my brothers."

Julia smiled as she sat up, looking into his eyes. He touched her face pulling her closer for another kiss. His kiss was soft, and she looked deep into his eyes. They were an intense brown, and she noticed tiny gold specks as she studied his features up close.

Randolph broke the silence, rubbing his thumb over her lips. "I could stay here all day with you, my beauty. However, we must go as I have your reputation to think about."

Julia acquiesced and got up from his lap. He offered her his arm, and they walked through the barn door to meet Mary. Julia could not remember having had such a wonderful time. She tucked the necklace into her gown to avoid any speculation from Sara. Julia went to hook arms with Mary, and Randolph escorted them back to the rest of the party.

Julia saw Sara drop Lord Jason's arm to come to her as soon as she rejoined the party. Turning away to avoid her, Sara hurried to stand in front her. Before she could speak, the prince appeared at her side. "Thank you for the walk, my lady. I will check on a few items with the staff and see you later." Julia smiled and curtsied, then finally looked at Sara's scowling face.

"What's amiss, Sara? You don't look like you feel well."

"Indeed." Abruptly taking Julia's arm, she whispered in her ear, "Can I speak to you privately?" Julia had a knot in her stomach but nodded her head as Sara escorted her to the side of the house.

"What's going on with you, Julia? I saw you escorted to the stable on the hill by Prince Randolph. People were talking and *speculating* at your involvement." She huffed, crossing her arms angrily.

"I had chaperones, Sara. I was not alone." Stepping back, she placed her hands on her hips. "How dare you accuse of me of any untoward behavior." Julia's face turned red. "I am *not* engaged to the duke. What is wrong with me spending time with the prince? We are just friends."

Sara stared at her cousin, seemingly trying to figure her out. Shaking her head, she raised her hands, exasperated by the obvious repercussions that would soon follow. "Bah! I am just friends with him, Julia. You are more than a friend, and everyone notices."

Julia shrugged her shoulders. "I don't care what they say."

Sara eyes widened. "How can you say that? You will ruin yourself and me."

"Stop it. I won't ruin you."

Sara started breathing hard, choking back tears. "You don't understand, Julia. When a woman acts untoward, the backlash is often extended to her whole family."

Julia huffed. "Sara, I was not acting untoward! I took a walk with a gentleman who happens to be royalty. I did not ruin my reputation. You are being impossible." Julia turned to walk away to end the conversation.

Sara grabbed her arm, pulling her back. "Promise me that you will be more careful. *Please*, Julia."

She did not like her accusations but did not want her to be on edge about her future. Besides, she needed Sara not to say anything to their parents. "Very well, Sara. I will make sure my indiscretions are more discreet." Julia laughed as she walked off. She couldn't help herself—the fact that a chaperoned walk with the prince could ruin Sara's reputation was ridiculous.

Sara went to stand next to Lord Jason "Where is Lady Julia going?" Sara shrugged her shoulders looking up at him. "I think we may need to leave. It's a long journey back."

Lord Jason nodded, giving his regards to the prince. "We had a pleasant day and thank you for your hospitality." The prince bowed, thanking them for coming. Julia was at the refreshment table pretending not to overhear. Prince Randolph walked beside her. "My lady, I hope all is well?"

She met his eyes, taking his arm as they strolled off toward the garden terrace. "My cousin says my behavior with you is scandalous."

He raised his brow. "Was she in the stable?"

Julia laughed. "No, she just saw us walking together. She would swoon if she knew we were alone in the stable."

Randolph laughed, leaning to whisper in her ear, "Then it must be our *secret*."

Julia shivered at his emphasis on "secret."

Sara and Lord Jason came to get her, and Julia let go of his arm. Sara gave Julia a threatening stare. "Julia, we must be on our way as the afternoon draws near." Julia nodded and bid farewell to the prince.

The ride home was long. Julia tried not to speak to Sara or Lord Jason. They were wrapped up in their own conversations, and Julia closed her eyes, feigning sleep. She did not appreciate Sara's insistence about her lack of propriety. The last thing she needed was more people telling her she needed to marry the duke. Even her own cousin was against her wishes.

Julia awoke as they were approaching the town house. She realized she must have fallen asleep for real. She sat up as the carriage turned on to the circular drive and hurried to be the first one off. Sara protested that Lord Jason should be the first one off, so he could assist them in exiting the carriage. Julia ignored her and jumped down, running to the door to get inside. Mary followed closely behind, and when they were both safely inside Julia's room, Julia collapsed on the bed.

Mary looked at her and smiled. "Does Miss Reynolds know?"

Julia suppressed a grin. "Not everything. She scolded me about taking a walk with the prince when I am to be engaged to the duke." She giggled covering her mouth. "She can't help herself, and I must try not to be so cross with her. She grew up in London society."

Mary laughed as she helped Julia dress for dinner. Julia told her all about the prince and the way he kissed her. Mary brushed out her hair and braided it as she listened to Julia.

Chapter 10

A FEW DAYS LATER, JULIA WAS awakened by her mother and Mary standing over her. Gasping at the intrusion, she was startled and jerked her head up. "What is amiss?" She could barely open her eyes as they pulled the curtains back, causing sunlight to stream through the window. Julia squinted at the blinding brightness, trying to open her eyes wider to focus on their faces.

Lady Savory held her hands close to her chest, sitting on Julia's bed, trying to catch her breath. "You, um... you received a package this morning. It was left on the doorstep."

Julia observed her mother's odd behavior and knew something was not right. "What kind of package?"

Her mother was trembling. "I wish your father was here. My nerves cannot handle this. Julia, I think you should get dressed immediately. Your uncle is waiting for you downstairs. He has called the authorities."

"Mother, you are frightening me. What is in the package, Mary?"

Mary's color drained from her face. She looked at Lady Savor, who nodded her approval. Mary took a deep breath, facing Julia. "Oh, my lady! There was a basket left by the front door. It was addressed to Lady Julia and had a blanket inside. When the footmen brought the basket into the drawing room, your mother lifted the blanket. She swooned! It was full of dead roses and had a bloody knife inside. There was a note… oh my lady! I can't say what it said. It is too awful."

Julia shivered, feeling her heart pound against her chest. "What did it say? Tell me now!"

Mary's voice cracked. "It said… 'Lady Julia will pay.'"

Julia gulped, looking at her mother in disbelief. Her mouth remained open as tears burned the back of her eyes.

Mary continued, "I told her we had noticed a few dead roses on your bed in the last few days, but we thought it was a jest."

Lady Savory covered her mouth and was visibly upset. Julia touched her mother's arm. "I will get dressed and meet you in Uncle's study."

Julia dressed in a hurry with Mary's help. They both kept glancing at each other with puzzled looks but stayed quiet. She left her room and hurried down to her uncle's study. As she rounded the corner, she almost ran smack into the duke.

"Forgive me, Your Grace. I was not aware you were here."

"I arrived late last night and wanted to visit you this morning. Your uncle told me of the horrible incident, and I was going to wait in his study for you." He reached for her hands. "I want to make sure you are safe and will personally hire extra help to guard you."

"Thank you, Your Grace. I don't think that will be necessary. My father has many footmen here." He raised her hands to his mouth, kissing them, and escorted her to the study. "I understand your need to be independent, Lady Julia, but my wish is that you will let me help you."

Julia remained silent as they entered the study. Her mother and aunt rushed over to her when she walked into the room. Her aunt took her into an embrace. "I am so shocked Julia—this is just awful!"

Julia's aunt went to stand near her sister, Lady Savory. She held her hand and squeezed it. They sat on the settee in the study. Julia noticed a chubby man with spectacles standing near her uncle. His mustache curled on the ends, and he walked with a cane. He walked toward her as she entered the room, motioning for her to sit on the high-back chair.

Julia's uncle introduced him as an investigator. He had called for his help to find out who was behind the dead roses.

He leaned over, smelling of pipe smoke. "My lady, will you answer some questions?"

Julia nodded. "Of course, I want to help in any way that I can."

She answered all his questions, watching the whole room hanging on her every word. She was not prepared for his questions. Going over the events in her head the last few months, she came up empty. Who would want her dead? *She had no enemies*! The investigator was looking at every possibility. He wanted to question all her acquaintances. Julia had very few as she was new to London. Lady Savory gave him a list of people she associated with and then gave the investigator Princess Mallory's name. Julia's chest tightened at the mention of the princess. She decided to keep quiet as she did not want the duke or anyone to know the amount of time she spent with Mallory was because of her brother.

The investigator stayed for tea before leaving. The duke asked Julia to walk in the park with him, and she reluctantly agreed with urging from her mother.

The ride in the park was quiet. Julia shivered when mist fell upon her face. It was not raining, but the cloud cover put a shadow on the afternoon. Julia kept scrutinizing the people within the park—wondering if they were watching her, wondering who wanted her dead. Everyone looked suspicious to her, and a chill ran through her body. She pulled her shawl closer wrapping in any warmth she could find.

"Are you cold, Lady Julia?" The duke's words shook her from her musings—she was so engrossed in her thoughts that she had not remembered he was there.

"No, Your Grace," she said more sharply than she realized. The carriage came to a stop and he helped her out, taking her arm and walking to the fountain. They were soon stopped by a group of people who must have been on friendly terms with the duke because they referred to him as Frank. Julia did not pay any attention to the group. She felt too nauseous, thinking about her fate.

The group's conversation suddenly halted, and she noticed their stares upon her. Realizing they were all waiting for her response, she turned helplessly to the duke. He smiled. "They asked you if you are enjoying London."

How could she answer them? No, she was *not* enjoying

London. But not wanting to explain, she lied. "Yes, thank you."

They all smiled, nodding their heads. Julia recognized one of the women in the group as Lady Janel. She stepped from behind one of the men and introduced herself.

"Hello, Lady Julia. I am Lady Janel. I did not get the pleasure of making your acquaintance at the ball. This is my cousin, Lady Sophia."

Julia stared at her and the other women in the group. They were dressed very fashionably, their greetings very proper, but had a condescending air about them. She could feel them looking her up and down, sharing quick glances with each other. The men continued with their conversation while Julia let go of the duke's arm. He glanced down at her as she took a step to the side.

She nodded. "Very nice to meet you both." Julia pasted a forced smile on her face and then patted some pretend dirt off her dress to break the stare from Lady Janel.

The duke's friend Lord James smiled at the exchange, and turning to Julia said, "I must say, Lady Julia, we are happy to *finally* make your acquaintance. You were preoccupied at the last few balls, and we have not been properly introduced." Her face felt warm at his direct stare. "You must tell us how you know His Grace as he told us that your families are old friends." He gave her a slight wink.

She looked between the duke and Lord James, evaluating his teasing. She captured the group's attention as they waited for her response. The duke stared at his friend, a disapproving frown forming at his face.

Julia would not take the bait as it seemed obvious that Lord James was aware of privileged information of their possible betrothal. Instead, she smiled with grace. "I am afraid that I don't remember him much." She shrugged. "I was a child when we left for America. We have been reacquainted since my return to London as he visits my father."

Lady Janel smiled, touching the duke's arm. She practically bumped Julia out of the way. "Let's finish our walk together, Frank. You have been very naughty. I must say you owe me something nice for not telling me you were leaving town. You missed my mother's dinner party that you had promised to attend." She giggled and continued, "Imagine my surprise when James told us that you were otherwise engaged on business." She kept smiling and rubbing his arm. The duke looked uncomfortable, and Julia felt Lady Janel's behavior was inappropriate toward a man who insisted on propriety.

James sensed the tension and walked to Julia to offer her his arm. "I would be honored to escort you, my lady." Julia wavered but took his arm. She felt the duke should have rescued her because these were his friends and not hers—especially Lady Janel, who insisted on putting Julia in her place.

The others followed closely behind, including Lady Sophia, who kept glaring at Julia. She wondered if those looks were because of her cousin or if she had a *tendre* for Lord James. They walked for a while, and Julia felt fatigued. She sighed in frustration at their conversations about their accomplishments, weather, and other people of the *ton* whom she did not know. Julia found them all boring and proud. She could not imagine spending any more time with the group and tried to think of any excuse to avoid their company. Letting go of James's arm, she approached the duke. "Your Grace, I am not feeling well and wish to leave."

The duke looked at her, concerned, letting go of Lady Janel. The entire group stopped walking as Lady Janel began protesting. "Oh no, Frank. The walk can't be over. I was looking forward to feeding the birds with you."

Julia opened her mouth in shock. She could not believe this woman! Had she not made it clear that she was not feeling well?

Tugging on his arm, she tried to steal his attention back. "I don't wish to ruin your fun." She drew her shawl around her shoulders. "Perhaps your carriage can take me home with my maid and you can stay with your friends?"

Lady Janel smiled. "Oh, yes, please stay, Frank. Lady Julia insists, and the poor thing just doesn't feel well." Lady Janel gave her a half smile as she pulled on the duke's arm.

The duke looked at Lady Janel. "I will not hear of it. I escorted Lady Julia here and will escort her home. I am a gentleman and will make sure she is safe."

Lady Janel's smile dropped as she glared at Julia. The duke kissed Lady Janel's hand and told her he would call upon her soon. Offering Lady Julia his arm, they turned to walk the other way after saying their goodbyes. Walking in silence until the group was out of sight, Julia let go of his arm. He turned to her with a surprised look. "What is amiss?"

Julia flipped her hand in causal protest. "I do not prefer your friends' company."

The duke lowered his brow. "Why? You seemed to enjoy their company. You were chatting with James."

She lifted her chin with defiance. "You *forced* me to spend time with them without asking my permission."

He straightened his shoulders, smoothing his jacket. "Those friends are from very distinguished families, and they are my most loyal companions. You could learn a lot from them, *Lady* Julia."

Julia stopped walking.

Her nostrils flared in anger. "I don't care who their families are—they are rude and proud. I don't wish to be acquainted with them." She took a step away from him, crossing her arms. "As far as *Lady* Janel, *her* behavior would be more welcomed in a local tavern. I could never learn anything from her unless I wanted to throw myself shamelessly at a man." Julia turned around and stomped off, choking back tears. She heard footsteps behind her before the duke grabbed her arm.

"Lady Julia, you will not speak to me this way in public. You will not disparage my friends as they deserve your respect. I have made excuses and tolerated your outbursts, but I refuse to allow you to act this way any further."

Julia jerked her arm away. "You will not touch me, sir. I can find my own way home."

Mary saw her distress and rushed for her. Julia embraced her maid's arm and asked if the footmen could escort her home because she felt like walking. The duke insisted they take the carriage and told them he had an errand to run. They could return to the park to get him after seeing Lady Julia home. The footman helped her into the waiting carriage, and she never looked back once.

Chapter 11

J ULIA WAS QUIET IN THE carriage, holding back tears. She could not believe how much of a watering pot she had become since arriving in London. She cried over everything! Her life was complicated—she felt lost and unsure of what her future held. Her gaze fell on Mary, wondering what it would be like to be a maid, having no marriage expectations. Mary held her hand, not speaking. Julia appreciated her discretion and was grateful for such a friend.

She arrived at the house and was immediately tackled in a hug by Sara. "Oh, cousin, I am so happy you are well. I heard the awful news after I awoke. It's dreadful!"

They entered the drawing room, and Lady Savory offered Julia some tea as they sat, exchanging pleasantries. Sara practically sat on her while Julia's mother took the seat on the other side, hovering over her. She was exhausted with everyone's attention and asked to retire to her bedroom. All she wanted to think about was Randolph and when she could see him again. The pressure was mounting on when she would decide about the duke. It wasn't fair! She was not any closer to securing an alternative plan of action and was running out of options.

Julia's bedroom was locked. She remembered the extra key the security guard kept and went back downstairs. After she retrieved the key, the butler gave her a missive that had arrived for her. She thanked him, taking it with her to her room. When she arrived, Mary was waiting for her in the hallway. They both entered the room, and Julia showed her the missive. The seal was not recognizable to either of them, and there was no indication who it was from. The butler said it was left by a footman he did not know. Mary volunteered to open it, so Julia passed it to her. Mary carefully cracked the seal, and they both stared at it as she carefully opened the sides, handing it to Julia.

Julia started to read carefully, a smile forming across her face. Mary begged her to read it out loud. "Very well, Mary. It's from Randolph, although he signed it 'Wooden Horses.'" She giggled as she remembered their afternoon together.

Julia continued. "He wishes to see me tomorrow and asks if we can meet him at his house." Julia looked at Mary's frightened stare as she knew they were being carefully guarded.

"Please, Mary, you must go with me. I need you to deliver a message back to the prince's guard. We need to think of a good excuse as I am being watched like a hawk."

Mary twisted her hands. "I think it's too risky. You shouldn't chance it right now."

"I have to see him, Mary. My mind won't settle until I do. We can use his sister as an excuse again. Maybe we can talk fast and go to the bakery. We will ask the Princess to accidentally run into us and invite us to tea. I will leave a message with my mother that we accepted her invitation.

She will be upset but won't have a chance to tell me that I can't go."

Mary shook her head. "I don't like it. It could be dangerous to leave the house."

Julia protested. "I received the threatening letter *at* the house. At least at the Prince's manor, we will be safer than anywhere. Royal guards are the best in the city."

Mary's shoulders sagged in defeat. "I will do it, but I don't like it."

Julia clapped her hands, jumping up to hug Mary. "We will be home by dinner. It's the perfect plan."

Chapter 12

JULIA TOOK EXTRA CARE THE next morning to dress. She wore her rose-colored gown with lace flowers, adding a silver bracelet to finish her look. She carried the locket in her reticule to put on after she left. Her nerves were overwhelmed all morning, although she was still looking forward to seeing Randolph.

Everyone seemed to be busy that morning. Sara announced during breakfast that she was meeting Lord Jason at the bookstore. Lady Savory skipped breakfast altogether to visit a friend. Julia took the opportunity to casually tell her aunt that she was going to the bakery down the street and would bring two footmen and Mary. Her aunt agreed and did not insist on accompanying her. Julia breathed a sigh of relief.

The smells of the bakery filled the shop. Julia smiled as she entered the store and thought she could probably eat four cinnamon buns if no one would stop her. She decided to order only two—one for her and one for Mary. They treated themselves while waiting for Princess Mallory to show up. But they didn't wait long as a beautiful carriage soon approached the bakery, and they watched the princess step out.

Princess Mallory's mouth formed a knowing smile as she opened the door to the bakery. They smiled back as they exchanged pleasantries in front of the footmen. Julia had brought parchment paper and quickly wrote a note to her mother that Princess Mallory had invited them to her home and they would be home by supper and that Princess Mallory would provide a carriage and she did not need to worry. They agreed to take one of Julia's footmen for extra protection before embarking on their journey.

Inside the carriage, Julia thanked Princess Mallory profusely.

"Julia, it's my pleasure. I assure you that my brother is already indebted to me and promised me I could ride his prize horse when we return home next week."

Julia's smiled faded. "Next week?"

By the look that crossed her face, Princess Mallory had realized at that moment that she might have revealed a secret that she should not have. Trying to recover from her blunder, she reached out and touched her arm in comfort. "Forgive me. I am sure Randolph may be trying to stay since he has found such a wonderful distraction in London. But I'm not sure if my father will allow it. I am sure he will tell you soon. Please keep this between us and let him tell you himself."

Julia took a deep breath, trying to hide her disappointment. "Of course. I am sure he will tell me today."

Her heart broke a little at the prospect of him leaving.

The prince rushed to greet her as soon as she stepped out of the carriage.

"My lady, you are even more beautiful than the last time I saw you."

She curtsied. "Your talk is sweet, Your Highness."

He took her hand and brought it to his lips. "I have the day planned for us, starting with a picnic in the gardens."

She accepted his arm and followed him through the grounds. Mary followed behind them but was interrupted by one of his footman that she had met a few weeks ago. The footman offered to show Mary the grounds at Prince Randolph's request with a promise to catch up with them later. That left Julia without a chaperone, alone with no protection.

Julia took Prince Randolph's arm, trying to calm her stomach. She walked next to him down an overgrown path. His familiar scent tickled her nose, causing her head to spin. She did not want to think about the dead roses or the duke. Trying to concentrate on her time with Randolph, she was happy to have no interruptions. The prince led her through many twists and turns. They finally approached a secluded wooded area, and he held back tree limbs to help navigate her through. There was a clearing in the middle of the brush, with a blanket already set up with a basket. Julia enjoyed the intimate setting, looking forward to spending time with him.

"Please have a seat, my beauty. I will fix you a drink." He pulled out two glasses and poured her some wine. He kissed her softly as he handed her the glass.

She smiled, sniffing the drink. "I am not used to drinking wine. Only champagne on special occasions."

"I won't tell anyone. It will help you relax."

She swirled the drink in her glass and then took a sip

of it. The sour taste made her cringe, but she managed to swallow it.

He moved closer to her, burying his face in her neck. "I missed you."

She bit her bottom lip. "I missed you too."

He touched her hand, slipping off her gloves while sneaking looks at her. He removed his gloves, holding her hands with nothing between them. The intimate skin-on-skin contact gave her goose bumps. She felt so close to him at that moment as he laid his head in her lap. She ran her fingers through his hair, smiling down at him.

"Tell me about your week, Julia. You were consuming my thoughts." She didn't want to tell him about the threats she received. Choosing to keep the secret to herself, she chose to speak of her mother.

"It was a full schedule, and my mother kept me busy."

Randolph grunted. "I bet she did." He paused. "She is probably hoping to announce your engagement soon."

She lost her smile as he sat up, turning to her with a serious gaze. Looking down at their fingers intertwined, she felt her stomach drop. She did not wish to discuss her pending engagement—she preferred to pretend it did not exist.

He did not let go of her hand and looked directly into her eyes. "There is much for us to discuss and some news I must share with you."

Julia interrupted him. "I know, Randolph. Your sister informed me that you depart next week." She bit her tongue, forgetting her agreement to keep it in confidence.

He was silent, looking away from her. "I never thought I would feel this way."

Julia's heart jumped into her throat. She was so overwhelmed by his words that she found it difficult to say anything back. He looked back at her. "I think I have fallen in love with you, and I don't wish to leave you. I will find a way for us to be together." He looked down, visibly fighting his emotions.

Julia reached out to touch his face gently. "I love you too." She couldn't believe that she had said it. Leaning over, she kissed him on the cheek.

Pulling her into his arms, he crushed his mouth to hers, raising his hands to cup her face. Their kiss was full of passion and intensified as he moved his tongue into her mouth. She opened her mouth widely, allowing him to lean her back on to the blanket. He moved his mouth to the curve of her neck and nuzzled her with wet kisses. Lightly touching her shoulders, he nipped at her ear as his fingers ran up and down her arms.

She knew that she should stop this recklessness, but she hesitated because she wanted it to last a little longer. Finally, as though he had read her mind, he broke the kiss. "You are so beautiful, my love."

He sat up on his elbow, moving his index finger over her cheeks down to her chin. He placed gentle kisses all over her face—her eyes, nose, and chin. Touching his hand to her chest, he made small circles with his fingers. Moving his head down, he placed light kisses on her chest while he stuck his finger inside the neckline of her dress. He was slowly lowering her dress, continuing to kiss her, when Julia reached for his hand to stop his advancement. She gasped and sat up. He stopped, looking at her with desire in his eyes.

"I am sorry, Randolph. I am not ready to share such liberties until we are married." Julia began straightening her dress with her hands.

Randolph's expression changed suddenly. "I don't understand. When we are married, it will be much harder."

Julia was confused by his words.

He grasped her hand. "Don't worry, my love. I promise we will be together. I can visit England a few times a year and secure us a town house for our meetings. We will make this work because we love each other."

Julia ripped her hands from his grip. Fury burned in her chest as she reached for her gloves and pulled them back on. Randolph sat in silence, a look of bewilderment on his face by her behavior.

She glared at him. "I am not the lady you think I am, *Prince* Randolph." He reached for her, trying to stop her from moving away from him. She couldn't stop the tears from falling as she put her hands on his chest to push away from him.

After pulling harder, he stopped his resistance, and she stood up. "Are you proposing that I become your *mistress*? Is that what you think of me?" Indignation ran through her veins. "I am an earl's daughter, not some courtesan that you picked up at a ball!"

Randolph reached for her again, but she jumped back out of his reach. "Don't touch me!" Julia grabbed the locket he'd given her from around her neck and tore it off, breaking the clasp. She threw it at him.

"Don't do this, Julia—you talk about things you don't understand." Randolph choked on his words. "I would marry you tomorrow if I could. In my country, all royal marriages are arranged. It would affect an entire country if I married outside of my family arrangements."

Julia rubbed her temples as she felt a headache coming on.

He took a long breath and then pleaded with her. "I could not break my betrothal and keep any of my inheritance. They don't recognize morganatic unions. My children would not be entitled to anything. I could not fulfill my duty as a provider for you or our children. I would not subject you to such a life. You are very young, Julia. You have yet to learn the ways of the world. My upcoming marriage is not a love match—my relationship with you would not have to change."

Clutching her stomach, she suddenly felt violently ill. Taking a few steps, she wretched by the bushes. It was too much for her. She felt Randolph come up behind her, offering his handkerchief. She accepted it to wipe her mouth. Reaching for her glass of wine, she took a sip. Wiping her mouth again, she put his handkerchief inside her reticule.

He kept looking at her through the awkward silence.

She composed herself and looked him in the eye as she spoke. "I may be young, but I know when you love someone you don't treat them the way you have treated me. I am so tired of people making decisions for me. I may be naïve, but what you ask from me belongs to my husband. I will never give myself to another man." Her words were choking her. She coughed, trying to maintain her breathing. Catching her breath, she put her hands on her hips. "When I fall in love with someone else, it will be my choice, and he will accept me for who I am." Julia took another deep breath, and Randolph took a step toward her.

Julia jerked her body away from him and held her hand up. "I need to leave *now*." She took a few steps and looked back at him. "If you love me, then you will let me go. Please do not follow me." She went toward the bushes and moved the limbs out of her way. He sat in silence as he watched her leave.

The prince clenched his fists at his sides. He battled within himself to run after her. He longed to wrap his arms around her and give her what she wanted, but images of his father—his king—kept him from moving. He felt his legs buckle as he grabbed hold of the tree, not able to believe he'd let the love of his life walk away.

Mary noticed Julia appear in the garden alone. She was visibly upset, and she ran to her. "Mary, we must go, now!"

Mary motioned to the footmen to bring the carriage around. They quickly boarded without saying goodbye to their hosts. Mary again sat in silence as Julia looked out the window with tears falling.

Chapter 13

JULIA TRIED TO SNEAK IN through the back of the residence but was caught. Sara rushed to her side and said, "What's amiss? Why are you entering through the back?"

Julia turned to her cousin, and Sara noticed her red eyes and immediately stopped questioning her. "Come with me."

She took Julia's hand, escorting her through a side entrance that was only used by servants. They snuck up the staircase with Mary behind them. Mary stood as a lookout as Sara took Julia to her room.

"Thank you. I just need to rest, if you could give me some privacy?"

Sara stalled before saying, "Julia, I will tell your mother that I checked on you and you were taking a nap. That should buy you some time."

Surprised by her gesture, Julia looked at her. "Thank you. That means a lot to me."

She smiled and closed the door behind her.

Mary helped Julia out of her dress to get ready for a nap. "Do you want to talk about it?" Mary stroked Julia's hair as she lay on the pillow.

"I just hurt so badly. He said he loved me, but he was going through with his arranged marriage."

Mary stopped stroking her hair and squeezed her shoulders. "I am so sorry. He has no idea what he has lost."

Julia turned around to face her. "That's just it, Mary. He does not feel he would lose me. He wants to go through with our marriages as our obligation but still be together. He even offered to buy a town house for our indiscretions. Can you believe that? He said he loved me and that was all that mattered. I can't ever face him again."

"Do you love him?" Mary asked Julia as she picked up her dress to put it away.

"I thought I did, but I must admit that I don't know what love is." A knock on the door silenced their conversation. Mary went to the door and found Lady Savory. She curtsied, leaving her in the room.

"Julia, what is wrong with your eyes?" Lady Savory moved in front of the bed, and Julia covered them with her hands. She did not want her mother to know that she was crying.

"I got something in them and am just trying to rest, Mother." Julia turned away from her mother, asking her to leave her alone to rest before supper.

"I am very cross with you, Julia. You should not have sent a messenger to me without any prior explanation. You're not allowed to take outings without securing our permission first. We also need a minimum of two guards with you at all times as we wait to see if any other threats come." Lady Savory took a breath and stood up from the bed. "I expect you to be on your best behavior tonight. We invited the duke and his mother to dine with us because your father is back in town. He was disturbed by your absence and met with the investigator this morning. I expect you to be dressed and ready to meet our guests in a few hours."

Julia shivered at the news. She could not imagine spending an evening with the duke after their incident in the park. She was not in the mood for her father either. Trying the only excuse she could come up with, she rubbed her stomach. "Mother, I am afraid I am not feeling well and must decline supper." Julia held her breath, hoping her mother would allow her this one wish.

"Don't test me—you will be dressed and ready to receive our guests as I demand it. Your behavior has not been acceptable lately, and I will not be toyed with. You don't wish for me to tell your father about your refusal, do you? I expect your compliance." Lady Savory turned to the door and let herself out. Julia began to cry and eventually fell asleep.

Julia sat in the drawing room with her family as the duke and dowager duchess were announced. Her aunt had invited a few others, including Lord Jason. It was a small dining party of twelve guests with enough food to probably feed half of London. Her uncle had spared no expense as her father and he had closed some big shipping deal.

Julia curtsied to the dowager duchess, who smiled at Julia as she sat by Lady Savory. The duke took Sara's hand and bowed to it. He addressed Julia with coldness, and in return, she curtsied, putting an emphasis on "Your Grace."

No one seemed to notice the exchange, and they were quickly given before-dinner beverages.

Julia made a point to engage in conversation with Sara and Lord Jason to avoid speaking to the duke. The last thing she needed was another confrontation. It was bad enough she was going to have to tolerate his presence during all the courses.

The couples entered the dining room. Due to the small group, they made it more informal and did not enter by rank. Julia knew she would be pushed toward the duke for an escort. She tried to make a beeline for Lord Jason but was not fast enough because Sara was already hooked to his arm, giving her a puzzling look. Feeling resigned, Julia walked to the duke and took his extended arm. As they entered the room, she quickly viewed the seating arrangements and realized there was no graceful way to switch seats to avoid sitting next to him. She accepted her fate and moved to sit beside him. The footmen pulled out the chairs, and Julia seated herself, taking special care not to look at the duke.

She focused her attention on the couple in front of her, Lord and Lady Dancy. They were an older couple and were friends with her uncle. Lady Dancy grinned. "Lady Julia, what a beautiful necklace you have on. I have never seen that color, and it closely matches your eyes."

"Thank you, Lady Dancy. I actually received it as a gift from my father in Boston." Her father heard her mention him and glanced at Julia and smiled. He was carrying on a conversation with the couple beside him.

The duke's brother made an appearance, apologizing for his tardiness. Julia offered him her seat, but he declined. The duke made no acknowledgment of her presence. The footmen added another plate, and Lord Jacob sat on the other side of Lady Dancy.

After what seemed like hours, the first course was finally served. They enjoyed their soup while carrying on conversations regarding the new plays at the theater. Julia thought back to Prince Randolph, wondering what a dinner with him would be like. She remembered the cream éclairs and the way he had wiped her chin. Tears threatened her eyes again, but she kept them at bay. Looking up, she saw her cousin staring at her. She realized she was lost in her thoughts again and hadn't heard a question.

Julia looked at the guests. "Forgive me. I didn't hear your question."

Sara saved her cousin. "Lord Jacob asked you if you were going to attend the premiere of *Romeo and Juliet* tomorrow evening. He wanted to know how many open seats they would have in their box." Julia looked at Lord Jacob across the table. She had not been aware of the premiere and realized that he might not know that she and the duke were no longer speaking.

The duke cleared his throat. "We have not decided on our attendance yet." He scowled at his brother, taking a drink of water.

Julia did not appreciate him answering for her. "Lord Jacob, if I decide to attend the theater tomorrow night, my uncle has a box, and I can use those seats. Please feel free to invite any guests you wish for your family box." There was no reaction from the duke—he refused to even look at her.

The footmen served more courses, and the conversation remained very casual. Julia mostly listened and only contributed to the conversation when she was asked a direct

question. Toward the end of the final course, Lord and Lady
Dancy had a brief disagreement regarding the napkin on
the floor and whom it belonged too. Lady Dancy accused
Lord Dancy of stealing hers and demanded he pick up the
one under the table. The footman offered to help, but Lord
Dancy refused. He stood up and bent over to pick up Lady
Dancy's napkin, and at that moment, his pants ripped at
the seams. He seemed not to notice and sat back down.

The rest of the table was in deep conversation, oblivious
to his pants. Julia's eyes swept across the table as she covered
her mouth with a napkin. She peered over at the duke, and
he too was holding back a smile.

He quickly reached for his glass and took a deep drink
of water. Julia could not take it any longer and started to
giggle. The duke finally looked at her for the first time all
night, and they both let out a laugh together as the rest of
the table looked at them questioning their merriment. Julia
quickly looked down at her meal to avoid the stern look
from her parents. The duke saved her and explained that he
had told her a jest. The rest of the table seemed to accept
that and went back to their conversations.

The duke leaned toward Julia's ear. "I hope his coat will
cover the damage."

Julia smiled at him, whispering near his ear, "Please stop,
Your Grace. My parents keep looking at me, telling me with
their expressions how very unladylike I am behaving." The
duke playfully winked at her and went back to his meal.

After supper, the men retired to the viscount's study to
have cigars and port while the ladies went into the drawing
room. Sara suggested they play whist when the men came
back inside. Julia couldn't help but suppress a grin every

time she glanced over at Mrs. Dancy as she thought about her husband's ripped pants. The laughing was good for her—it did make her feel better about the whole situation.

The men finally appeared, but only a few couples agreed to play the game. The earl and the viscount went to play cards with a few of the men in his study. The duke refused the men's offer to join them and agreed to be Julia's partner for whist. They played and laughed throughout the evening. She saw a different side of him and liked him more and more. But they lost both games to Sara and Lord Jason. The night wore on, and finally the games wrapped up. The duke bid Julia good night but did not attempt to make further conversation. Julia wished him a good night in return.

She went to her bedroom and fell on her bed. Relieved to be alone, her thoughts took her back over the day. Just as she slipped off her shoes, a knock came at the door. A little frustrated, she opened it and saw Sara standing in the doorway. Julia opened the door wider as Sara entered, walking to the wing chair. Julia sat on the end of the bed and looked at her.

Sara hesitated and wrung her hands. "Julia, I want to speak to you about why you were crying earlier today. Is there is anything I can do?"

Julia looked at her cousin and bit her bottom lip. "I believe I am a little melancholy, nothing more."

Sara raised her brow as if questioning her honesty but did not press her. They sat in silence for a few minutes as they listened to the wind howl outside of the window. Julia walked over to stare out the glass onto the London streets. Sara finally let out a breath. "Julia, I know you don't love the duke, but the two of you looked very content tonight. I couldn't help but think you may fancy him a little."

Julia smirked. "I must admit that his behavior tonight was tolerable."

Sara snorted. "He even caught a few glimpses from your father when he was laughing with you."

Julia laughed out loud. "I know. He does surprise me sometimes."

Sara laughed as well. "He must have forgotten he was a duke." They giggled, speaking about the play tomorrow night. Julia decided she might attend as the story of *Romeo and Juliet* was one of her favorites.

Chapter 14

THE NEXT NIGHT, THEY DRESSED in their finest for the theater. Julia knew that sometimes royalty attended premieres in the royal box, and she could not help but wonder if she would see Randolph again even though she was angry with him.

The theater was crowded, and she recognized a lot of the faces from the balls. Thinking over the previous night, she was a little surprised the duke had not invited her to attend with him. After they'd played whist, the tension had seemed to subside, and they'd gotten along well. Perhaps he did not like the theater or had other plans?

Julia's parents met some business associates as they made their way toward their box. She stood beside them, taking in the atmosphere. The walls were covered in red velvet wallpaper with hanging portraits of the playwrights and actors. Patrons nodded their greetings toward Julia's family, and she curtsied more times than she could remember. Feeling excited about being at the play and enjoying people-watching, she noticed the duke out of the corner of her eye escorting none other than Lady Janel. They were surrounded by their group of loyal companions that included Lady Sophia and his brother Lord Jacob.

They were walking their way toward her! She tried to dash behind her parents and hide—to no avail. Her father kept moving, giving away her folly. Looking for the ladies' drawing room, she thought about a quick exit. But she was too late. Lord Jacob made his way around a group of people to greet her. "Oh, you came, Lady Julia."

He took Julia's hand and kissed it. Julia's face lit up at his attention. "Thank you, Lord Jacob. It was a last-minute decision, and my uncle had some extra seats available."

Julia's parents exchanged pleasantries with him and turned to greet the duke and Lady Janel.

The duke turned to Julia and said, "Lady Julia, you are looking lovely as usual."

Lady Janel forced a smile at Julia's parents and turned to her. "It was so nice to see you the other day in the park, Lady Julia. We must have tea soon."

Julia's mother gave her a tight smile, noticing her attachment to the duke's arm. "Indeed." She hurriedly said their goodbyes for her family and turned to her daughter saying, "Julia, we must find our seats."

Julia curtsied to the group, turning to take her leave. Lord James stopped her with a grin, "Would you care to join us? I do believe we have an extra seat in our box."

Julia inwardly grinned at the look on Lady Janel's face but declined his offer. He smiled teasingly at her, giving her a wink as if knowing what she was thinking.

She caught up with her parents, and they walked around the crowds, finally arriving at their box. It didn't seem that her uncle and aunt had arrived yet. As they opened the door, Julia was eager to see their view of the stage. She moved to take a seat and noticed a box wrapped in gold paper resting on top one of the chairs. Her mother noticed it as well and picked up the box. It had a card attached to it that read "To Lady Julia." Her mother smiled, handing her the box telling her it might be from His Grace. Julia crinkled her nose, knowing how her mother exaggerated at times.

Julia unwrapped the paper as her cousin and Lord Jason entered their box. She slid the ribbon off to open the wrapping, feeling giddy with anticipation. The paper dropped, and pleasure turned into a scream when dead roses fell out of the box onto the floor. Dozens of spiders were crawling up her arms, and Julia cried out and threw the box away from her, swiping the spiders off her frantically. Lady Savory helped her daughter as the crowds looked up into the balcony, wondering what was amiss.

Lady Savory steered her out of their private box while the earl removed a yellow note that had fallen on the floor that read "SOON." He raised his brow in question at Julia, but she had no idea what it meant and was petrified. The blood rushed from her head, and feeling nauseous, she tried to hold herself together as everything suddenly went black.

Julia awoke with four guards surrounding her as the earl carried her in his arms. She was taken through the hall to the theater exit with her parents. The whole family was leaving as they were too upset to stay and their box needed to be cleaned of the spiders.

The earl was visibly shaken and walking out the doors when the duke and his brother came running toward Julia. The duke said, "What happened? I heard Lady Julia screaming from my box."

The earl told the duke there was another incident, and

Lord Jason filled him in on the rest of the story. The duke could not take his eyes off Julia and offered his assistance in carrying her. The earl held his daughter close but relented, handing Julia to him. She was too exhausted to argue. The earl asked the duke to help escort her home by riding in their family carriage for protection because he wanted to stay and speak to the investigator. He knew they would want to check out the theater box. The viscount had to stay too since it was his private box.

Lord Jason escorted Sara and her mother to their carriage while the duke asked his brother to give his regrets to Lady Janel. Julia shifted in the duke's arms but made no comments. She buried her face in his chest and for the first time noticed how nice he smelled. The duke told the earl he would wait for him at the viscount's town house and offered the use of his personal carriage to his use when he was done in the theater.

He carefully placed Julia in the carriage after the footman opened the doors. Lady Savory took her seat next to her daughter as she entered, and he sat on the other side of Julia. He rubbed her arms, keeping her close to him but trying to keep propriety at the same time.

The ride home was in silence, and the duke offered to carry Julia into the house, but she declined. He did escort her, and she leaned on him more than usual. He was very attentive, keeping her close but allowing her to set the terms. When they arrived inside, they went into the drawing room, and Lady Savory asked the guards to stay near whatever room her daughter was in. She could not take any chances with her only child. The duke sat beside

Julia, and Lady Savory called for some tea. She asked the duke to stay with Julia while she looked for her sister.

The duke caressed Julia's hand and kissed the inside of her wrist. She did not resist him, and she placed her head on his shoulder. She stared at the fireplace as their hands intertwined. The duke broke the silence. "Lady Julia, do you want to talk about it?" She shook her head and kept her eyes on the fireplace.

"No, I just want to forget about it." The duke didn't answer back and just squeezed her hand.

Julia was enjoying some quiet alone time with the duke. The door was slightly open for propriety. "I don't know who could be doing this to me. I have no enemies and thought in the beginning that it must be a jest. But now it has happened so many times that I just want to go home to America where I was safe. My parents won't listen to me, and I may never see Boston or my friends there again." She tried to stop the tears but couldn't, and the duke touched her face to wipe them away for her.

"Please don't cry. I will protect you. We will find out who is doing this. I will hire the best detectives in London."

She looked at him and smiled. "Thank you, Your Grace."

He took her hands and brought them to his mouth to kiss them. "I am at your service, my lady."

Lady Savory appeared at the door, and the duke let go of her hands. He stood as she entered the room. "Please sit, Your Grace. Do you need anything more than tea and biscuits to eat?"

The duke smiled at Lady Savory. "I am well, your ladyship. However, Julia should be taken to her room. She looks exhausted and probably needs a hot bath and rest. I will wait here for the earl to return."

Lady Savory nodded her head in agreement and escorted Julia up to her room. Julia accepted her mother's arm, walking to the doors of the drawing room. Before they walked through, she turned back and smiled at him.

The duke waited for the earl and viscount to return home, so he could volunteer his services. They came back to the residence about an hour later and asked him to accompany them to the study. The earl poured them all a drink. "Your Grace, I must thank you for your help tonight. I have never seen my daughter so distressed. As you can imagine, I am concerned for her safety."

"Indeed, my lord." The duke took a drink, looking out the window. "I wanted to invite your family a few days before the official house party begins. Perhaps a trip out of London will take Lady Julia out of danger. It could be good that she doesn't follow her usual schedule. This may cause her follower to back off. I thought it might be someone she knows because they knew where she would be tonight and whose box she would sit in."

The earl took a drink of his brandy. "Great idea, Your Grace. I had not thought of that, so I will notify my family in the morning. A few days out of London may be best. We should depart by lunchtime."

Chapter 15

JULIA WOKE THE NEXT MORNING to find Mary packing her bags. She sat up in bed and took a drink of her chocolate that Mary had left on the nightstand. "Oh good, you're awake, my lady." Mary smiled at her as she was pressing some of Julia's gowns.

Julia yawned. "Why are you getting such an early start?"

"Your father wished to depart early today for the duke's house party. He said to send you to him when you awoke. I think he is in your uncle's study. I overheard him telling your mother that they think it would be best for you if they leave town for a while to keep you safe."

Julia let out a sigh. "I assume they are trying to be cautious. I just don't like having to give in to fear. I find myself suspecting everyone in the house. These notes did not start until after we arrived, and I don't know whom I can trust. The only ones I know for sure I can trust are my parents and you." Mary smiled at her and helped her into her day dress. Julia went downstairs to talk to her father and break her fast.

Her father was in his study, and he motioned for her to enter. "You wanted to see me, Father?"

"Yes, my girl. I have a few precautions that we must discuss."

"What kind of precautions?"

"You are to have guards with you all day and night. Shallot suggested that you always stay at the house or on the grounds, and I agree. You are to always have an escort with you. I need your promise that you will comply with our wishes."

Julia nodded her head. "Of course, Father. I don't want you to worry about me. I am sure that everything will be fine." Julia stood and kissed her father's cheek. Her father reached for her hand, and Julia looked at him with surprise.

He looked at her with affection as he patted her hand. "Julia, I just want you to know that I only had your best interests in mind when I brought you to London. I hope you can be happy here."

A slow smile tugged at her lips. "I know, Father."

The earl looked at her for a few seconds more, then released her hand. "Very well, I will let you get back to your morning."

Julia looked back at him, slowly walking out of the study. Bewildered by his show of affection, she thought back to memories of her childhood. She had feared her father when she was younger because he was a source of authority and his loud, deep voice frightened her. Never a gentle man, he always expected his wishes to be honored. She didn't remember him teasing or playing with her as a child as many fathers did with their children. He had brought her occasional gifts when he traveled abroad but always made her mother give them to her. Julia sighed as she thought about her father's concern regarding the dead roses. He had carried her through the theater until the duke came for her. Her chest tightened as she thought about his regards for her well-being. Perhaps he did love her and just didn't know how to show it.

Julia was headed to the breakfast room when she noticed movement in the back parlor. She snuck around the corner and spotted Mary with Kashan. They were wrapped up in each other, and his hand was touching her cheek. Mary put her hands on his chest as they stared into each other's eyes. Kashan leaned down, whispering in her ear. Julia felt like she was intruding but couldn't bring herself to look away. Mary's face was glowing. She was so happy for her maid. Julia kept watching as Kashan embraced Mary's waist, pulling her in closer for a kiss, and Mary wrapped her hands around his neck.

Julia took a few steps to leave but couldn't help but look back one more time. She was curious about their attachment. Julia knew that Mary wanted to marry someday, and she hoped Mary would get that chance. Mary had met Kashan when they arrived in London because he worked for her uncle. The other footmen had given him a tough time at first because he was new, but Mary had introduced herself to him as she was new as well. Julia chuckled as she thought about them comforting each other. She finally broke her eyes away from their display of affection and went to find her mother to break her fast.

Julia's mother embraced her daughter as soon as she saw her. Julia could tell by her mother's swollen eyes that she had not gotten a lot of sleep. Her heart ached over her mother's worry. "Mother, I am fine. Please don't fret about it. Father has hired many extra guards for my protection. I promised not to leave the duke's grounds."

Her mother took a deep breath, shaking her head. "I

hope that is enough protection. Perhaps we should miss the season and just go to Savory."

Julia shook her head in frustration—she did not like the sound of that. If they skipped the season, they would not need to wait for the marriage, and Julia was not ready for that commitment. She knew she was losing time to come up with an alternative plan, but to skip the season would mean an ultimatum.

She looked at her mother. "I don't think we need to avoid the season. We are not even sure if I am in any true danger." Julia tried to shrug off the incident and took a bite of her eggs. Her mother's brow rose as she sipped her tea, shaking her head. The rest of the breakfast was in silence until she excused herself to get ready for the journey to the duke's home.

Chapter 16

JULIA WAS IN AWE OF the massive estate as her family's carriages full of people and trunks pulled up to the duke's residence. The rolling hills were a backdrop to the huge lake surrounding the main house. The duke had sent a missive to his staff earlier that morning announcing the earl and his family's early arrival. As they exited the carriage, the staff notified the earl that the duke would meet them later that evening as he had some business to complete in town first. Security was heightened as Julia's father had hired extra protection for their caravan to the estate, and the duke had also hired extra footmen to be stationed throughout the house. Julia was given strict instructions not to travel the grounds alone and to never be outside of the stone walls. She agreed, assuring everyone that she would comply with the security measures.

Julia was escorted to a beautiful room that overlooked the gardens. Royal-blue curtains fell gracefully from the windows onto navy-blue carpets covering the floor. The wooden columns on the four-poster bed were engraved with intricate flower designs, and the scent of flowers filled the room with fresh fragrances. Julia eyed a chaise lounge chair that was near the window—she knew it would serve as her escape. Mary joined her shortly afterward and told Julia about her room in the servants' quarters. It was huge as well and had vases of flowers. After the long trip, Julia was physically drained and decided to rest before dinner.

The duke had arrived shortly before dinner. He invited them into the parlor for some pre-dinner drinks. The earl spoke to the duke regarding the security layout of the house. The duke kept stealing glances at Julia as he spoke to her father. Julia hadn't been paying too much attention to their conversation, so when her father interrupted her woolgathering, asking her if she understood the security measures in place, Julia nodded her consent at him. Julia's mother paced the floor in front of the parlor window, visibly nervous regarding the conversation. When the footman announced dinner and the family made their way to the dining room, Julia felt relief at something else to think about.

They were served turtle soup for their first course. The second course offered roasted duck with potatoes. They topped it off with pudding for dessert, a favorite of Julia's. Her family kept the supper topics very light, sharing a few laughs. Julia's mother played the piano while the men drank their brandy. The official house party would begin in a few days, and Julia welcomed the sereneness now without the crowds of people. She was not looking forward to spending time with the duke's friends, especially Lady Janel. Julia's parents had some friends in the area and made plans to visit them for a luncheon in the morning during receiving hours. Julia declined to join them, and the duke told them he would see to her safety for the day.

The next morning, Julia woke late to break her fast. The duke was waiting for her in the breakfast room, reading. "Good morning, Lady Julia. You look well rested."

Julia smiled as she helped herself to some toast with jam. He put his book down and moved to sit in the chair next to her. "I have a surprise for you today. I thought we could do some riding. Would you like to change after you have eaten and meet me on the terrace, so we can walk to the stables?"

Julia nodded and quickly finished her food. She ran up the stairs to put on her riding clothes. She couldn't wait to feel free in the country without anyone watching her every move. Mary helped her with her riding habit.

She walked to the terrace and saw the duke waiting for her with a smile. He was holding a brown bag. Julia grinned taking his arm. "What's in the bag, Your Grace?"

The duke chuckled. "It's your surprise, and you must wait until we get inside the stables to open it."

The groom was waiting for them when they arrived in the stable. The duke dismissed him, nodding toward the door. The groom tipped his hat as he took his leave.

He guided Julia to a bench, asking her to sit for a moment before their ride. A little apprehensive at his change of behavior, she felt nervous. He sat beside her, holding the bag in his lap.

"Lady Julia, my gift to you is for one day only. You can never mention it to your parents, and this must be our secret." His normal stiffness had vanished, replaced by a playfulness she was beginning to like to see in him.

"A secret from my parents? A little brazen, Your Grace."

He rolled his eyes. "I am not always so proper, my lady." She giggled, and he placed the bag in her lap. "Open it."

Julia hesitated, unsure of what it could be. She slowly opened the bag to find brown paper wrapped around a soft object. Lifting it out of the bag, she took the paper away and gasped, looking quickly at the duke in surprise.

He smiled down at her, visibly enjoying her reaction,

She could not believe her eyes. It was a pair of woman trousers. *How shocking!* The "proper" duke had given her a scandalous gift that her mother would have surely swooned over.

"This is the best gift I have ever received. Thank you, Your Grace!" She laughed with exhilaration.

He smiled at her giddy reaction. "I hope I got the size correct."

She held them up, hugging the pants.

He pointed to an empty stall. "You can change in there. I will wait outside. There is a boys' button-up shirt inside the bag as well."

Julia looked around the stable. "What about the groomsmen?"

He smiled. "I gave them the morning off. I was well prepared, my lady."

Julia took her trousers to the stall. She was so thrilled to change that she had forgotten one important detail of the dress she was wearing—the dress was too tight for her to untie the back by herself. Mortified, she realized she had no choice but to ask the duke for his assistance. Peeking out of the stable door. "Um… Your Grace? We have a problem."

The duke moved to the door to see the problem.

She looked down, biting her bottom lip. "I can't untie my dress." She tried to hide her face as her cheeks flushed a light shade of pink in her embarrassment. Worse than that, she hadn't worn a corset today to go riding.

The duke felt warmth rise to his face at the thought of her undressing. He had forgotten about the most important part of a lady's wardrobe. He had not planned for this but was a little amused by the predicament. He felt he should volunteer to help but did not want to come across too untoward.

Looking around him, he realized no one was around. Stepping into the stable, he closed the door. "Did you need me to help you loosen the laces?"

She nodded, and lifting her hair, she turned around, giving him access to help remove her gown.

Holding his breath, he took in just how beautiful she was. He'd imagined this moment for many nights but had a different scenario in his head. His first observation was the very feminine curve of her neck. He had to hold himself back from kissing her. Her silky skin was enticing him as he tried to loosen the laces. The intoxicating smell of her lavender perfume clouded his senses, and he wanted to embrace her. Just one taste of her beauty was all he needed.

He knew he had to get a hold of himself. The laces were not as easy as they looked, and he struggled to keep his hands from shaking. He was finally able to loosen the first couple of holes, and the dress loosened down her back.

His voice cracked like a schoolboy's. "I think you will be able to get rest of it now," he whispered, leaning toward her ear unconsciously. He felt her shiver, but she quickly turned around, holding her dress as best she could.

"Thank you, Your Grace. I will be only a moment."

Looking at her in her state of undress, he had to force himself to leave the stable. She was a vision of complete beauty with her dress undone, showing more of her silky skin, and her hair was loose with pieces of hair coming out of the pins. She had a glowing complexion with feminine curves that would have brought any man to his knees. He ran his fingers through his hair before exiting the stable.

Julia appeared a few moments later with a huge smile on her face. The duke had to take in a deep breath as the pants accented her feminine curves in such a way that made him forget he was a gentleman. How much could a man take to be in her presence? He needed to remember who he was.

Julia felt so free and elated. She turned around to show him the pants. The duke complimented her on the look. He helped her mount, taking some extra time to make sure she was secure in the saddle. She took a deep breath and grabbed the reins. He quickly mounted his horse, and they rode into the country.

"Oh, Your Grace, I just feel so free. I want to ride all day."

The duke laughed in pleasure as he rode beside her. The landscape was incredible, and Julia admired her surroundings. One of the servants said a famous battle had been fought nearby, and her eyes filled with wonder. "Is it true that soldiers once fought on this land?"

He nodded. "Yes, my little brother and I used to look for arrows when we were kids."

"That is fascinating. What kind of artifacts do you think we could find?"

"Perhaps chain mail or maybe the famous Mackenzie sword used to defeat the Scots."

Julia's eyes widened. "Sword? Do you really think we could find it?"

He cracked a smile.

She realized he was teasing her. "Forgive me if I am driving you mad with all my questions." English history interested her, although she would never admit that to her father. He had "Americanized" her, as he called it, and thought she had no awareness of her heritage.

The duke chuckled as they approached a stream. "I enjoy your questions. I just wish I would have taken more time with my history studies at Oxford. Would you like to take a walk and let the horses have a drink?" It was then that she noticed he seemed more relaxed around her and not so uptight. His guard must have been down, and she liked this side of him.

She nodded, and he helped her dismount her horse. They led the horses to the stream, and she stopped to watch some fish jump. "I bet there is good fishing here."

"The best, my lady. We decided that the house party must have a fishing contest, and my mother is awarding prizes for first and second place." They walked along the stream, talking about the upcoming events for the party. Julia found herself looking forward to some of the games that his mother had planned. She felt at ease in the country, enjoying it more than London. The formalities were more relaxed, and she could be more herself.

"Lady Julia, I would enjoy nothing better than to spend the day with you, but your mother will be back in a few hours, and I don't want her to be cross with me. Before we head back, you must definitely hide the pants." He gave her a big smile that showed his perfect teeth.

"Of course, Your Grace. But I am keeping them." She wrinkled her nose in a playful display of feigned defiance.

He took her hand. "I like you in the pants." His gaze fell on her mouth, and she swallowed hard, bracing for his kiss. Slowly, she closed her eyes, feeling him brush her cheek with his lips. Letting the breath out she was holding, a little feeling of disappointment invaded her. Would his kisses move her like Randolph's did?

"You may keep them, my dear. Don't fret. I will find a way for you to ride in them again soon. Meanwhile, I will trust in your discretion. We were without a chaperone today, and you were dressed as a man." He winked at her, holding out his arm.

The time went by fast. They mounted their horses again to head back to the stables. Julia hurried, not wanting her parents to catch her wearing the trousers either. When they arrived back at the stables, she asked him to wait by the door to help her tie her dress. Looking a bit pale, the duke helped her button up her dress. Pulling the laces tighter, he purposely brushed his fingers across her back. The intimate touch caused her to shiver, and she quickly moved away as he finished. She hid the pants in the bag to conceal her gift, hoping to find a hiding place that her mother would not find.

He snickered as they climbed the hill back to the house. "I think I may have found your weakness, my lady. Most men buy women diamonds, but you prefer pants."

Julia let out a small laugh as she shook her head. Pausing halfway up the hill, she pulled her arm away. He gave her a puzzled look and asked, "What is amiss, Lady Julia?"

Julia looked up at him. "I have reconsidered your earlier request."

The duke tilted his head. "Which request would that be?"

She beamed at him. "I would like very much to call you Frank instead of Your Grace, and I wish you would call me Julia. I do consider you a friend."

He felt a tug within his chest because her request pleased him. He wanted to be more than her friend, but he felt it was a good start. "I oblige, Julia, and look forward to being your friend."

Chapter 17

THE NEXT DAY FLEW BY as the servants were busy preparing for the house party. There were many deliveries and extra staff to help with the growing list of people. The dowager duchess had originally said it was going to be a small house party, but more people were invited daily. The new expectations included over one hundred guests, causing them to open an additional wing to accommodate the extra people. It was sure to be a crush. They also secured two inns in the local town for guest overflow. Some of the neighbors offered their homes for accommodations if needed. The duke and his family were well respected, and many people volunteered to help.

Julia did not see much of the duke the next day as he had scheduled a lot of business meetings. He was also occupied with her father going over security details. House parties gave excuses for new business ventures—many aristocrats as well as business associates were attending, hoping to secure some new shipping deals. Julia found the conversations dull and kept away from the group. Most of the ladies sought other amusements while their husbands engaged in business matters.

Julia and Mary did their best to stay entertained as

Julia was not allowed outside of the gates. She was bored of playing chess and did not think she could look at another chessboard again. Most of the guests were due to arrive the next day, but a few close friends as well as the business associates would be at dinner tonight. Julia and Mary snuck into the library to get better views of the carriages approaching. They wanted to see when Lady Janel would arrive and who else was considered a close friend of the duke's family. His brother had arrived that morning and brought a school chum with him. Julia's aunt and uncle would arrive tomorrow with most of the other guests as her aunt had a previous engagement.

Julia took exceptional care with her appearance. Wanting to look older, she stayed away from pastels and wore a navy-blue gown with golden buttons. She knew there would be prominent members of the *ton* present as the dowager duchess was highly favored. She heard they were having music after the supper for entertainment and hoped for some dancing. Her melancholy had subsided since there had been no incidents during the last few days. The safety she'd found in the country was a breath of a fresh air. Feeling secure reminded her of her days on their farm outside of New York she'd visited as a child. Perhaps the perpetrator did not know she had escaped to the duke's estate? Would the investigators find who was responsible?

Looking back at her reflection, she paused to redden her cheeks with pinches. The pain women had to go through to look good always went unappreciated in her opinion. She wished that Sara were there, so she could accompany her when all the duke's friends arrived. She felt like a child having to be escorted by her parents.

A knock at the door pulled her from her thoughts. Her mother told her it was time.

The drawing room overflowed with guests who spilled out into the foyer. Julia did not recognize all of them as some people were local gentry familiar with the dowager from the country. Julia took a glass of lemonade from the footman, walking around the room greeting people with her mother.

Her mother became engaged in a conversion with an acquaintance when Julia turned around, eyeing Lord James and Lady Sophia approaching. "Good evening, Lady Julia. It's so lovely to see you again." James took her hand to kiss it.

She curtsied to them both. "It's nice to see you both again too."

"I hope you are feeling better. I know the duke was concerned for your health when he left the theater."

Julia did not want to give them too many details, and Lady Sophia looked uninterested in the conversation. In fact, she seemed distracted by looking around the room. Julia refocused her attention on him. "Oh, yes, Lord James. Thank you for your concern." The duke approached their small group then and welcomed them into his home.

He slipped his hand over Julia's arm. "If you will excuse us, I must steal Lady Julia. I have something to show her in the library."

They said their goodbyes, and she took his arm. As they were walking through the foyer, Lady Janel approached them. Julia took in her appearance, assessing the gold dress with a plunging neckline. Her assets were on display, and a bit of anger flooded Julia's chest. Holding her tongue, she held the duke's arm a little tighter.

Unphased by Julia's presence, Lady Janel lifted her hand, waving her fan. "There you are, Frank. I thought you might be hiding from me after leaving me stranded at the theater." She took his other arm and did not acknowledge Julia.

The duke grew tense, and Julia let go of his arm, refusing to fight over him. Lady Janel tilted her head toward Julia, "Oh, Lady Julia, how nice you could make it. I heard you were not feeling well. I am glad you could still come."

Julia smiled tightly and remained quiet. She took a sip of her lemonade, relieved as she saw Sara approaching. Julia embraced her, surprised that she had made it early. "I thought you were not coming until tomorrow."

Sara smiled. "Mother finished up her engagement early, and my parents decided to come instead of waiting an extra day."

Sara curtsied to the duke and acknowledged Lady Janel with a nod. Lady Janel smiled at Sara and turned to Julia.

"You must excuse us—my mother wants to see Frank. She has not forgotten that he owes her an apology for missing her party."

She pulled the duke with her as he looked back at Julia. She made eye contact with him, holding his stare as he mouthed the words, "Forgive me?" She nodded, locking Sara's arm with hers to take a turn around the room. She knew this was going to be a long week and didn't want to forget her manners the first night.

Chapter 18

THE FESTIVITIES WERE UNDERWAY, AND Julia was caught up in a game of charades with Sara and Lord Jason. Earlier in the day, she had met some of Lord Jason's friends, including his cousin Lord Bernard—a marquis who was *very* flirtatious. A handsome man if you liked his type. His dark hair curled at the ends, and he wore it unfashionably longer than society dictated. He had a bit of a rebel tendency that Julia admired. His large stature and demanding presence filled the room. Julia learned that his mother was from Scotland, and she had not met him before at any of the London's balls as he had been out of London at his mother's estate for the season. He had come to visit his cousin for the next month, so he'd obtained an invitation to the duke's house party. Julia found him very entertaining because he knew the best jests. However, she had to be careful as she did not want to encourage any romantic intentions toward him.

Lord Bernard asked Julia to partner together as they created a new game of couple charades. The couples had to act out an action, and the others had to guess. Julia chose the word "asylum," and they had to act it out. Lord Bernard whispered in Julia's ear, and she nodded her approval.

Trying not to laugh, she watched him mess up his hair with his hands, rubbing the strands until they stood straight up. He raised his eyebrows making odd faces, causing Julia to lose her breath from laughing so hard. She swung around to run from him as he pretended to chase her and plowed straight into the duke.

His face hardened as he balanced Julia with his arms.

She stumbled over her words. "Forgive me, Your Grace." The whole group stopped laughing, staring at him.

The duke observed all of them as he swept lint off his gloves. "Pardon me. I must take Lady Julia from you. I have a pressing matter to speak to her about."

Sara nodded her head, and the group sent her their regrets and told her they would see her later.

Julia took his arm as he escorted her to his study. The door was kept slightly open for propriety reasons. Taking a seat behind his desk, he paused to comment, "You appeared to be enjoying yourself."

"Indeed, Your Grace." Julia noticed his agitation but made no comment regarding it.

He sighed, tilting his head to the side. "I thought we were friendly terms now and calling each other by our given names?"

"Was there a matter you wanted to discuss with me, *Frank?*"

He studied her, fumbling with the button on his coat. "Yes, as a matter a fact, there was. I wanted to invite you to be my partner in the rowboat races tomorrow."

Julia brought her brows together, puzzled. She thought back to the pressing matter he had told the group and realized there was none. He was just jealous of the attention she was giving her new friends. She snorted, pushing aside the frustration of him interrupting her game of charades. "Partner?"

He raised his brow. "Yes, I need someone to help me win."

She lifted the corner of her mouth. "Hmm. How good are you at rowboats? You know I am competitive." Squinting her eyes, she gave him a serious look.

He tried to suppress a grin. "You know I don't like to lose, Julia."

She placed a finger on her chin. "Then it is settled. I will be your partner on one condition."

"What would that be?" he said, leaning back in his chair.

She smiled at him coyly. "You have to tell Lady Janel before the races."

He grunted. "Very well, it's a deal." He rose, walking around his desk to offer his arm. She took his arm, standing up as they entered the terrace and watched the crowds in the garden. The activity bustled around them as hordes of guests were arriving.

He stood gazing at the flurry. "Julia, this is going to be a busy week. I hope you can have a wonderful time and relax."

"Thank you, Frank. I hope you will not have concerns about me and enjoy your guests."

He raised his brow, and leaning toward her, he whispered, "You are my *special* guest, Julia. I will always have concerns over you."

She blushed, looking away.

"Well, my dear, it's time to ready ourselves for supper. May I escort you inside?" She tore her gaze from the crowds.

"As you wish." She took his arm, and he guided her toward the staircase.

The formal supper that evening was a grand event—every detail had been taken into consideration. The tables were set up in the formal dining room accompanied by trays of food that were full of delicacies. Julia chose to wear her pastel yellow gown with gold earbobs. Her mother had let her borrow a yellow-stone necklace, which highlighted her green eyes. Julia finished her look with long, white gloves and a spray of lavender perfume. She descended the staircase into the foyer.

The foyer was full of guests preparing for the dinner bell. Julia searched the room for a familiar face, hoping to see Sara. She finally found her cousin chatting with her parents, and Julia joined them for some drinks. Julia's uncle looked concerned, and he reminded Julia again of the safety precautions. Julia appreciated everyone looking out for her well-being, but she was feeling overwhelmed by all the attention. She was gracious to her uncle, agreeing to always be escorted on the grounds.

Julia took her leave to look for her father, but she was stopped by the duke's brother, Lord Jacob, who asked if she had an escort for supper. Julia shook her head, taking his arm. They entered the dining room together, and she sat at the head table with the duke's party. The duke glanced at her, smiling as she sat next to his brother. Julia enjoyed sitting by Lord Jacob because he reminded her of some of her friends that she had left back home. As a second son, he did not have the weight of nobility on his shoulders, allowing him to be freer with his relationships. On the other side of her was Captain Crawford, who was an old friend of the duke's. He was a jovial fellow—he must have been a few years older than the duke as his hair was showing signs of gray. He was very polite, sharing some war stories with Julia. She found him fascinating, asking many questions regarding the conditions during war. Lord Jacob also took part in the conversations, offering his questions as well.

Frank was mostly silent during dinner, making polite talk with his mother and her friends. Julia noticed Lady Janel shooting daggers at her from the table next to theirs. She decided to ignore her, instead focusing her attention on Captain Crawford. The dinner served seven courses, all delicious, but she was growing tired of eating. She looked forward to the activities after dinner as the dowager had arranged for music and singing.

After the music show, she spent most of the evening with Sara's friends, only occasionally seeing the duke. He was preoccupied most of the evening with some business associates that he had invited to the party. Most of the men excused themselves after the evening entertainment to retire to the card room. Julia's mother insisted that she excuse herself and get some rest. A card room was no place for a young lady.

Chapter 19

JULIA WOKE EARLY THE NEXT day to break her fast. She went downstairs and walked onto the terrace, where tables were set up with buffets. She took a plate, helping herself to some fruit and toast with tea. She spotted Lord Bernard and Lord Jason eating alone at a table. She looked around for her cousin or other female companionship, but Lord Jason waved her over to eat with them. Julia walked to the men as they stood up to greet her. She smiled as Lord Bernard held out a chair for her.

"You look well rested, my lady." He bowed to her. Julia thanked him for the chair. Lord Bernard grinned, taking his seat. "What plans do you have today?" he asked as he took a bite of his eggs.

Julia cleared her throat. "We have the rowboat races later, and they will be followed by a picnic. I was going to take a nature walk guided by Professor Donaldson this morning, who is a friend of the duke's. My maid is finishing up her morning chores to chaperone me."

Lord Jason stood up as Sara approached with her mother. Her mother greeted the group but decided to sit at a different table with some friends. Sara sat beside Julia. The four of them had a fun time and giggled over some of the other guests. One guest fought with some birds over his food, and unfortunately, the bird won the battle, claiming the bread as his prize. Julia enjoyed Lord Bernard's animated faces—it was hard to concentrate on eating. He'd missed his calling as an actor for the theater.

"What do you say that we partner up for the rowboat races?"

Julia lifted her chin, challenging him. "I don't know, Lord Bernard. I can be a fierce competitor."

He raised his brow. "Then we would make an excellent team, my lady."

Julia crinkled her nose, laughing. "I would, but I already promised His Grace."

Lord Jason and Lord Bernard looked at each other with raised eyebrows. Julia did not like their accusatory stares. "What?" she questioned them.

They both looked at each other again.

She protested. "Why those faces? Is it because of the duke?"

Lord Bernard moved his plate out of the way, looking directly at Julia. "What's the story with you and the duke?"

Sara choked on her juice. Lord Jason looked at her. "Are you okay?" Sara nodded.

She did not make eye contact with Lord Jason as she covered her mouth with her napkin.

They all looked at Julia. "I don't know what you mean. He is our host and asked me yesterday. I didn't think it would be polite to turn him down."

"Hmm," said Lord Bernard. "You don't seem like his usual type. That chit, Lady Janel, has her hooks set in him—she may not take kindly to you being his partner. If you need me to rescue you, then only say the word."

Julia laughed at him. "What type would that be?"

Lord Bernard squinted his eyes. "He is just so pompous. Always has a serious face. He looks bored most of the time. When he comes into a room, you know he is a duke, and he enjoys that."

Julia felt a little defensive over the duke. After all, they were friends. She shrugged her shoulders. "It's just that he is a lot older than us, and he probably doesn't appreciate our humor. He is a family friend of my father's, and he can be very kind."

Julia hoped that would end the conversation as she didn't want to speak too much of her obligations or association with Frank. They seemed to accept her response and started talking about horses and their newest purchases.

A few minutes later, the duke entered the terrace. Julia caught his eye almost immediately with her beautiful strawberry blond locks and womanly curves accentuated in her light-green gown. Not wanting to stare at her, he quickly turned away. She was with her friends, and he didn't want to interrupt. But they were distracting, cackling and being loud—it was almost rude. Trying to ignore them, he walked over to the buffet table and spoke to a few servants regarding the luncheon plans. All the while, his attention was distracted by the laughing of Julia's group. They were acting like school children! His gaze fell on Julia as she met his eyes with softness. She seemed at ease with her young friends. How could men that young be such an interest to her? He wondered if she would have preferred a man her own age as her immaturity did show at times. He stared at her, watching the wind blow her hair and admiring her natural beauty. Thoughts of her becoming his wife gave a tug at his heart. He turned away from the group to gather his thoughts as he saw Lord James approaching him.

"Frank, good to see you." Lord James patted him on the back. "Come join us at our table. We are sitting by the corner."

Frank paused as he saw Janel and Sophia looking at him expectantly. He did not want to appear to be with Lady Janel at the party, but he didn't know how to gracefully get out of the predicament, so he told Lord James he had made plans to break his fast with his mother in her private parlor and that he would see him later. The group looked disappointed as he made his way past the tables. On his way out, he stopped by Julia's table. "Good morning, ladies and gentlemen."

The group immediately lost their good humor and sat up properly. "Good morning, Your Grace," they said in unison. As soon as he was near the door, he could hear them all laughing again. He felt like he was a child trying not to look back at them.

Chapter 20

LATER IN THE AFTERNOON, JULIA joined her friends in the gardens as they all walked together to the lake. She had never been in a rowboat race before but was looking forward to it. Looking around for the duke, she found him speaking to his staff, making sure everything was coordinated. Many of the women were not going to participate, choosing to stand on the shore with their parasols, gossiping—a boring pastime to Julia, if anyone had asked her for her opinion. Sitting around looking pretty did not sound fun.

A few tents were set up with tables and chairs, and blankets were laid out under the trees. The dowager had announced that the teams must have one male and one female partner to make it fair. The men would do the rowing while the women sat in the front. Julia scanned the lake shore and noticed twelve boats set up with ropes pulled across. Many of the guests had started to make their couple teams, so she walked away from the group, trying to find the duke.

Walking around some trees, she spied him speaking to Lady Janel near the dock. From the look on her face, Julia could tell she was upset. She was waving her hands as she spoke while he was trying to calm her down. Lord Bernard come up behind her and, leaning down, he whispered near her ear, "I see that Lady Janel knows that you are his partner now." He started laughing as he walked away. Julia gave him a ferocious look although he spoke the truth. Not wanting to appear obvious, she walked away from her spying and went to find Sara—she needed an ally in her corner. Sara was partnered up with Lord Jason, and he was going over their strategy on how to balance the boat, so it could move the fastest.

The duke suddenly appeared at Julia's side and took her arm. "Are you ready?" Julia hesitated as she looked around for Lady Janel. Not able to see her, she accepted his arm, and they went to pick their boat.

Lady Sophia and Lord James followed along with the other couples to choose their boats. That left one empty boat that was not yet claimed. The dowager duchess made a final announcement to ask if anyone else wanted to participate.

Lord Bernard stepped forward. "I will humbly claim the last boat." He searched around the group tapping his chin. "Which lady would like to claim the winning prize with me?"

Silence hung over the crowd. After a few seconds, a sound beckoned from the middle of the crowd. It was a female voice, and people moved so she could walk to the front.

"I will." Lady Janel announced in front of the group. Her satisfactory smile did not go unnoticed by the others as she held her head high. "We will win together, Lord Bernard."

He smiled and took her arm. Looking back, he cocked

his brow at Julia and gathered his oars to compete. Julia covered her mouth, trying to hide her smile. This was going to be so much fun!

The couples climbed into their boats and waited for the signal to begin. The duke's immense size filled most of their boat, causing them to sit very close together. He was experienced using a rowboat, and when the race started, they quickly took the lead. Julia couldn't help herself—she cheered for Frank. Her heart warmed when she heard his laugh.

After more rowing, beads of sweat bubbled on his forehead. "Come on, Your Grace. We need to go faster. Sara and Lord Jason are catching up to us!"

He smiled, lifting his brow. "You may need to jump out. Your weight is slowing us down."

Her mouth fell open.

Laughter erupted. "I am only jesting. Now come on and lean forward. It will help us go faster."

Julia turned to watch Sara pass them. Looking back at the duke, she lifted her hand. "Come on! We need to catch up!"

The duke splashed her with the oar, and a little water to hit her in the face. She turned around, trying to be cross with him, but busted out laughing.

He cracked a smile. "Forgive me. You looked hot."

They giggled together until they heard a commotion.

They both turned toward the sound of two people arguing as Lady Janel took one of the oars, splashing water on Lord Bernard. She was yelling at him for going too slow and getting her wet. Lord Bernard jerked the oar away from her, causing the boat to rock. A look of rage fell over her face as she stood up to jerk the oar back and lost her balance. Julia grimaced as she watched Lady Janel fall into the lake.

Lord Bernard reached for her hand, pulling her back into the boat, and she screamed at him as he made their way to the bank. The dowager asked the servants to bring over a blanket for Lady Janel, and she wrapped it around her when they returned to the shore. She stomped off towards the house.

The commotion and their attention on Lord Bernard and Lady Janet had caused another couple to take the lead and win. Lady Julia did not care if they lost—she was exhausted from laughing so much. The duke took her hand and helped her out of the boat.

He bowed, "Thank you, my lady."

She curtsied. "Sorry we didn't win, Your Grace."

"Winning didn't matter. It was more fun watching you."

His compliment took her by surprise. Not knowing how to answer him, she didn't reply but instead allowed him to escort her to some blankets under the tree.

He stood for a moment quietly holding her arm, looking a little lost for words. "Would you like some lemonade?"

She nodded and watched him walk away.

In his absence, she joined Sara and Lord Jason. Lord Bernard joined them, dressed in some new clothes. They were laughing about the day when the duke approached with her lemonade. The men quieted, waiting for him to speak. He seemed uncomfortable but sat beside her. Surprised by his gesture, she sat closer to him, trying to include him in their conversation.

A few other young couples joined them as they spoke

about the competition and a possibility of a rematch before the party ended. Frank was out of his element, looking uneasy around the youthful group, but obviously trying to please Julia, he stayed.

After another hour, the picnic ended, and the duke escorted Julia back up the hill toward the house.

"This afternoon was the best I have had since I left America."

He pressed a kiss on her hand. "I enjoyed the day with you too. I will see you at dinner."

She smiled, watching him leave. On her way to her chamber, she spotted Mary in an empty hallway whispering to Kashan. Grinning to herself, she tiptoed past them, trying to go unnoticed. Along the way, she saw her security guard nod his head to her as she entered her room.

As she opened the door, a foul stench invaded her nostrils. She covered her nose, noticing clumps of mud trailing to her bed. Puzzled, her eyes spotted an object moving under her covers. She slowly stepped to her bed and gently pulled back her quilt, letting out a blood-curdling scream as she stumbled backward.

In her bed were many dead roses covered with rotting food and a live rat strapped to the bed. Julia backed away, falling onto a chair. The guard rushed into the room, shielding her as he tried to cover the rat. Julia was gasping for air, crying uncontrollably when her parents rushed into her room followed by other guests coming to see what had happened. Her mother rushed to Julia pulling her out of the room. The duke finally arrived followed by the dowager and Lady Janel. He rushed to her side, picking her up to carry her into the upstairs parlor so that she could lie on the settee.

"Are you well? What happened?" His eyes revealed his worry as his hand rubbed her arm.

Short gasps of air came out of her mouth as she tried to speak. "I… saw… mud…"

The duke raised his brow in disbelief. "Mud?"

She covered her face with her hands, sobbing loudly. They looked at each other, unsure of how much to press her. Uncovering her face, she sniffed loudly. "There were clumps of mud on my floor leading to the bed. Then I saw something move under the covers. Imagine my surprise when I lifted the quilt."

Lady Savory brought her hand to her chest. "I just can't speak of it."

Sara knelt in front of her. "You can sleep in my chamber. We can share my bed."

"Thank you, Sara. I will send Mary for my things."

Julia's father entered the room, visibly shaken. "Your Grace? May we speak privately?"

The duke looked up from the settee. "Of course." He turned back to Julia. "I will be back soon." He squeezed her hand.

He looked at some of the guards standing behind the guests. "Please post a guard outside of Miss Reynolds' bedchamber. We will cancel all activities and ask that guests remain in their rooms."

Julia widened her eyes. "Oh, please no. I don't want to ruin everyone's fun. Please don't cancel any activities. I will remain with my bodyguards always. I don't think anyone else is in danger."

The duke looked at her father. After a pause, he nodded. "I will send a missive to London and ask the authorities to join us as soon as possible."

Lady Savory stood. "Mary, we must start packing. I think it's best we return to London."

Julia lifted her hand in protest. "Mother, no. It will be the same in London. At least here, I have the fresh country air. I don't wish to leave yet."

Her father walked over to his wife and gave her comforting pat on the shoulder. "She is right. Until this culprit is found, she is not safe anywhere."

Lady Savory shivered. "I don't like it." He patted her hand and escorted her out of the parlor. "You need some rest, my dear."

Julia followed the guards to Sara's room. Both girls retired for the night.

Chapter 21

THE NEXT DAY, THE MEN went on a hunt, and the women took baskets of food to the families in the village. Julia couldn't leave due to her home restrictions, so she gave Mary the afternoon off to spend time with Kashan.

Bored to tears, Julia had the guard escort her to the library to find a book to read for the afternoon. He waited for her outside as she looked through the shelves. She told him she didn't want to spend all day in her room and would read on the settee in the library.

Slowly passing each book, she realized the duke had an interesting library—a little surprising for someone so conservative. Laughing to herself, she came across some romance novels. Imagine that! Reading the first few pages, she heard some scratching.

Looking around the room, she realized it was coming from the wall. Probably rats! She shivered, thinking about her encounter last night, but continued to read until she heard a knock coming from the same wall. Thinking it might be a game, she walked to the wall and knocked back.

Putting her ear up to it to listen, a hand covered her mouth with a cloth from behind, and she began to panic.

Her screams were muffled, and no one could hear her. Attempting to take deeper breaths, she struggled and kicked against the force holding her back. Despite all her effort, she could feel herself losing consciousness. Her eyes were so heavy, and her arms were numb. She had no strength to resist falling into the darkness.

Julia's vision was blurry when she awoke on a bed. Feeling out of sorts, she tried to focus on getting her bearings, but her heart was racing inside her chest from being so frightened. Her arms couldn't move and resisted each time she lifted them, and after a few seconds, she realized they were tied. Struggling to get them loose, she twisted and turned, feeling the burn of the ropes against her skin. *Where was she?* Frantic with worry, she tried to focus on her surroundings, but with her head pounding, she felt dizzy. After several seconds of struggling, she made herself rest and took quick breaths to calm down. Finally, her eyes landed on some shadows, and she deciphered it was a chair in front of her. An empty chair with old stains on it. Eyeing the rest of the room, she noticed it was sparse with only a small table in the corner. The air was damp, and she shivered from the chill.

She could hear faint movements coming closer. The door creaked open, and she quickly closed her eyes again to feign sleep. She heard shoes scrape against the floor and smelled smoke from a freshly lit candle. There was a musky smell coming from the person who was moving around the room, but she didn't recognize the scent. She felt the stranger touch her face and shake her. Julia pretended to sleep, hoping the stranger would leave soon so she could figure her way out of there.

Julia heard the scraping of a chair being pulled out from the table and placed closer to her. "I know you're awake, Julia. Open your eyes."

She knew that voice but couldn't place it. Keeping her eyes closed, the stranger moved even closer and pulled her hair hard, and she couldn't help but let out a moan of pain. Unable to keep her eyes shut anymore, she opened them. The vision before her was blurry as she focused her eyes, finally recognizing him.

"Jasper? Is that you?" Julia was shocked! She could not put the puzzle together. Why was he there? Why was he trying to hurt her?

"Hello, love. Welcome back to the land of the living." He smiled and sat back down in the chair.

"What is going on here, Jasper? I don't understand why you are here."

"Come on, Jules. You know exactly why I am here." He laughed and blew her a kiss.

"I am sure that I don't."

"I am here to make you pay for what you did to me, you little wench." He scowled at her.

Julia looked up at him, shaking her head. "I don't understand, Jasper."

"Stop playing innocent, Jules. I am not buying it anymore. I courted you for weeks and treated you like a princess." Jasper stood up and punched the table.

Julia gasped in surprise.

Jasper continued, "I offered your father a good home for you. I would have been a good husband to you. All my friends were convinced that we would be married. I even told my parents, and they were very happy for us."

He was silent for a minute and stared at her. Walking toward the window, he looked outside. "You can imagine my humiliation when I was refused and told you were already engaged." Turning around, the lines in his brow creased with murderous rage.

"My father gave me no choice, Jasper. I am only a woman. I am not allowed to make my own decisions. I am innocent," Julia tried to plead with him.

Jasper glared at her with disgust, "Nice try, my lady. You knew the whole time we could not be together, and you led me on. You probably watched as our friends whispered behind my back, laughing at me. I stopped receiving invitations after you left. You ruined me! That is why I sent you the dead roses. You killed my love for you, and now you must pay." He pointed his finger at her. "You will regret the day you crossed me, Jules."

"I did not know, Jasper. You have to believe me." Julia started crying.

"You are so pathetic. I have seen you at work. I followed you for weeks and know about your indiscretions with the prince. Does your betrothed know? How many other men were you seeing in Boston? I bet you have many that were left humiliated after making an offer for you. You disgust me."

Turning around, he came closer to her and rubbed his thumb over her chin. "You will give me a wedding night, Jules. I may not love you anymore, but I will take what belongs to me. I earned it." He kept touching her face, and she jerked her head out his grip.

"I can't marry you, Jasper. It would never work between us—my father would never approve."

"Marry you?" Jasper started laughing. "I don't want to marry you. Oh no, Jules... I want to ruin you. That is much worse."

He ran his index finger down her arm. "I will not kill you, Jules. I will take my time and go very slowly. I will take your innocence and leave you humiliated. Then no man will touch you again. Your reputation will leave you few choices." He laughed, reaching for her, as she kicked him, struggling to untie her hands.

He slapped her, and she fell back onto the bed. "You had better be nice, or I won't be so gentle with you."

Jasper walked back to the window. He alternated between looking outside and at his timepiece. Julia wondered if he was waiting for someone, but that thought was disturbing. He kicked over the chair and threw it across the room.

"It's your fault we are losing daylight. Little Miss Princess had to sleep in a different chamber last night. This could have been over by now!"

Julia kept quiet, trying not to make eye contact with him or engage in any conversation. It was important that she try to keep her wits about her. After a few moments of hearing him pace across the chamber, she could have sworn she heard dogs barking outside. The men had gone hunting, and she could hear the dogs chasing their prey. They were close by! Tugging at her binds, she tried to loosen the rope around her hands and realized that her feet were not tied at all. She could try to kick him if she had to, but she wasn't sure if she could run fast enough.

Jasper let out a sigh and left her alone in the room. Straining her ears, she could hear him going down the stairs. Desperately, she looked around the room, trying to find a way out. Julia pushed and pulled and with all her strength but ended up in tears because she could not find a way to get loose.

The hunting party made their way back to the house to freshen up. The ladies were still in the village shopping after having delivered the baskets. Frank and Lord James entered his study to smoke pipes.

Julia's father barged in a few minutes later out of breath. "Pardon me, Your Grace. Have you seen my daughter?"

The duke's smile faded. "I have not. Is she not with the guards?"

"No, and no one has seen her. Mr. Maxwell said she went to the library, but there was a misunderstanding and they thought she was with different guards. She has been missing for hours."

The duke's heart plummeted at the thought of her missing. "Guards!" The duke yelled as many men entered the study.

"I want every man combing the estate. Search every inch, and do not return until you find her!"

"Yes, Your Grace." The men said and unison as they ran out and barked orders to all the men standing around.

Frank excused himself to assist the earl. The group called for Julia's maid, and Mary showed up to answer their summons. Frank addressed her directly. "Where is your lady?"

Mary looked confused. "Lady Julia gave me the

morning off. She mentioned that she may go to the library in the afternoon."

The men looked at each other and ran out of the study and into Sara and Lady Savory. "What's amiss?" Lady Savory asked.

Julia's father looked pale. "Is Julia by chance with you?"

"No, she stayed behind to rest. Why are you asking me this? Is she not here?" Lady Savory grabbed her chest as if in pain. She ran upstairs to Julia's room and then to Sara's. The whole party was screaming her name.

Frank ran into the library and yelled for the earl. He pointed to the ground, showing overturned books and a bracelet. A pounding sound came from under the desk, and the men moved the desk away from the wall to find a guard tied up with a gag in his mouth.

The duke reached out, taking the gag out of his mouth. "Where is she?"

The guard shook his head. "I heard a struggle and came into the library. Then everything went black. When I woke, I was tied and gagged under the desk."

The duke ran his fingers aggressively through his hair. "I will leave at once and search around the estate."

A burly guard ran through the library doors. "We have the neighbor's hunting dogs. We need a dress of Lady Julia's that has not been cleaned to give the dogs her scent."

"I will get it." Lady Savory ran out of the room looking for Mary.

Frank hurried through the estate, finding no trace of her. The house was chaotic with guests, servants, and guards looking for Julia. The men showed up with the hunting dogs, and the duke followed them. The dogs picked up her scent and led the search party deeper into the woods.

Chapter 22

J ULIA DIDN'T REALIZE THAT JASPER had a partner in her kidnapping until she heard him finally show up with the pistol that Jasper had asked for. Jasper paid him for his assistance, and then she heard him saying he was leaving town because the duke's house was forming search parties with hunting dogs and he was frightened of getting caught. Julia listened carefully and recognized his voice, which grew louder as Jasper voiced his agitation.

"It's not time to leave yet! I will need your help in getting her prepared. Your job is not over, and you will not receive full payment until it is." The door opened, and she saw Jasper reach to grab the bag of coins from his partner. The partner grabbed the coins back, and they fell to the floor. The men shoved each other and punched each other. When the man punched Jasper and they crashed through the table, she gasped in recognition. It was Kashan, the footman Mary was seeing.

Her mouth hung open as she watched them fighting on the ground. She couldn't believe that he was helping Jasper. Julia knew Mary would be horrified when she found out.

Jasper pushed him into the wall, and Kashan lost his footing and slid to the floor. Julia yelled at him, "How could you do this to Mary?"

Kashan wiped the blood from his mouth, looked at Julia, and grinned, "It's business and nothing more, my lady."

He got up and lunged at Jasper again, taking him across the room and hitting the other wall. Julia closed her eyes as she realized his ruse. He must have gotten close to Mary to hurt her. Julia screamed as the men crashed into the window before tumbling onto the floor again. She finally pulled hard enough to get the ropes loose from the bed. With one hard push, she fell onto the floor. A knife had fallen out of Kashan's pocket and was swept toward the bed. Julia touched it with her foot and managed to pull it up with her tied hands. She quickly worked on cutting the ties while the men continued to roll on the floor, grabbing each other in a fight to the death. Julia did not wait or look behind her.

She ran.

Bolting through the bedroom door, she jumped down the stairs. The front door was locked, and she pulled frantically at it, beating against it, trying to unhook the latch that was stuck. She kept pulling on it until she felt the latch break. Hearing footsteps behind her, she ran as fast as possible. She didn't look back but ran, screaming at the top of her lungs. She lost her sense of direction, taking off with pure adrenaline through the woods.

The sound of dogs barking could be heard in the distance, and she knew they were getting closer. Running as hard as she could, she choked while fighting back tears. A rip of her gown jerked her backward, and a hand grabbed her shoulder. The force pulled her down, knocking the wind out of her as she hit the ground.

She tried to scream as loud as she could before a hand covered her mouth. Her captor held her down to the ground, and she looked up to see Jasper's face with bloodstains across his cheeks. She could smell the stench of body odor as she struggled with him. She didn't know what had happened to Kashan and quickly looked around to see if he was helping Jasper. She tried to push him off her, but he slapped her again, ripping at her clothes. The sting from the hit caused throbbing in her ears. She kicked him in his manhood and attempted to run again, but he seized her foot to pull her back. Julia clawed at the ground as he dragged her back to him and felt a rock under her hand. She picked up the rock and raised it, hitting him on his head. He screamed out, touching his head, but continued to hold her down with his body.

"You're going to pay for that, you little wench!"

Julia screamed again as she heard a commotion. The pressure of Jasper on top of her was relieved as someone knocked him over. Julia frantically tried to pull her skirt down as someone ran past her. There was suddenly a crowd of people staring down at her as dogs were circling her. She recognized Frank as he attacked Jasper with several punches and many of the men took over tying him up.

Frank looked back, reaching for Julia as she choked back tears, trembling. "I have you." She heard his words of comfort and fell limp in his arms.

With a shaky voice, she stammered. "Please, there is a footman. Kashan... he is in the hunting lodge. He helped him take me."

A group of men looked at each other and ran toward the lodge.

Frank held her tight. "It's over, Julia."

One of the estate workers came to the couple. "Please take my horse, Your Grace."

The duke lifted her onto the saddle and slid behind her, carefully holding her in his arms. When they reached the house, he grabbed a blanket and carried her to the family's private parlor. Julia's mother rushed to her side, but the duke did not let go of her.

"Let's give her some privacy." He looked at the housekeeper. "Please make sure she has no visitors. Only her parents."

The housekeeper nodded. "Of course, Your Grace. I will notify the guards and staff."

Julia leaned against the settee as her mother stroked her back. "I just need a moment before I can talk about it." The earl stood in the doorway, unable to speak, watching his daughter.

Lady Savory's eyes filled with tears. "Of course, my dear. Your father has already sent for the investigator."

After an hour, Julia's maid was allowed into the parlor, and the duke asked her to prepare a bath for Julia. He ordered a light meal and some tea for her too.

Mary escorted her to a private bedroom that the dowager had assigned in the family's private quarters. They wanted Julia to have as much privacy as possible. The water was steaming and ready when they arrived.

Mary's hands were shaking. "My lady, I have been so worried. Thank God you are okay. I can't believe it was Jasper."

Julia did not know how to tell Mary that the man

she claimed to love had also been helping her captor. She trembled. "He was completely mad."

Julia stepped into the warm steamy water, and her wrists stung as they hit the water. She rubbed the red marks from the ropes. Feeling dirty, she wanted as much soap as possible to clean off the grime that enveloped her body. Wincing with pain near her eye, she knew it was becoming bruised where one of his punches had landed. After Mary washed her hair, Julia reached for the towel and wrapped it around her. She walked to the bed to sit down. Mary took another towel, trying to dry Julia's hair, but Julia reached for her hand. "Mary, I need to speak to you."

Mary looked at her as fresh tears formed in Julia's eyes. Taking a deep breath, she tried to compose herself. "I have something to tell you."

Puzzled, she tilted her head. "Did he *touch* you—in that way?"

Julia swallowed hard. "No, it's not about me. Jasper was not alone…" She took another deep breath and bit her bottom lip. "It was Kashan. He was helping him."

Mary gasped, the blood draining from her face. "No!" she shouted, shaking her head back and forth.

Julia started crying. "Mary, I am so sorry. He was helping Jasper, and I saw him with my own eyes."

Mary's tears fell against her cheeks. Covering her eyes, she took a moment, unable to speak. A few shaky breaths later, she choked out her words. "I am so sorry, my lady. I just don't understand. How could he do this? He said he loved me." Mary clutched her stomach, rocking herself. "How could he hurt you? You mean more to me than anyone. I should have protected you."

Julia wiped a tear from her face. "No, Mary. You didn't know. He was working for Jasper, and he fed him all the information he needed. He was also the one helping Jasper with the dead roses. He knew everywhere that I would be."

Mary hugged herself, turning back around. She was breathing hard as she walked over and embraced Julia's hand. "I am so angry that I trusted him and thought he loved me. He listened to my secrets and dreams and used them against me. He was only pretending to love me."

Julia squeezed her hand. "I am sorry, Mary. He didn't deserve your love." They hugged and held each other tightly.

Frank stood to greet Julia as she appeared in the parlor. He escorted her to his study, where the investigator was with a constable. Julia's parents embraced her, and they all sat around the duke's desk.

The investigator looked at Julia with gentleness. "Do you feel comfortable speaking about it?"

"Yes, sir, I do." Peeking at her parents, she turned back to the investigator. "I went to retrieve a book from the library and heard a noise. When I investigated the noise, I felt someone grab me and place a wet cloth over my mouth before I blacked out. I woke up in a room that I did not recognize and felt dizzy, trying to focus on my surroundings. My hands were tied to a bed, and I struggled but could not move." She closed her eyes. "I was so frightened."

The earl shifted during her questioning and rushed over and put his hand on her shoulder. "That is enough. This is too difficult."

She patted her father's hand on her shoulder. "No, Father. I need to speak about it."

Julia took a breath. "I did not know who my captor was at first. I heard him moving around the room, so I shut my eyes to feign sleep. He struck me and told me to get up." Julia covered her face, letting out a cry.

Frank rushed to her and took her hand. He looked up at the investigator. "She needs to rest."

"No," Julia said as she tried to steady her breathing. "I wish to finish my story."

Frank let go of her hand and stood beside the earl. Lady Savory took her daughter's hand to hold. Julia continued. "It was then that I recognized him as a boy that I was acquainted with in Boston. He had asked my father for my hand in marriage, and my father refused." The earl huffed in annoyance. He was visibly angry and upset at the same time.

She looked at her father. "Father, it's not your fault. He thought I had ruined him on purpose by declining his offer. He said that I caused him humiliation and I was going to pay with my virtue, so I would be ruined too."

Lady Savory gasped and rubbed Julia's arm in comfort as Frank started pacing back and forth with his fist clenched at his side. Julia quickly tried to calm the room down. "He didn't get a chance to touch me in such a way."

Julia rubbed her temples for a moment and then continued, "Jasper had help from a footman who was courting my maid Mary. It was the perfect way to get close to me." She looked around at everyone, watching them hang on to her words. "I saw them fighting with a knife. It was kicked near me, and I used it to cut the rope around my hands, and I ran. I could hear them coming after me, but I ran as fast as I could until he caught me and threw me to the ground."

The room stared at her in silence as they waited for her next words.

"What happened to Kashan?"

The investigator gave her parents a look, and the earl nodded his head. Then the investigator gently leaned over. "My lady, Kashan has been killed by Jasper."

Her eyes widened. "Oh no! What will happen to Jasper?"

"He will be tried and probably hanged for murder and kidnaping."

Julia looked down as a tear dropped from her eye. "It was all a misunderstanding, and now people's lives are over. It's my fault."

The investigator stood. "No, my lady. Jasper was disturbed, and Kashan was greedy. None of that is your fault."

"I need to be alone. If you will all excuse me." She couldn't help but feel guilty although she knew there was nothing she could have done differently.

"Of course, my lady. We will finish up with your father."

"I will escort you." The duke held out his elbow and escorted her back to the family parlor.

When they reached the parlor, they were alone, and the duke took both of Julia's hands, gazing into her eyes. He hugged her then. There were no words spoken. He just held her as tears streamed down her face. He gave her his handkerchief, and she smiled as she accepted it. "I am here for you anytime you may need me."

She looked at him. "I don't know how to thank you."

The duke rubbed her shoulders, and Julia thought he may kiss her, but he pulled back.

He took a breath. "I will let you know someday." He bowed and left as Mary came into the parlor.

The next day, Julia woke up early. The dowager came to check on her, and Julia appreciated her concern.

"I think it's best we cancel the ball given the recent events. It will give everyone the chance to depart early."

"Your Grace, if it's acceptable to you, I would like to have the ball and forget about the incident. Not having the ball would end the house party on such a sour note, and the guests may forget what a wonderful time they had. I think the ball should go on."

The dowager reached for her hand and patted it. "As you wish, my dear. We will have the ball."

Julia smiled. "Thank you. That would please me."

The dowager smirked. "Well then, if you will excuse me, I must notify the staff."

Julia left and tried to find Sara. She was downstairs and embraced Julia when she saw her. "I was so worried. They would not let me see you."

Julia rubbed her shoulder. "I am well."

They were soon joined by Lord Jason and Lord Bernard. She smiled at both and thanked all of them again. "Please, everyone, I can't bear to keep speaking about the attack yesterday. Can we please just focus on the day's events?"

Lord Jason smiled. "Of course. They are playing pall-mall in an hour. Do you want to join us?"

She nodded but noticed a small tear on the sleeve of

her dress. "I will meet you there shortly. I need to change my dress."

Their eyes fell on the tear, and Lord Bernard laughed.

When Julia reached her bedroom, she saw Mary crying on her bed. Rushing over, she put her hand on Mary's shoulder. Mary sat up quickly. "Forgive me. I thought you were playing games."

Julia reached over and hugged her. She knew this could not be easy.

"I have a tear." A quick giggle escaped her lips. "I feel so clumsy." Mary gave her a guarded grin, and Julia wished she could take her pain away. Mary had dreams of owning her own cottage someday and being a wife. Julia wanted this for her as well and would try to find a way to help her.

Mary wiped her face. "I don't wish to speak about it anymore. You caught me in a moment of weakness. Come, let's get you changed."

Julia hesitated but complied with her wishes. They picked out a rust-colored dress, and she laced it up in the back for Julia. Julia turned around and rubbed Mary's shoulders to comfort her friend. "Would you prefer to leave the house party? I could ask my father."

Mary refused and began straightening up Julia's room. "I will be well. Don't fret about me. I will see you later and help you prepare for the ball."

Julia reluctantly said goodbye and headed for the south lawn.

The dowager duchess called for partners to compete, and Julia had promised Lord Bernard that she would be his partner as she knew the duke was away for the day meeting with his business associates. The game was fun, and it attracted many observers. Lord James and Lady Janel were also partners, and Lady Sophia sat and watched. Julia imagined that Lady Janel had bullied her into not playing. Lady Sophia seemed soft-spoken and looked to Janel to tell her what to do. Studying her features, she noticed she wore her hair parted down the middle and swept back in a bun. Conservative for London standards, no tendrils and no braids. She was very classical looking and reminded Julia of a porcelain doll. A bit older at around twenty-five. Rumors were that she had been unsuccessful in her previous seasons, but her father had recently come into some money, causing her to be back on the marriage mart. If a woman had a nice dowry, then her marriage prospects became more appealing. Looking at Lord James, she'd heard he was the second son to an earl and probably needed to marry money. He had gone to school with the duke at Eton, and they had remained friends. She wondered if they would make a match or if their closeness was due to Lord James's infatuation with Lady Janel. Julia could not figure out the triangle as Lord James often accompanied Lady Sophia, but his eyes were always on Lady Janel. Julia thought back to the duke and wondered about his feelings for Lady Janel. He allowed her to flirt with him yet never acknowledged anything more than friendship. As far as Julia knew, they had not courted, but the scandal sheets spoke of them as a couple. Lady Janel was around twenty-two and would be officially on the shelf within a year or two. She may have been getting desperate for a match soon, and Julia thought she would keep her eyes wide open to make sure nothing got by her. Julia's thoughts were interrupted by Lord Bernard.

"Stop woolgathering! I need you to focus." He bent down and whispered, "Don't overhit the ball and have to chase it. It's better to hit softly."

Julia nodded as he handed her a mallet. "Don't worry. I don't plan to lose." He rolled his eyes as they joined the others. Bernard had requested to take their turn last, so they could observe the other players. She laughed at the seriousness of his expression.

The game was well advanced when Julia missed her mark. Biting her bottom lip to help her concentrate, she tried unsuccessfully to get the ball back on the playing field. At the third try, she finally got it back onto the field. Watching the competition intensify, she grinned when Lady Janel missed her ball. Holding back a laugh with a ladylike cough, she noticed Lord Bernard watching her with a raised eyebrow. Julia looked away, trying not to smile. He then took his turn, and she heard a splash as his ball went into the pond. Julia was laughing so hard that she bent over to hold her stomach. He shrugged his shoulders and handed his mallet to her. They had to officially forfeit the competition.

They walked together down the hill and went to cheer on Sara and Lord Jason. Sara was very good and had played many times before at her grandmother's estate. They easily won the competition, and Julia hugged her as they were announced the winners. The dowager duchess gave them both a ribbon and told the guests there was tea available on the terrace.

Julia and her friends took some biscuits and tea and

found some shade to sit down under. They were talking about the day's events and having an enjoyable time when Lord James approached their table and congratulated Lord Jason. Lady Sophia and Lady Janel glared at the group as they made their way past them. Julia smirked, looking at Sara's face, and she rolled her eyes. "She is just jealous, and I would pay her no mind."

"I feel sorry for her because she doesn't know how to enjoy herself."

Lord Bernard laughed and looked at Julia. "I don't think that it is the problem. I think she would have enjoyed herself plenty if you were not here." Julia pretended not to understand and shrugged her shoulders.

Lord Jason looked at his cousin. "Julia, what is between you two? The duke follows you around, and you claim you are just friends. Lady Janel tries to insert herself at every chance she can with him. Do you think he will make an offer?"

Sara paused and tried to help. "Come on, Jason. The season is not over yet. Who knows if the duke will make an offer to anyone? According to the paper, he has been linked to many different women."

Lord Bernard looked at Julia for a reaction. "So, tell us, Julia. Are *you* going to marry this season?"

Julia laughed. "After the last few days, I think I will take a break from the opposite sex." They all laughed and let the conversation go on to different subjects. She then excused herself, so she could rest before the ball.

Julia rested inside her chamber. It was the first time she had been completely alone since the incident. Sitting up in her bed, tears blurred her eyes. The thoughts played over in her mind of what could have happened if she had not run. Would she be ruined? Would the duke still want to marry her? The memories of his fury at Jasper made her tremble. Her attraction to him was growing, and she didn't know how to feel. Her heart still ached for Randolph even though his intentions were misplaced. She was confused and felt her eyes grow heavy. Lying back on the bed, she fell into a deep sleep.

She woke a few hours later feeling refreshed. Excited for the ball, she hopped out of bed, looking for the perfect dress, finally deciding on a light-green one that matched her eyes. Her mother had lent her an emerald necklace that made the dress shine, and sparkles showed in the dress as she walked. Mary fixed her hair in a style that allowed part of her hair down, showing off cascades of curls. The rest of her hair was braided and twirled around the top of her head. She used some perfume that had been a gift from her father and smelled like fresh flowers. Mary found a looking glass for Julia and told her how beautiful she appeared. Julia smiled and told Mary to take the rest of the night off.

Julia waited for her parents to escort her to the ball. The dowager duchess had invited many of the local gentry from the county, and Julia was more relaxed than at the London balls as it was a less formal atmosphere.

Julia could hear the crowds of people laughing and talking while complimenting each other on their latest attire. Her parents soon ran into Julia's uncle, and she took Sara's arm as they made their way around the room. Sara looked very beautiful in her blue gown and white gloves. Her hair was up off her shoulders with a few curls hanging down. They giggled as they took in all the people and beautiful decorations. Julia realized they did not have dance cards available and was happy not to have such obligations.

The duke approached Julia, and Sara curtsied and prepared to leave to speak with Lord Jason. Julia gave her the side-eye stare as she knew Sara was trying to leave them alone.

Julia curtsied to him. "Your Grace." He smiled down at her.

"You're breathtaking, my lady." She took his extended arm, and they went to the terrace. He stopped and offered her a seat on the bench.

He looked at her with concern. "Are you well?"

She nodded her head and looked at the crowd.

He whispered to her, "I had thoughts of your welfare all day."

Julia looked back up at him, noticing how handsome he was. His eyes were a green with specks of blue. His hair had a slight curl on the ends, accenting his high cheekbones. Thinking back to when she first met him, she realized she'd tried so hard to hate him. But now the hate had dissolved to affection.

The duke stared back and rubbed her hands. "May I have a waltz later?"

A smile lit up her face. "Of course, I shall look forward to it."

He leaned over and whispered, "Hmm. I may request all the dances to be a waltz, and then you would be forced to dance with me all night."

She looked coyly at him with a flirtatious grin. He escorted her back to her parents, then bowed to take his leave.

Julia danced country dances with Lord Bernard and a few others. She shared the waltz with the duke and the supper dance with one of his business associates. The duke looked helplessly to her when Lady Janel claimed him for the supper dance. She gave him no chance to refuse her. Julia smiled and looked away.

Julia joined her group of friends for supper, and the duke joined his group at a different table with Lady Janel. Julia felt a little empty as she viewed the couple sitting together, looking very cozy. Lady Janel kept laughing, and it irritated her. They seemed engaged in a close conversation with Lady Sophia and Lord James. A few older lords met with them and joined their group. Julia couldn't take her eyes off them as they all conversed like old friends. The duke seemed very comfortable, and a twinge of jealousy coursed through her. Quickly dismissing the feeling, she looked away to see Lord Bernard complaining about one of his dance partners who had stepped on his foot. Lord Jason was laughing at him as he stroked his foot with a frown. Julia excused herself and told them she was ready to retire for the evening. The men stood as she left, and Sara offered to escort her. Holding out her hand, she told Sara she could find her own way back to her room.

Julia went to her parents' table to bid them good night, and she made her exit, deliberately not looking at the duke's table. Climbing the stairs, she fantasized about being the duchess of this magnificent house. She glanced back at all the people below and took in the scenery—dreaming of a future there.

The private quarters were beautiful, and her room was exquisitely decorated. She wondered about the other guests who may have stayed in that same room. Julia undressed and washed her face. She put her jewelry away and pulled the covers off her bed. She sank down on the mattress and replayed the week in her head. Tossing and turning, she finally fell asleep.

The next morning was a hustle and bustle of many carriages leaving. Servants were packing and moving people out of the door. The house party had only been a small diversion from the London season. Julia could not imagine what a large house party looked like if this was a small one. She met her mother and father to break their fast as her bags were carried and delivered outside. She looked around for the duke and the dowager duchess to give them her thanks but could not find them and went upstairs to gather her reticule, so they could leave for London. Sara and her family had left earlier that morning.

Julia saw Frank as she came back down the stairs. He was standing beside Lady Janel, and they both were telling people goodbye together. Julia stopped her descent to stare at them. An outsider would have thought they were a couple bidding farewell to their guests. Lady Janel was very gracious and thanked people for coming like she was the duchess. Julia's stomach took a turn, and she wished she could find a way down the remaining stairs without being spotted. She tried to be as quiet as she could, but the duke looked up and saw her. He walked over to the staircase and offered her his hand to help her down the last couple of stairs.

He smiled back at her. "You look well this morning, my lady."

Lady Janel turned around and walked beside the duke.

"Oh, yes, she does. Poor thing, I am so happy you are feeling better."

She gave her a huge smile. "We thank you for coming." Lady Janel took the duke's arm and motioned him toward more guests. The duke took her hand off his arm. "I will escort Lady Julia to her carriage."

Lady Janel took a deep breath and pasted a fake smile on her face. "Of course, I will see you afterward." She nodded to Julia and walked away.

Julia took the duke's arm, and they walked along the parked carriages. She was quiet and tried to hide how furious she was at Lady Janel's blatant attempt to insert herself into the duke's household, but she chose not to mention it to the duke.

They approached her carriage, and she turned to him. "Thank you for everything."

He lifted the corner of his mouth. "You don't have to thank me, Julia. I feel it's my duty to protect you." He kissed her hand and helped her into the carriage. "I will call upon you soon."

She took a seat and looked out the window as he walked away.

Chapter 23

A FEW DAYS LATER, JULIA WAS in the drawing room embroidering. Her parents had appointments in the city, and Sara had taken a ride with Lord Jason. She wondered if there would be an announcement soon regarding them. The butler interrupted her thoughts. "Prince Randolph is here to see you. Should I escort him in?"

She inhaled sharply and pricked herself with her needle. Wincing at the sharp pain in her finger, she looked up at the butler. "Um, yes, please show him in."

Julia stood as Prince Randolph made his appearance. "Your Highness. This is a surprise." She curtsied.

He gave her a bow. "My lady, please forgive me if this visit is unwelcomed. I couldn't part London without speaking to you again."

She thought he looked very handsome with a black waistcoat that showed off his muscular build. His hair was styled perfectly, and the smell of his shaving cream lingered near her. It was a woodsy musk that tickled her senses. She noticed he was carrying two small bags. He placed them on the table and reached for her hand to kiss it. Picking up one of the bags, he handed it to her. She took it from him, giving him a puzzled look.

He smiled at her. "Please open it."

She hesitated and slowly untied it. She smiled as she took in the smell of cinnamon buns. "You must know my weakness."

He laughed. "It's a peace offering."

"You are brave to come to call on me. You must have good luck because my parents are not in residence. I thought you had left London already."

"I must confess that I waited for your parents to leave." He gave her a sly look, grinning. "I am actually leaving London tomorrow. I had heard rumors of your awful experience and could not leave without assuring to your well-being. I wanted to rush to help you but did not think I would be welcomed at the duke's house party."

She looked away, not able to make eye contact. The prince took a step closer, still holding a different bag. He asked, "Do you think we could take a stroll in the garden?"

She agreed and walked toward the terrace doors. "I have another present for you but only ask that you put it somewhere safe until we return from our walk." He handed her the mystery bag. "I don't want to be here when you open it."

Julia thought he was being secretive, but she called for Mary to put it in her room until she got back. She took his arm, and they strolled through the garden pathways until they reached the fountain, and they sat on the bench. They rested in silence for a minute, and he turned to her.

"Julia, I just want to apologize for that day of our picnic. It was not my intention to hurt you or treat you badly." His eyes locked with hers, and she could see hurt in them.

She stiffened but kept her gaze on him. He continued, "I haven't slept well since you left, and I find myself miserable without you. I was horrified to hear that someone tried to hurt you, and I wanted to be your protector, not the duke. I feel like you belong to me and not him. I was wrong to suggest that you marry him. I know now that there is no way I could let you marry another."

Her heart skipped a beat as she was desperately trying to understand what he was saying. "I don't understand, Randolph. Have you changed your mind?"

He stopped walking. "I have, Julia. I want you to come with me to my country. I love you."

Julia's heart tugged in her chest. She had longed to hear him say it, but a part of her heart had warmed to the duke. Leaning against him, he slid his arm around her, holding her close to him.

"Randolph, we have to speak to my parents."

He smiled. "Of course, although they might not understand that I have good intentions. I can provide for your every need and give you luxury accommodations in my country." He held on tight to her hands as she gazed into his eyes. "We can tell them you will be visiting Mallory."

Julia stared at him. "I don't understand."

He held her hands close to his chest. "We can be together every day after my obligations are complete. We will need to be discreet before the obligations are fulfilled, but I will take care of you because I love you."

Julia's throat went dry. She realized at that moment that she was never going to be with him as his wife. Looking away from him, anger bubbled up inside. *How dare he suggest this again?* But the anger quickly turned to pity.

"Randolph, I love you too. But I will not live a life like that with a man that I am not married to." Julia pulled her hands away. "I am not the girl for you."

She shifted away from him and sat on the bench. "I want to have my union recognized by the Church and my children to have their father's name. I may not find love again, but I want to be respected. Respect is better than love."

Randolph was shaking his head back and forth. "Is that what your duke gives you?"

Julia hesitated to speak about him. "I am fond of him, and yes, he respects me. My views have changed, and I don't need love anymore to be married. I need someone who cares enough about me to give me his name."

Randolph looked away—he was struggling with his emotions and sat down beside her. "Julia, you're asking me to choose between my right arm and left arm. You are my right arm—my soul mate. My country and family are my left arm. I can't give up either of them."

She leaned over and kissed him on his cheek. "Randolph, I want you to try to fall in love with your wife. She deserves all of you and will give you the heirs you desire." Sliding away on the bench, she put a little distance between them. "I don't regret our time together, but it's come to an end. I understand that your duty comes first."

"Julia, my heart will always be yours. I wish you a lifetime of happiness. If you will excuse me, I must go." He stood up and walked away.

Julia nodded her head slowly as he stood up and bowed. She watched him walk away and felt a burning in her throat. Staying in the garden, she couldn't stop crying.

Chapter 24

An hour later, Julia was still in the garden thinking about her life. A sound startled her, and she quickly turned around, surprised to see the duke approaching her with a smile on his face. "You look so beautiful in the garden, but you must be chilled." He took off his coat and put it around her. She smiled back at him as he sat down.

Julia felt guilty that the prince had just been there but chose not to mention it. The duke took her hand, turning toward her. "Julia, I have to talk to you, and I am not sure if I can find the right words to say."

She faced him, studying his features, watching concern draw on his forehead as he looked at her more closely.

"Your eyes look red."

Not wanting him to know she had been crying, she sniffed her nose and touched her eyes. "I have been rubbing them. Maybe something in the air?"

He seemed to let it go and fidgeted with his gloves. "As you know, the season is ending soon, and our parents have asked us for a decision regarding our engagement. I know you had reservations, but I hope I have convinced you that I would make a good husband."

Standing up from the bench, he bent down on his knee in front of her. "I want to be your husband. I could provide for you, and you would never want for anything. I also think we could be great friends."

He smiled as he took her hands in his. "I have affection for you, Julia, and wish you to be my wife. Please tell me you will accept." He brought her hands to his mouth and kissed them. "Julia, will you have me for your husband?"

Julia was taken aback but not surprised. She'd known this day would come but found it odd that she did not hate the idea of marrying him. She had respect and fondness for him. Perhaps they could have a good life together. And an added bonus—he wanted her for his wife, not just a mistress. That was more than the prince could give her. The man she loved had never given her an honorable offer. She may not have loved Frank, but romance was not always practical.

She smiled down at him and nodded her head. "Yes, Frank. I accept your proposal."

He smiled as he kissed her cheek and pulled her up to stand. Julia held her breath, thinking he may kiss her for the first time, but he did not pursue more. She wondered how she would feel about his kisses—if she would feel weak at the knees or if it would feel like kissing a friend.

The corners of his mouth turned up into a smile as he kept rubbing her hands to keep her warm. "You have made me very happy, Julia. I can't wait to tell our parents at dinner tonight. We must dine together. I will have my staff arrange it. I will have a ring for you, so we can make it official. Please invite your family."

They turned to walk back to the house. He leaned

down and whispered in her ear, "Our fathers chose well even if we didn't want to admit it."

She laughed and waved goodbye as he left.

Julia confided in Mary but had promised Frank she would not tell anyone else until tonight. Mary was cautious but relayed her congratulations. She waited for Julia to finish tea with her family and met her in Julia's bedroom.

Julia entered later, wanting a bath to get ready to go to the dukes for dinner. She could tell Mary was wary but didn't want to say anything.

"Mary, stop sulking. I know you think I don't want to marry the duke. But he is a good man, and that is enough for me. Prince Randolph did not love me as he claimed he did. He would not give up his royal life and wanted me only as a mistress. I was not raised like that. He asked more of me than I could give."

Mary brushed her hair as she prepared for the supper at the duke's home.

Mary sighed. "Perhaps the prince will change his mind. What if you are married to the duke and can't be with him?"

Julia looked down, taking in a deep sigh. "Mary, this is not a fairy tale. He made his decision, and I will accept it."

Mary looked worried. She braided Julia's hair, looking toward the bed. "Oh, my lady, we almost forgot—I hid the bag from the prince under your bed."

Julia had completely forgotten about the other bag. Mary bent down on the floor and retrieved it for her. They both sat on the bed, and she opened the bag, taking papers out. She uncovered a box that was a carefully wrapped in tissue that contained a small statue. She smiled, laughing out loud. It was a table with carved horses that spun around. Julia untied the note that came with it and read the letter out loud.

> *My Dearest Julia,*
>
> *This miniature represents the best day of my life, and I wanted you to have it. I never thought I would know what love was until I met you. I wanted to protect you and be with you every minute of the day. You once told me that you dreamed of having the ability to live the life of your choosing and not what your parents wanted for you. My gift for you is inside this miniature. It's yours to keep and will give you the ability to choose your own life. If you ever need my help, I will always be there for you. My heart is yours.*
>
> *Your servant,*
> *Randolph*

Julia found a small hidden latch at the bottom of the table. She unhooked it, turning it upside down as her locket fell out, and she caught it. She smiled, rubbing the heart with her thumb. Looking inside again, she drew out a black velvet bag hidden inside, pulled it open, and watched a handful of diamonds fall into her palm. *He has left me a small fortune!* She gasped, watching Mary's eyes get bigger. She looked at the jewels in her hand and counted ten in all.

Mary cried. "Oh, my lady, you're rich! You don't have to marry the duke."

Julia rubbed her forehead. Dumbfounded, she stared at

jewels for a few seconds, finally realizing that she couldn't keep them. "I can't accept this."

Looking around the room, her hands slightly shook as she put the jewels back into the bag. "Mary, we need to hide this somewhere safe so that none of the servants find it." She walked to the bed and took the covers off. "I will put it inside of the mattress cover, and you make sure that no one else makes my bed. Tell the other servants that only you can. I need time to think, Mary, but I must go for now."

Mary nodded. "It's what the prince wants, my lady. You can't give the money back. It's your chance."

Julia bit her bottom lip. "Perhaps we can keep it. I don't even know how to give it back. He leaves in the morning. It's our secret, Mary. You must not tell anyone."

Julia's family took the new carriage to the duke's house. It was white with black trim and had darkened window shades. The cushions were light-brown with embroidered flowers on them. The earl had spared no expense with his new luxury transportation. He was also looking for a town house to purchase as their family residence in London.

Her cousin and the rest of her family followed behind in the viscount's carriage. Julia looked out the window and tried to enjoy the ride. She'd expected to feel nervous but found that she was more excited than anything.

A knot formed in her chest looking at her parents and realizing how much she loved them. Pleasing them was more important than anything. Their love for her had been apparent when Jasper abducted her. If she refused Frank, she may be forced to be separated from them. She had also grown fond of Sara and was becoming accustomed to London society. Besides, she didn't always have to be in London and knew that she could also enjoy country life. Frank had several other estates. Her mind settled on her decision—she would marry him. She would learn to accept her fate and be surrounded by people who cared about her. It was better than living in a cottage alone.

The duke's residence was full of people when Julia arrived. The dining room was set up with many tables. Julia realized this was not a small intimate supper but was a large-scale celebration. Her hands began to sweat as she knew all eyes would be on her tonight. She wished she had some close friends in London as most of the guests were acquaintances of his mother.

She entered the foyer, and the duke's face lit up. "Julia, you look exquisite this evening."

She smiled, giving him a curtsy. "You are too kind, Your Grace." He laughed and put her hand on his arm. She gave him a coy smile and rubbed his arm.

He whispered to her, "Are you nervous about our announcement?"

"A little," she whispered back.

He touched her other arm and bent down closer to her ear. "I will be by your side."

She smiled back, and he excused himself as his mother was calling for him. Julia curtsied as he took a bow. Turning around, she saw Lady Janel glaring at her. She was with Lord James and Lady Sophia again. Julia smiled at her and walked into the drawing room to find her parents. She refused to play her games. She ran into Sara and Lord Jason and was happy to find some friendly faces.

The dowager duchess welcomed all the guests and told them her son had an announcement and was keeping it a secret. She looked as puzzled as everyone, but Julia suspected that she knew and was only playing a part. The Earl and Lady Savory also claimed to know nothing about the announcement. Julia purposely avoided the duke to try to throw people off. She made sure not to look for him while they waited for the dinner announcement.

When dinner was announced, the duke escorted his mother to the table, and Julia was escorted by his brother, Lord Jacob. After taking their seats, she thanked them for coming. She asked her son to come forward to make his announcement.

The duke stood up and looked over the crowd of people. He smiled, and there was complete silence as the room full of people rested their eyes on him.

"Friends and family, we invited all of you here this evening to enjoy a very special moment. Earlier today, I asked for Lady Julia's hand in marriage, and she has agreed. She has made me a very happy man."

There were a few gasps but mostly cheers. The duke turned to Julia and helped her stand. He held up his hand for the crowd to calm down. "Lady Julia, I want to put my grandmother's ring on your finger as a pledge to our commitment. We are now officially engaged."

Julia smiled and gave him her hand. He slid the ring over her glove and kissed her hand. She looked up at him and knew she had made the right decision. Her mother stood up to hug her, and so did the dowager duchess.

They all sat back down and enjoyed a grand supper fit for the king.

Julia's family and friends rushed to her side after supper. They were all very excited to see her ring. The duke kept his hand on her lower back as people approached them to offer their congratulations.

As they received the well-wishers, Lord James and Lady Sophia congratulated the duke. Julia noticed that Lady Janel did not wish them well. She didn't see her at all after the dinner. Lady Sophia was insincere and quickly made an exit. Lord James patted the duke on the back and then walked away. The duke introduced Julia to some of his business associates, and soon the crowd began to separate.

They all moved into the music room to enjoy some entertainment before retiring for the evening. Julia couldn't stop staring at the duke. He was always smiling or winking at her, and she enjoyed seeing him happy.

Chapter 25

THE NEXT FEW DAYS FLEW by—Julia's mother kept her busy at dress fittings. The papers said it would be the wedding of the year, and her mother wanted everything to be perfect. Their engagement ball was the following Saturday, and the dowager duchess had insisted on hosting that party. Her mother would host the wedding breakfast. They were hoping their new town house would be ready by then. There was even more pressure to hire staff to make sure that the house could accommodate and entertain all the guests. The wedding list kept growing, and Julia felt she needed a break from all the attention. She escaped with Mary, and they took a trip to the bakery for cinnamon buns and tea.

Mary laughed in the carriage. "How were you able to get away?"

Julia smiled. "I had to bring in some reinforcements and asked Sara to help me. She kept my mother busy with flowers. My father was engrossed in business papers, and I told him I was leaving for the afternoon. He nodded his head, and I took that as a yes."

Mary giggled. "My lady, it's hard to believe you will be duchess soon."

She shook her head. "Hmm, hard to believe that in a few short months, I won't need their permission to leave the house. I will be a married woman."

The carriage pulled over by the bakery just as it started to rain. Julia pulled her cloak over her head, walking into the bakery. She noticed Lady Janel, Lord James, and Lady Sophia were also there upon entering.

"Oh drat! It is Lady Janel," Julia whispered pointing toward the group. She quickly hid at the back table facing the wall, taking a seat. She asked Mary to sit on the other side, facing the counter. There was a pole that blocked a partial view, and if she kept her cloak on, she didn't think they would see her.

Mary waited in line to purchase the bread as the group did not recognize her as being Julia's maid. The group sat at a table not far from Julia, and she heard them gossiping about their day. Mary returned soon with the buns and tea. Julia took a bite, thanking Mary as they enjoyed their treat without much talking. Julia heard some whispers and then heard her name. Mary took a drink of tea, raising her brow in question at Julia.

Lady Janel was speaking about the duke. "I don't understand is all I am saying. She acts like a child and is very plain looking. It can only be because of the business dealings with her father. Her manners are horrible—I can't imagine her being a duchess."

"Everyone knows how the duke feels about you. He will be bored with the chit within three months, and then you can resume your relationship." Lady Sophia said reassuringly.

"I just don't understand it. He was practically courting

me, and the papers talked about our pending engagement. I will call on him tomorrow—he will probably want to talk about our relationship."

Lord James looked surprised. "You're still trying to see him, Janel?"

She looked at Sophia, and they giggled. "You know the duke—he can't settle for a child."

Julia felt she would be sick. She couldn't listen any longer and slowly got up from her hiding spot behind the pole. Sneaking through the back door, she ended up in the storage room. Eyeing an exit on the side, she slipped through the alley with Mary close behind.

They found their carriage and stepped in. Julia noticed Mary staring at her with concern.

"I just want to be left alone. I need to think." She turned away, looking out the window.

Mary looked at her friend with sympathy. "I think she is lying to her friends. Even Lord James looked surprised that she would still try to see the duke."

Julia shrugged at Mary's suggestion, feeling her insides come apart. Lord James could have feigned surprise because he wanted to court Lady Janel. The scandal sheets had showed a cartoon this morning regarding the love triangle. She didn't know whom she could trust and decided to trust no one until she could find out for herself.

Julia's mother was meeting with the dowager duchess when the girls returned home. They were making final plans for the engagement ball the following Saturday. Julia's heart sank when she saw the excitement on their faces.

The women practically giggled as they went over colors and flower choices with her. The dowager duchess asked her about the menu and any special request that she may have. Julia politely allowed her to take over the process and agreed with all her recommendations.

She tried to excuse herself, so she could freshen up. The women hardly noticed when she took her leave as they were engrossed in the planning of the ball. Julia thought about the wedding as she went to her room. Her family was inviting half of London. She was overwhelmed and wondered if she could go through with the wedding. Chastising herself for letting her emotions get her guard down, she realized the afternoon was slipping away. There wasn't much time to rest as she was supposed to meet the duke soon for a trip to the museum. She took a deep breath and washed her face in the basin. She rang for Mary, so she could change and get ready to meet him.

Frank was prompt picking her up for their excursion. Julia thought he looked handsome in his new brown coat but quickly dismissed the feelings, remembering Lady Janel's conversation in the bakery. His face lit up when he saw her, his usual scowl turning to a warm smile. He complimented her dress, offering his arm. She took it as they headed toward the carriage.

Her parents allowed her to go alone with him to the museum now that they were engaged. The footman drove them, but Mary did not accompany her. Julia was nervous to be alone with him inside the carriage. She was unsure of his intentions and how she felt about him. Lady Janel and Lord James's conversation kept playing in her mind repeatedly. She wanted to know if he was only marrying her because of their family's business arrangement.

She thought back over the last several days and admitted to herself that she had grown an attachment to him since he had rescued her. Could it all be a farce so that he could get his heir, then live his own life without her? Did he love Lady Janel? Most of the *ton* had thought she would be his duchess. They felt Julia's father had provided a lucrative offer and that was the only reason he is marrying her. Julia felt the insides of her stomach coming up in her throat. All these thoughts were consuming her, and she needed to keep focused. Finally reaching the carriage, she took his hand as he helped her inside, taking the seat opposite of her.

"You are very quiet today, my dear."

"I apologize. I have a lot on my mind."

"There is a lot of planning, and I know my mother is overwhelming with all the arrangements."

Julia forced a smile but remained quiet. She did not know what else to say and did not feel comfortable asking him about his feelings for her or Lady Janel. She was hoping the day would go by fast, so she could be alone with her thoughts in the safety of her bed. The rocking of the carriage was soothing, and Julia straightened her skirt with her hands. She tried not to look at him but briefly looked up, finding him looking directly at her.

"Are you feeling ill today?" Frank looked concerned as he reached for her hand.

Julia tensed as he touched her, shaking her head. "I am feeling fine." She hesitated as he rubbed her hands.

"I have something for you, Julia." He bent down and

from under the seat pulled out a box. She looked confused as he handed it to her.

He rubbed his lips. "Today's gift is something very special to me, and I want you to have it."

Julia couldn't help but smile and unwrapped the box. She looked inside and saw a bracelet that was made from an unusual rock. It was beautiful. Holding out her arm, he placed it on her wrist.

"It was my grandmother's, who was very special to me. She was my maternal grandmother and gave it to me for my future wife. She gave one to me, my brother, and my mother to remember her by."

Julia thanked him as she looked down at the rocks— they sparkled as she moved her wrist. It was exquisite. Feeling guilty, she gave him a weak smile, not knowing if she could be his wife. There was a tug on her heart. He moved seats and sat beside her in the carriage. He took her hand and intertwined his fingers with hers. Lifting their hands together, he twisted them around to see the bracelet. The carriage finally slowed, and they made their way inside.

The museum was crowded as they strolled through many exhibits. Frank kept her hand in the crook of his arm as he introduced her as his fiancée to many lords and ladies. Julia enjoyed the museum and tried to forget about the doubts in her mind. The duke purchased them some pastries as they looked for a table on the terrace to eat. Julia felt a chill when she went to sit down and remembered she must have left her shawl on the bench at the exhibit. She excused herself and insisted on getting it herself. Frank stood and offered to help her, but she held up her hand

and told him she knew exactly where it was and would be right back.

She walked to the history exhibit and found it lying across the bench. Picking it up, she placed it over her arm and walked back out the terrace doors. As she approached her table, she hesitated, seeing a woman talking with the duke.

Julia stared at the table for a few minutes. She noticed a familiarity with the woman and Frank, and she walked slowly toward them to hear the exchange. She did not know who the woman was, but there was a flirtatious exchange, and she felt a twinge of jealousy run through her.

As she approached the table, he stood up nervously. "Lady Julia, this is Miss Crawford." He looked at the woman. "Miss Crawford, this is Lady Julia."

The lady nodded. "My lady."

Julia gave a guarded smile. "Miss Crawford."

Julia took note that he did not mention she was his fiancée. The woman checked her out from head to toe and smiled at her as Frank pulled out Julia's chair. The woman bid him farewell and made her exit.

Julia looked up him with a questioning look. "Who was that woman?"

He brushed off the comment, quickly looking away. "She is an acquaintance from a long time ago."

Julia did not like his answer. "What kind of acquaintance?"

Frank shifted in his seat, loosening his collar. He took a bite of his tart as Julia stared at him. He met her eyes and let out a frustrated breath. "I barely knew her. She is a friend of my brother's."

Julia let the awkward exchange go and began to eat her food. There was some music playing on the terrace and some birds landed close to her. She fed the birds some crumbs and joined Frank in pleasant conversation.

The ride back to her residence was very quiet. Julia could not help but wonder who the lady was and why he had not introduced her as his fiancée. She concentrated on looking out the window and hoped to arrive quickly. Julia did not invite the duke in for tea but told him she needed to rest. He walked her to the foyer and kissed her hands. She curtsied to him and took her leave.

She went to her room and found Mary there when she arrived. "Mary, I want you to find out some information about a woman named Miss Crawford. She is apparently acquainted with the duke, and he was most uncomfortable when I was introduced to her."

Mary nodded her head slowly and fidgeted with her apron, looking at Julia with concern. "My lady, the other servants have told me some upsetting rumors."

Julia sat on the bed. "What rumors?"

Mary took a breath. "Apparently, the dowager brought a few maids with her today on her visit. They were very talkative."

Mary sat beside Julia on the bed. "Well, one of the maids said that there were rumors that a match was planned for Lady Janel and the duke. They said the duke is in love with her and had refused to marry you. But apparently, his family had put enormous pressure on him to marry you instead, and he finally agreed. The rumor is that his father had threatened to take away all of his inheritance that was not entailed if he didn't marry you in his will, so he finally relented."

Julia closed her eyes, feeling the back of her eyes burn with the threat of tears. "I don't understand, Mary. Why go through with an engagement to me if he loves her?"

"The staff thinks he will leave you once you give him an heir and perhaps a spare. They said his relationship has not stopped with Lady Janel." Mary rubbed her lips together, pausing for a second. "I am so sorry."

Chapter 26

THE NEXT WEEK FLEW BY, and Julia was successful in avoiding the duke. It was not easy, and she had to keep herself busy, but she managed to keep her distance. Nevertheless, avoidance could not last forever, and the night of the engagement ball had finally arrived.

Unfortunately, no revelation came regarding how to handle the duke. Confusion muddled her mind as she was still unsure of how to move forward with her plans to marry him. Most would probably have told her to accept her fate, that once an heir was born she could live a life full of social events and extended trips to Boston. That would fulfill *her* life while the duke had his dalliances. Eventually, he would grow old and tire of having a mistress. Some said the women of the *ton* could have their own relationships once they were finished having children. Her thoughts took her to Randolph. Perhaps she could reconsider his offer later? No, she knew in her heart she could never accept those circumstances. *What a miserable life!*

Julia took a bath and waited for Mary's help. When Mary arrived, she ran to Julia.

"My lady, I know who she is!" she said breathlessly.

"Who?"

"Miss Crawford. She was an opera singer, and there were rumors about her and the duke being together a long time ago."

Julia stepped out of the tub, wrapping a drying cloth around her. Disheartened, she thought about what Mary said. Frank had lied to her about who Miss Crawford was to him. She was not sure of anything anymore. The only thing she was sure of was that she did not want to go to the ball tonight. Her stomach felt queasy, and she ran to the chamber pot to vomit. Mary pulled back her hair and patted her back as she relieved her stomach.

Julia wiped her mouth, and tears burned her eyes. She didn't know this man at all. Looking at Mary, she cried. "I feel like a piece in a chess game, and the enemy is closing in on me."

She walked to the window to look outside. "I am trapped, Mary." She breathed hard on the inside of the pane and watched the window fog up. Touching her finger to the window, she drew a heart. Lifting her finger, she sliced through the heart. Turning around, she accepted a damp cloth from Mary and rubbed her eyes.

She composed herself. "I will find out the truth tonight."

Julia arrived early to the duke's house. The dowager duchess had a room made up for her to freshen up in, so she could make an entrance with the duke after the guests had arrived. The room was beautiful with cream-and-pastel-green drapes with a matching bed covering. There were also golden statues and wrought iron dressers along the walls with a pastel-green settee standing near the huge window.

Julia was impressed with the marble flooring that led to a huge dressing room. She walked into the dressing room and noticed a door on the far side. Curious, she opened the door and realized it led to another dressing room that she imagined was the duke's. Quickly closing the door, she latched it shut. It suddenly came to her that this was the duchess's chamber. She knew the duke's family was trying to welcome her by letting her use the chamber tonight, but she felt out of place and uncomfortable in a room meant for his wife.

Julia waited for Mary to return with some chocolate to drink. Julia paced around the room, trying not to think about the obligations of the night ahead. She decided to speak to the duke about his relationships with Lady Janel and Miss Crawford. Seeing him face to face would tell her if the rumors were true. She knew in her heart that rumors from servants usually had some merit, and she didn't want to be naïve. Julia could not calm her nerves and paced around the room, wearing down the carpet.

Mary smiled at Julia and gave her the chocolate and a cinnamon bun. "The kitchen had cinnamon bread—maybe this will calm your nerves."

Julia enjoyed the treat and tried to soothe the nauseous feeling she had in her belly. Mary put some finishing touches to her hair and put some lavender perfume on her wrists and neck. There was a knock on the door. Mary opened the door wide to show Julia that the duke had arrived.

"May I have a private word?" He raised his brow awaiting her reply.

Mary curtsied and left. Julia smiled. "Of course."

He gazed upon her as appreciation shined in his eyes. "Can you join me in the family parlor?"

She took his arm and walked down the hallway to the parlor. Upon entering, he leaned down to kiss her on the cheek and guided her to the fireplace. There was a jewelry box on the mantle, and he handed it to her.

Surprised at another gift, Julia opened it, and her mouth dropped open in awe. "It's beautiful!" Inside was a sparkling diamond necklace with matching earbobs. She gasped at the beauty of it and shook her head. "I can't accept this."

He looked at her with such admiration. "Nonsense, you are worth every stone and more." He helped her put on the necklace, and she slid the earrings on her ears.

His eyes brightened. "I can't believe how great they look on you. I ordered them last week, and they came this morning. They look better than I imagined." He smiled and leaned down to put his forehead on top of hers. Julia tensed, thinking he may kiss her, but he didn't. He walked to the door and asked the footmen to ring for some tea.

The dowager duchess and Julia's parents joined them for tea and biscuits before the party. They complimented Julia on the jewelry the duke had given to her and talked about the guest list for that evening. Julia was lost in her thoughts again, wondering about her future. She did not know if she could forget about the rumors, and she had to find out if the duke was in love with Lady Janel.

The duke had never told her that he loved her, although he did seem to care about her. Was that enough for her? Could she live as most aristocratic wives did and share her husband? Her stomach was nauseous. Not able to settle her stomach, she excused herself from her family and told them she had to attend to some private needs.

Chapter 27

THE PARTY WAS CROWDED—MOST OF the guests had arrived when Julia heard a knock on the door. It was Mary telling her that the duke was ready for her. The dowager duchess was going to make the announcement. Julia walked to the door slowly. She saw Frank outside the door and took his arm.

When they arrived at the landing, the dowager duchess asked all to congratulate the happy couple and officially announced their engagement. There were cheers from the audience, and everyone lifted their glasses in a toast. Julia tried to smile. Frank lifted her hand as the audience congratulated them. The music began, and he led her to the dance floor for the opening waltz.

Many spectators watched their dance and clapped for the couple. Julia was nervous to have everyone watching her, but she tried to concentrate on her steps to not think about it. Focusing on his chest, she refused to look up and make eye contact with him.

He leaned down to whisper. "You look stunning, my dear. I am so happy that you are going to be my wife."

Julia did not know what to say in return. Her feelings were changing, but they confused her. The dance came to an end, and Frank bowed to her, taking her to her father, who had asked for the next dance.

She was happy to dance with her father. He twirled his daughter around the dance floor and seemed so proud that this union had made his little girl happy.

Julia danced with some of the duke's friends and some of her own. She had started to finally relax when she noticed Lady Sophia whispering into Frank's ear. He shook his head no and walked away. She watched as Lord James also approached Frank, saying a few words in his ear. Frank's frustration was visible as he walked toward the back hallway.

Julia could not help herself—she casually walked to the refreshment table and told Sara she had to leave for a moment to attend to some private needs. She followed the duke down the hall, hiding behind some columns so he wouldn't see her. Thankfully he was far ahead of her and was walking fast. He opened the library doors and entered. Julia quickly walked to the room on the other side of the library and opened the door in between slowly so no one would hear her. Inside the library, she saw Lady Janel speaking to the duke. Straining to hear, she could not make out what they were saying, but Lady Janel was crying. She tried to get a little closer and could hear the duke saying, "It's going to be okay. It will work out."

Julia's heart fell. Not able to take it anymore, she slipped back through the door. She ran up the servant's staircase to avoid her family. She had to get to the duchess's chamber before anyone saw her crying. Not able to face anyone, she just wanted to go back home to Boston and live a normal life. She didn't want to be a duchess and live with a man who did not love her.

Lying on the bed for several minutes, she knew she must clean herself up before people came looking for her. She splashed water on her face and pinched her cheeks. There was a knock on the door, and Julia did not know if she should open it. She was afraid it could be the duke. The knocking continued, and Julia finally said, "Who is it?"

Sara whispered. "It's me, Sara. Are you okay? The duke and your parents are looking for you."

Julia took another deep breath. "I will be right there. I was not feeling well." Julia slowly opened the door.

Sara looked at her. "Is it your stomach? It must be making you nervous to be in front of all these people."

Julia nodded. "Indeed, my cousin." She took her arm, and Sara escorted her back down the stairs.

The duke smiled when he saw her. He asked her for the supper dance, escorting her to the table. She tried to keep the conversations casual as they ate with friends and family. Julia had decided what she must do and began to make the plans in her head.

When the ball came to the end, the dowager duchess offered the family a room to reside in for the night, but Julia asked her parents to return to the town house. She told them she felt uncomfortable staying until they were married.

Her parents graciously declined their offer and they said their goodbyes. The wedding would be within a few months, and now all Julia's mother could talk about on the way home was having their new London residence ready for the wedding breakfast. Julia remained quiet and told them she was tired. She was relieved to arrive home and quickly went to her room. Mary helped Julia undress, and she went to bed shortly thereafter. Julia could not sleep as she tossed and turned all night. In the morning, she got up and prepared her plans. She knew what she must do and rang early in the morning for Mary's help.

Chapter 28

MARY SCREAMED IN PROTEST, "LADY Julia, you can't run away. The streets are harder than you think, and you will have no protection."

Julia did not care if the streets were rough—she would find a way out of this marriage. "Mary, I can't pretend any longer. I saw them and know the duke loves Lady Janel. Please understand that I can't marry a man that is in love with someone else."

Julia's heart hurt so much as she thought about her predicament. "I was wrong. Affection and admiration are not enough." Julia had tears in her eyes. "I have pin money saved and the jewels from Randolph."

Mary pleaded with Julia. "Lady Julia, please don't do this. You need time to plan."

Julia crossed her arms stubbornly. "My mind is made up."

Mary dropped her shoulders in defeat as Julia began to pull out her dresses to pack. "My lady, I may have an idea that could work if you are determined to leave."

Julia looked at Mary suspiciously. Mary told Julia she would be right back and left her in the room alone. Julia stopped packing and sat back on her bed. She wanted to be careful not to accept too much help from her. Julia didn't want her actions to cost Mary her position or livelihood. They could punish Mary and let her go without references. Julia could not allow her actions to hurt her.

A few minutes later, Mary returned to the room with a piece of paper. It was an advertisement for a horse show with some writing on the back. She handed it to Julia.

"My brother came to London with his wife. He works as a groom raising horses. I am to meet him tomorrow for a visit. I could ask him to take you with him when he returns home. He could help you settle and offer you protection."

Julia viewed the paper. Thoughts raced through her head. "I don't know. Do you think he would help me? If I go, you would have to stay here. At least for a while, no one can suspect that you helped me. I didn't know your brother lived so close. Why didn't you tell me?"

Mary shrugged he shoulder. "I haven't seen him for years. I went to America with our mother when I was young. He stayed behind in England. He misses me—his letter asked me to move in with him and his wife. They own a small cottage near the farm with a room for me. You can stay in my room."

Julia nodded. "Yes, Mary. I think this could work. At least for a while."

Mary met with her brother at the horse show in London the next day and was gone for most the afternoon. Julia tried to keep herself busy waiting for her return. She had to talk fast to avoid the duke earlier when he came by for a visit. She told him that she had promised Sara a trip to the bookstore and would speak to him later. He had a business appointment later, so they agreed to meet the next day for a ride in the park. Julia felt guilty when he left because she knew she may not be there tomorrow or ever again. She canceled on Sara, so she could be there when Mary returned. Julia was growing tired of her own deceptions.

Julia's parents were harder to avoid. She didn't want to lie to them but had no choice. Sadness consumed her thoughts about the way they would feel about her tomorrow. Julia understood that, in society, once an engagement was announced, it could ruin the girl if she broke it. Her reputation would be shattered. She bit her lip anxiously, thinking about the consequences of her actions. No man would make an offer for her again—society would turn its back on her. She would no longer be received in polite company. Her family would likely suffer as well. She would be doomed to the life of a spinster with no connections.

Julia could not help but think about her father and how her actions could affect his business dealings. She reasoned with herself that he would not suffer because the duke needed him for his land as well. Most of the earl's wealth was from America, which did not rely on the *ton*'s acceptance. She did wonder about Sara, but they were only cousins. Surely, they would not hold her responsible. Julia knew Lord Jason loved her, and Julia's actions should not affect that.

A few hours later, Mary arrived and met Julia in her room. Her brother had agreed to help, and so had his wife, to Julia's relief. The girls made their plans all afternoon. They decided that Julia would go by the name of Rachel— she would be a distant cousin. An unemployed lady's maid who was visiting for a few months. Mary would tell her brother and his wife to tell no one as it could put Julia in danger.

Julia insisted on helping Mary pack her bags. "No, let me help. I must get used to taking care of myself. I don't think your brother would let me have a maid."

Mary smirked. "I would not get to use to it. I will join you soon."

She borrowed a few of Mary's dresses to blend into her new station in life and hid some money in her stockings. The girls' excitement had slowly diminished as they finished their packing in silence. They were both growing weary thinking of their separation. Julia had to write goodbye letters, and she asked Mary to return the duke's gifts back to him. Mary left her alone and told her she would return later to help her get ready for bed. They had to be up early the next morning to meet her brother.

Julia sat at her desk to compose letters to the duke and her parents. She also left a small note to Sara and a fake note to Mary. She could not let them suspect that Mary had anything to do with her departure, so she made Mary promise to keep working for the family until she sent for her. They had to allow enough time to pass so that no one would know that Mary had anything to do with her disappearance.

Julia's stomach churned with anxiety. She felt her throat tighten with sadness as she thought about her decision.

There was no turning back.

She imagined her parents' faces as they found out about her betrayal. Julia had given them her word and was now running away. Her thoughts turned to Frank. Would he be humiliated? Would he hate her? She had begun to care for him. Her heart hurt when she thought about his rescue, his kind words, and the pants he'd given her as a gift. She knew he didn't love her, but he'd tried to make her happy. It was an honorable match, living up to his aristocratic expectations. Julia put it out of her mind and concentrated on breathing. She was her own woman now, and she would change her life.

Chapter 29

MARY'S BROTHER, JOHN, WAS TALL with similarly shaped eyes to Mary's. He smiled with kindness, making her like him instantly. His wife, Laura, was short and a little plump with big, brown eyes that matched her hair color. They both smiled when they saw Julia and Mary approach.

"John, this is my Lady Julia."

He took off his hat. "Nice to meet you, my lady."

Julia swished her hand. "Please don't call me by my title. I am now a maid."

Her brother loaded the luggage onto his cart. Their visit had to be short because they were late for a meeting with another worker from the estate who was riding the new stallion that they'd purchased.

Mary explained their concocted story again to her brother—Julia was staying with them as her employer had gone to America, and he was to treat her like his cousin Rachel. She was their distant cousin from Bath and would be staying for an extended visit. Julia's childhood of practicing impersonations would benefit her new English accent. She had to be careful not to give away her American pronunciations.

John laughed. "Don't worry, I will take good care of

my cousin Rachel." He winked as he checked the wheels on the cart.

She hugged Julia with tears in her eyes.

Julia took her hand and said, "Thank you so much for all of your help, Mary. But now you must hurry. You have to be back at the house before everyone wakes to find their notes. They can't know you had any part in helping me."

"I know, my lady. It will be fine."

John helped Julia get settled into the back of the cart, and they were off, leaving Mary waving to them before heading back to the house.

Mary sneaked back in through the servants' entrance and went to her room to feign sleep. When it was time to reveal the story that she and Lady Julia had created, she picked up the box and the note for the duke that Julia had left behind and took them to the footman, asking him to deliver it to the duke.

A few minutes later, Mary rushed to find Lady Savory. "My Lady, Lady Julia is not in her room. I found pillows stacked up under her covers imitating as her person."

"What?" Lady Savory questioned.

Mary nodded. "I also found notes left on her desk addressed to family members."

Lady Savory ran up the stairs.

She entered Julia's room, screaming for her sister and Sara. They both rushed in to find a hysterical Lady Savory. Sara's mouth hung open, looking around the room.

"She is gone." Lady Savory choked out the words.

Her sister wrinkled her nose. "Are you sure?"

Lady Savory nodded and picked up the notes on the table. She kept one and handed the other two to Sara and Mary. Taking a deep breath, she walked over to the chair and opened the letter.

Dearest Parents,

I hope you can forgive me for leaving. I have tried to be the daughter you wanted me to be, but I can't pretend anymore. I found out that the duke is not who I thought he was, and I can't go through with this arrangement. I know that I will lose your favor and no longer be welcomed as your daughter. I don't want to cause any problems with the family and will honor your reputation by staying away. I am of the age now to not be a burden and have chosen a different life. Please don't worry about me. I have found a safe place to live and will need no assistance. I hope one day you will want to see me again when you are no longer angry.

I love you both.
Julia

"She has run away!" Lady Savory began to cry as she finished the letter, and her sister walked over to hug her.

Sara sat on the bed and cracked the wax seal to open her letter and began to read aloud.

Sara,

I have enjoyed our friendship and think you are a loyal cousin. My actions are my own, and my confidence is that these actions will not affect you. You have my permission to disown me as your relative, so my behavior will not reflect upon your reputation. I hope you have a happy marriage with Lord Jason and wish you many joyful years.

Your cousin,
Julia

Lady Savory looked at Mary to give her permission to read her letter.

Mary,

Thank you for all your dedication over the years, and I apologize that I no longer need your services. You are a wonderful lady's maid, and I know my parents will give you a good reference if you should want to leave. However, they have other positions in which you are more than qualified and can probably keep you on the staff. Please tell the other staff members goodbye for me. I have chosen a different life and wish to be left alone. Good luck to you, and I wish you well.

Julia

Mary tried to contain her tears and asked to be excused. Lady Savory waved her hand in dismissal, and Mary took her leave.

The others remained quiet until the earl entered the room a few moments later. He looked pale and angry at the same time. He turned to his wife. "The staff is spreading rumors that Julia has run away?"

Lady Savory let out a cry, handing the letter to him. He took the letter and read it. The earl shook his head when he was finished. "Does Shallot know?" They all looked at each other and shrugged. The earl grunted. "I need to go see him. She will be ruined once this gets out."

Lady Savory cried out, "She will be ruined!" Her sister tried to hold her hand, but she ran out of the room.

The earl went to his study and wrote a message for the investigators that he had used before. He wanted them to meet him in private at his new house. Wiping his brow with his handkerchief, he was hoping he could save the family's reputation if he could find her and make her change her mind. *How could she do this?* He threw the pen across the room, watching ink fly over the floor.

"Gregory!" The earl called a footman. "I have had an accident."

The footman appeared and helped clean up the mess. The earl left the study, putting on his coat to visit the duke. He should have never agreed to let her wait until the end of the season to comply with the marriage. All the trouble could have been avoided if she had been safely married.

Taking a few deep breaths, he tried to brush aside the twinge of remorse as a distant memory came to him. He remembered Julia as a small child wearing his shoes in the foyer. He was a strict father, but the memory brought a small smile to his face. She had always had a mind of her own, and as angry as he was with her, he also wanted to protect her. She was his only child and had no idea the dangers that lurked in the city.

He knew he would have to speak to the duke and it was not going to be easy. He had made allowances for Julia, but this stunt would ruin her. The duke would surely ask to be released from the marriage contract—he would not be able to secure further protection in London. His dreams of living in Savory would be over, and they would have to take Julia back to Boston and pray that she could find a match there. Her dowry was big, and there was probably someone who would agree to marry her. The earl put the thoughts out of his mind and opened the door to leave.

The duke was eating breakfast when a footman told him he had a delivery and a missive. The duke stood up and took it from him. He cracked the seal on the letter and began to read:

> *Your Grace,*
>
> *It is hard for me to write this letter to you. I have struggled with my decision and know my actions will hurt many people whom I care about. I hope you can forgive me someday, but I can't marry you. I know this will ruin me, so I have decided to leave London before the scandal gets out. I fear I will no longer be welcomed in society. This is not the life for me, and I would not be a good wife to you. I am not like other women in the* ton *and don't wish to share my husband. I understand that it could affect business with my father, and I have explained to my parents in their letter that this was my decision alone and not to hold you responsible. Your friendship meant so*

much, and I will never forget how you rescued me. I am indebted to you for that. I hope one day you will understand my actions. I want a love match, and I know you don't feel that way about me. Your heart belongs to another, and I am setting you free.

Forgive me,
Julia

The duke dropped the letter to the floor. He opened the box, finding the diamond necklace, earrings, and the engagement ring. Throwing the box across the room, he watched it crash against the wall. His fist landed hard on the table as he kicked the chair across the room. The servants jumped back, and the duke straightened his jacket, breathing hard. He bent down to pick up the letter and asked his butler to put the box of jewelry in a safe place. The duke left his house to find the earl.

Chapter 30

Pain shot through Julia's back, she had been in the same position for too long, and her back was aching for a break. She was not accustomed to riding on a cart but counted her blessings for help with the escape. After a few hours of relentless riding, they pulled into a small village to meet with one of their friends from the horse farm who worked with John.

"There is Matthew. He is talking to the merchant." Laura pointed to a large man on the steps.

Julia took in his appearance, noticing how tall and muscular he was. She could tell he worked outdoors, he had a golden tan and dark, curly hair. He must have been only a few years older than her, but his face showed a lot of maturity.

Matthew waved as he motioned for John to come join him. "I will be back in a minute." He handed the reins to Laura as he hopped off.

Laura turned around to look at Julia. "You will like Matthew. We have known him for years, and he and John have plans to train their own horses one day."

Julia smiled, watching the man approach. John looked

at Julia. "Rachel, this is my friend Matthew Barnaby." He looked at Matthew. "This is my cousin, Rachel Johnson."

Matthew took off his hat. "Miss Johnson, it is a pleasure."

She had heard John talk about his fellow worker, who was also his best friend, throughout the ride. He'd told her that Matthew had worked on the farm since he was a child and his father was the head groomsman.

Julia smiled back, trying to remember her new name was Rachel. They rode for another few hours while she snuck looks at him riding beside them. He reminded her of one of the heroes she read about in her romance books as he handled the stallion with such experience, showing off his rugged good looks. He caught glimpses of her staring at him, and she quickly jerked her head, trying to look away so as not to appear so obvious. His presence took her mind off her hurting joints—she was relieved when they decided to take a break under some trees.

They let the horses rest and drink water from the stream down the hill. Julia went to sit down, forgetting she had no maid. Quickly getting up, she helped Laura with the blankets and food. They had bread, cheese, and apples. Julia ate it all, washing it down with cider. She had been too nervous to eat before they'd left this morning and now felt ravenous.

Matthew sat beside Julia. "Tell me, Miss Johnson... how is someone so pretty related to John?" He chuckled.

She smiled and looked away, guarding her secret. Trying to mask her American accent, she answered him. "John's a handsome cousin." She laughed. "But I am closer to his sister, Mary—she is a lady's maid too. I lost my position because my employers went to America, so now I am visiting John. I was grateful that he and Laura offered me a room."

Matthew looked at John and smiled. "I am glad they are adding beauty to the place."

Julia blushed, taking a drink of cider.

Once they were done resting, they rode into the night, stopping at an inn to sleep. They had no rooms available for them upstairs as it was reserved for those with more funds or titles, but the woman who owned the place offered a servant's room by the kitchen that was unoccupied. The servant who used it had to take care of a relative. They paid the lady, and the girls shared the room while the men slept in the stable.

The next day, they started out early, driving all day again. Matthew was entertaining, and Julia enjoyed his horse stories. He offered to let Julia ride with him on the stallion to give her a break from the cart.

Julia accepted his offer, yet she felt shy as he put his hands around her waist to lift her up onto the horse. He threw his leg over and settled in behind her. Embarrassed by their closeness, she tried not to lean too much into him but eventually lost the battle because of her hurting muscles and rested comfortably against his hard chest. She found the ride to be relaxing as he was very much the gentleman.

Julia marveled at the beautiful scenery as they approached the farm—the rolling hills, the many horses. As they rode closer, Julia saw several white stables and a huge mansion in the background. They rode to the side of the stables to the cottages under the trees. Matthew slid off the stallion, and helped Julia unmount. He bid the group good night and promised Julia he would give her a tour the next day before going to a small stone house by the stables. Julia thanked him as she got into the cart to go to John and Laura's cottage, as they lived a few miles from the farm.

John and Laura's cottage was set back in the woods—it boasted two stories and huge windows. The stones were chipped—a few repairs were needed—but it looked very cozy. John said there were two bedrooms upstairs and a chamber downstairs. Mary's room did not have a bed but a pallet on the floor with a table and dresser. Julia was just looking forward to anything she could sleep on. John unloaded the cart, carrying Julia's luggage upstairs. A musky odor filled the room, but Julia tried not to let it affect her. She lifted the window to air it out while putting her luggage away.

She went downstairs after a while and helped Laura make some bread with a slab of cheese for a quick dinner. Laura laughed at her attempt to help. "Have you ever cooked before, my lady?"

Julia blushed. "Forgive me, I have never cooked. But I do know how to pour tea and offer sandwiches."

Laura laughed. "I can teach you a few things if you plan to live on your own."

Julia smiled at her. "Thank you, and please don't call me 'my lady.'"

Laura looked at Julia in awe. "I have never met a real lady before. I can't believe your father is an earl."

Julia had tried not to think about her family during the trip. Putting their faces out of her mind, she did not want to talk about them. She knew Laura was being kind and didn't want to appear to be rude. "Yes, but I grew up in

Boston. The titles are not so proper there—I did not grow up around the *ton*. It's not as glamorous as it sounds."

"Sounds better than farm life."

Julia smiled. "You would be surprised." They walked to the settee and started talking about the neighbors instead. Julia was happy to have a diversion to the conversation.

Julia woke early the next day and went downstairs to fill the basin with water. She needed a bath and didn't see a tub around the house. She asked Laura and was told that they used a wagon bucket and she could heat up some water or use the creek down the road. Julia took a bucket of the freezing water up to her room and undressed again. Taking soap and a washcloth, she cleaned up as best she could, leaving her hair unwashed and dirty. Deciding that she needed to clean the grime out of her hair, she dressed and took a blanket with her to the creek, along with some rose soap she had brought from London. The creek trail was marked with strips of cloth, and she could hear the running water. Laura had assured her that there would be no one around this early as everyone was working.

Julia paid for room and board but tried to help herself as best she could. After all, she could not treat her landlords as servants. The walk was brisk, and she tried not to pay attention to the chill in the air. The water would be cold, but her hair needed attention—she couldn't remember it ever being so dirty. Finally approaching the creek, she hesitated before undressing. Looking around the area, she saw no one nearby, but just in case, she kept her chemise on.

Her first step into the water was so cold it hurt. She thought back to London and her steamy hot baths with scented water. Smiling to herself, she pushed those memories aside and took a few more steps before holding her breath to dunk her face into the bone-chilling water. Releasing her hair, she took the soap and started to scrub and rinse her hair, her body slowly acclimating to the temperature. Now that it was too cold to get out, she kept her body submerged and took in the scenery. It was beautiful—very private and quiet. After a few moments of enjoying the water, she heard some footsteps. Julia turned around quickly and gasped. She spotted Matthew leaning on a tree, smiling. Julia yelled, submerging herself under the water with just her head peeking out. "Go away. I thought I was alone."

Matthew laughed and said, "You look even more beautiful wet."

Julia glared at him, and he put up his large hands in a sign of surrender. "Forgive me, Rachel. I came out early to bathe myself. This swimming hole is known as the best place to bathe, so I took a ride out here. I did not know you would be here." Julia did not say anything but waited for him to leave.

He stopped smiling and looked seriously at her. "I can turn around, so you can dress, and then I can take my turn."

Julia hesitated. "You promise you won't turn around?"

He crossed his finger over his heart. "I promise."

Julia slowly stepped out of the creek with her eyes on the back of his head. Matthew started to whistle while Julia dressed in a hurry. She gathered up her drying cloth. "You can turn around now." Her face burned with embarrassment.

He smiled slyly. "You can stay and watch me bathe if it will make you feel better." He chuckled.

Julia threw her towel at him, stomping away. He laughed at her again. "Don't forget our tour later—I will pick you up in a few hours." Julia did not turn around as she marched toward the house.

Julia helped Laura gather eggs after she returned, trying to keep herself busy. She found farm work fascinating and wanted to learn more about it. Laura laughed and said, "It is fascinating now, but wait for a few days, and you will tire of it."

"I would like to be useful. Unfortunately, I am not trained in the kitchen."

Laura smirked. "What are you good at?"

"Besides shopping?" She chuckled. "I can make curtains. My old governess showed me, and I was good at it. Maybe we can buy some material in town soon and I can make some for you."

"I would like that. I will ask John to take us soon."

Later that afternoon, Julia read in her room while Laura finished her chores. Matthew came by, bringing a horse for Julia to ride. He had free rein at the horse farm to ride and exercise any horses that he wanted. Julia was excited to ride as they took off into the fields. Matthew was a very experienced rider, and Julia was impressed. He handled the stallion well, making it difficult for Julia to keep up. She realized that Matthew had finally caught on that her expertise was not in horses, and he slowed his pace, taking it easier on her.

He pointed out landmarks to tell her more about the history of the land. Their ride took them across an old stone castle that had been built hundreds of years ago. The old structure was crumbling apart with many overgrown plants and broken limbs, but Julia was very curious to explore.

Matthew helped her off her horse, tying both horses up

as he took her hand to guide her through the old gates. It was not too big in size but built very well.

"This is one of my favorite places to come. Just to think sometimes."

Julia could relate to him and thought about her adventures as a child. Finding an abandoned castle had never been far from her thoughts. "It has always been a childhood dream of mine to play in a castle."

"Oh, then I must make your dreams come true. Come on! Let's explore your castle." She ran after Matthew and was having a wonderful time climbing up the stairs. She enjoyed looking through old hallways that were in ruins. Matthew thought that a royal family had used the castle as some sort of retreat. He guided her out to a garden area in the courtyard of the castle and sat on a big stone while Julia sat across from him.

Matthew looked at Julia questioningly. "I find it difficult to believe that you were a lady's maid."

Julia panicked. "Why not?"

He took a deep breath. "You're too pretty—no lady would have the competition."

Julia blushed. "The aristocrats don't look at their maids in that way."

He moved over and sat beside her. "I think you would be surprised."

He reached over and ran his fingers through a piece of her hair. Julia pulled away to stand up. "I am sorry, Matthew. I don't want to give you the wrong impression."

He sighed. "You can't blame me for trying."

Julia smiled, a little amused. "I will not, but I think we should start out as friends. I have recently broken up with a man, and I am not ready to trust anyone again."

Matthew nodded and took her hand. "I can be your friend—for now."

He walked her toward the horses. Matthew helped her mount, and Julia thought of the time she went riding with the duke. She smiled at the memory of him giving her the trousers. Thinking back to that day, her heart ached at the memory of their secret adventure. His gift was nothing she had imagined—her heart had changed for him after that.

Matthew led them back to the cottage, and Laura asked him to stay for supper. He agreed and went to help John outside. Julia offered to help Laura prepare the beef stew, but Laura was already finished. She was just preparing some fresh bread to serve with the stew and setting the table. Watching Laura work in the kitchen, she admired her attention to detail. Her kitchen was organized, and she knew where every spice and kitchen tool were located. Feeling a bit useless, she compared her life with Laura's. She had been raised to be a lady and a wife. Being a duchess was her destiny—the host of elegant dinners and the supervisor of the staff. Julia took a deep breath as she pulled out her chair at the table. Realizing she had a lot to learn on how to survive without the assistance of her father, she trembled with fear at her lack of training in the real world.

Dinner was full of laughter—it was less formal than any supper she had ever attended. Julia offered to help with the dishes, but Laura refused. This was probably just as well because she did not know how to wash dishes. Laura told them to go to the drawing room and she would bring out some apple tarts for dessert. Julia admired how hard Laura worked—between farm work and taking care of the house, she had no rest.

Matthew challenged Julia to a game of jacks when she arrived in the drawing room. She had not played since she was a child but enjoyed getting her mind off other things. Matthew was a good competitor and offered a few wagers. However, Julia refused his wagers as he could have beaten her easily and the stakes were too high. Matthew took his leave after dessert as they had to wake up very early to go to work. Julia bid Laura good night after Matthew left and went upstairs to her room.

Julia tossed and turned, finding it difficult to sleep. Her deceptions were consuming her as she lost count of how many lies she had told over the last few days. She knew Matthew was becoming attracted to her, yet she enjoyed his friendship. How could she remain friends and discourage his affections?

The bedroom temperature was freezing—the fire had gone out a long time ago, and she didn't have a servant to keep it going. Julia wrapped herself in the blanket tighter, trying to adjust herself to a comfortable position. To make matters worse, her mind was racing and kept returning to think about the duke. She thought about him more than Randolph. Trying to push those feelings away, she knew he must hate her. But it was too late to have any regrets. Besides, she thought he was probably already with Lady Janel and they were undoubtedly counting the days for their announcement.

Julia must have finally fallen asleep because she woke up to light streaming through her window. Her heart was beating fast as she remembered her dreams. They were full of the duke, and Randolph. She remembered that she had been falling because Randolph had dropped her. Then the duke was trying to catch her, and she fell on Matthew, knocking him down. She found it all very strange and went to get water to wash her face. The water was freezing, and she shivered as she tried to dress.

Matthew had joined them to break their fast. He said that he had come by to ask John some questions about the farm. But Laura nodded suspiciously because she knew that Matthew could have waited for John to go to the farm. He was giving some riding lessons and could have spoken to John then. Laura suspected that Matthew had some feelings for Julia. She knew from Mary that Lady Julia had been involved in a scandal in London and needed some refuge, and she did not want Matthew to get tangled in the mess. Julia appeared very gracious, and she would not tell Matthew the truth due to her promise to Mary, but she was worried that Matthew would suffer heartbreak.

Chapter 31

THE NEXT FEW MONTHS FLEW by for Julia. She and Matthew went riding almost every evening to explore their castle. They'd started calling it *their* castle as their adventures turned up secrets every time they visited it. Julia loved exploring and discovered that she was growing an attachment to the farm. She now knew how to gather eggs and milk the cows without Laura. She had even learned how to make bread and was so excited to show Mary how domesticated she had become.

Julia enjoyed her time with Laura away from the farm. They often went into the local village on Saturdays. The village was a few miles from their cottage, and the closest city was twenty miles away. The men had promised to take them one day soon to the city, so they could take in the local entertainment. Julia smiled as she thought about her outings in Boston and London, where social events were held almost every night of the week. She had not packed any ballgowns or fashionable day dresses and wore the same dress to breakfast and supper. Her mother would have swooned if she knew that Julia only owned a few dresses. The girls were always window shopping and talking about what they would buy one day if they had enough money. Julia felt a pinch of remorse for the lifestyle she had previously lived. Being spoiled by her father had not prepared her for how the rest of the world lived. She had been blessed by wealth and never known the difference.

John and Laura grew attached to Julia. Matthew was always at their house and coming up with fun ideas of things they could do. He had built a wooden swing that hung on a rope from a tree and would push Julia in the swing after supper while they talked. They were always full of chatter during supper and discussed the dreams of owning their own horse farm one day. John would take care of the business side, and Matthew would be the trainer. They even dreamed of expanding the cottage, and Julia would help Laura come up with more ideas for decorating the extra rooms. Laura dreamed of filling the rooms with children and teaching her children during the day. Julia enjoyed encouraging her friends to pursue their dreams and tried not to feel melancholy over hers.

It was on a Friday morning when Julia saw John running down the path with a smile. He had been given a day off as a reward for working hard. He was excited to take Laura into town to celebrate at a real restaurant. They had always thought it was too expensive, but he had some savings and wanted to treat his wife. He invited Julia to join them, but she told them to go alone.

Matthew came by later that evening. He took her to the swing, so they could talk privately.

"I am missing my youth with this swing. We had one in Boston." Julia leaned back looking into the darkened sky.

"Boston?" He asked her inquisitively.

Julia's eyes widened. "Bath. I said Bath."

He chuckled. "I thought you said Boston."

"Perhaps you have been working too hard." She laughed it off nervously.

"Perhaps you are right. I need a day off, and I thought about joining John and Laura. Would you like go to the restaurant too?"

Julia did not want Matthew to spend his hard-earned money on her, but he insisted. She shook her head, "It's too much."

"Nonsense, It's a treat for all our hard work. I insist that we go too. I have some money put away. I have been saving for the horse farm that John and I will pull together. We plan to breed a racehorse."

Julia stopped the swing and stood up. "I am so proud of you, Matthew."

He stepped in front of her as she met his eyes. Panicking, she realized he was going to kiss her. She quickly turned her face as his lips brushed against her cheek. For a moment she saw the duke instead of Matthew, and she blinked her eyes, trying to recover.

He looked at her and touched her chin. "I should take you back inside." Julia smiled weakly and walked with him back to the house.

Julia could not sleep that night. She felt empty inside—the void in her chest could not be filled. Realizing she missed her family and Frank, she wondered if she would ever see any of them again. Her heart ached to know if they were well.

Reflecting on her life since arriving in London, she finally admitted to herself that she had tried to hate the duke just to defy her parents. Although, she would never admit that to anyone. Turning her pillow over, she looked out the window. There was a quarter moon that night that lit up parts of her bedroom. She fantasized about what it would have been like to have gone through with the marriage to Frank. Perhaps she could have fallen in love with him if he was willing to make the ultimate commitment.

The blankets were caught underneath her, and Julia rose to pull the blankets off her and straighten out her pallet. Throwing the blanket over her shoulders, she walked to look out the window. Darkness and mist came off the fields, and she shivered as the wind blew across the grass. How many weeks had gone by? Her stomach fluttered when she thought about Frank's smile and how gently he'd spoken to her. She often thought of the day in the parlor when he'd kissed her cheek and forehead. Julia's mind briefly went to Randolph—such time wasted on her infatuation with him, confusing his attention for what she thought was love.

Julia walked back over to her pallet and tried to go back to sleep. She wished Mary could write her, but she had insisted that she did not notify her of what was happening with her family. She wanted no trace of her whereabouts. A letter could have been followed, and they may have found her. Although she doubted that any of them were still looking for her. It had been almost three months since Julia had left, and she knew she would have to go back to London to get Mary soon. They had made a promise, and Julia would keep it. She could have just asked Mary to come visit her brother and had him send a letter. But deep inside, she wanted to see her parents again, and this was an excuse to see them one more time.

Waking up with the sun shining through the window, she realized sleep had not evaded her completely. Today was her special date with Matthew as they were finally going into town. Julia was looking forward to a change of scenery and was hoping that it would brighten her melancholy. Stretching her back, she walked over to her trunks in the corner. Wanting to find something special to wear, she went through her belongings. As she was moving around things in her trunk, she spotted a purple velvet bag in her perfume box. Julia looked puzzled as she opened it and found the bracelet that the duke had given her. It was the one that had belonged to his grandmother. She had forgotten to give it back to him and knew she could not keep it. Putting it safely away, she thought to return it when she returned to London to retrieve Mary.

She found some blue ribbons, hoping they would match the dress she was saving for a special occasion. A twinge of nervousness entered her thinking about Matthew. Aware of his attachment growing for her, she thought about speaking to him about his attempted kiss. Although she loved their friendship, they could never be together. It wasn't fair to him.

Her stomach growled, reminding her that she needed to eat. Going down the stairs, she saw Laura working in the kitchen. "Good morning. I hope you slept well." She offered Julia some toast with jam and hot tea.

"Thank you." Julia took a seat at the table. Laura was cleaning up the breakfast dishes as both John and Matthew were in the barn, planning the new horse farm. Laura wanted to sew the hem of her dress and make it ready for tonight's outing. Julia offered to help, but Laura told her she could handle it and that she should relax. Julia returned to her room to read a new book she had received from a lady at church.

The night finally came, and the girls giggled as they got dressed up. Julia found it difficult to fix her own hair as she was used to Mary helping her. Laura offered to tie her hair up in a bun and let some curls hang down. Julia wore the duke's bracelet and pinched her cheeks for some color. Laura borrowed some of her rose perfume, and before long they were both ready to go into town.

They made the men wait below so they could make their entrance together. When they went downstairs Matthew's, eyes lit up when he saw Julia. He had a huge smile and complimented her beauty. She took his extended arm to guide her outside to the carriage. John whistled at his wife when she made her way behind Julia, and she could see the love he felt for her.

Matthew had borrowed an older carriage from the farm, and the men had hired their friend Eli to drive the carriage, so they could ride on the inside with the ladies. They had a fun time talking and laughing during their trip. The group arrived in town, and John helped the girls out of the carriage. They walked to the stores, and Julia enjoyed looking through fabrics for the curtains. Matthew helped her pick out some he thought would match the cottage. They went to a candy store and bought some sugar treats for later. John and Laura wanted to look at some new bonnets, and Julia wandered to the bookstore. Matthew had to deliver some papers to a friend at some offices across the street, so Julia had agreed to meet him at the restaurant with John and Laura. Julia looked through the bookstore and purchased a new book. She was excited to go home later and start reading it.

Julia spotted Laura and John and met them outside.

"Where's Matthew?"

Julia shrugged. "He said he will meet us at the restaurant."

The restaurant was in the downstairs ballroom of an inn. It was nice and had white tablecloths with candles at each table. Julia spotted Matthew in the foyer and smiled at him. She noticed his grin was strained, and there were some visible worry lines creasing his brow. John went to speak to him, but the conversation was brief. Matthew approached Julia and offered his arm as they were escorted to their table. Julia tried to make light conversation with Matthew, but his answers were short. Julia wondered what type of business he'd had with his friend and why his mood had turned so sour.

The dinner was wonderful—they were served roasted chicken with peas and potatoes. The dessert was flaky apple tarts with cinnamon and sugar sprinkled on top them. Julia could have eaten two but tried not to indulge too much. They finished their meal with tea and milk. Julia enjoyed the meal but was disturbed by Matthew's behavior and demeanor.

John tried to speak to Matthew on the carriage ride back, but he only nodded and kept his answers brief. Laura snuck looks at Julia with a questioning gaze, but she shrugged her shoulders, as confused as they were. The ride back was long, and Julia looked out the window, mostly thinking about London and how she should get back there to retrieve Mary. She may have to hire a driver because John had his work at the horse farm and probably would not be able to escort her.

The carriage pulled up to the farm, and Matthew helped Julia step out. "May we speak privately?"

Julia nodded, trying to hide her wariness over his stern look at her. John and Laura said their goodbyes as they took a horse back to the cottage. Matthew asked Julia to wait at the entrance of the carriage house until he could unhook the horses from the carriage. Julia nodded and walked toward his house. It was a small house with two rooms and stone walls. There were two chairs outside on the porch. Julia sat in one while she waited for him to finish. She was perplexed by his behavior and a little curious. Leaning back in the chair, she closed her eyes, feeling the breeze as she waited. She soon heard footsteps and opened her eyes.

He rubbed his chin with his hand, pausing before he spoke. "Did you rest well, Lady Julia?"

Julia was silent. He had used her real name—her mind was racing. She didn't know what to say and gave him a blank stare.

Leaning against a tree next to the porch, he sniffed loudly in agitation. "Your silence says a lot."

Julia looked down and bit her bottom lip. She was tired of lying and had to trust someone. Matthew had been very nice to her—he deserved to know the truth. Finally making eye contact with him, she asked, "How did you know?"

He took a deep breath and handed her a piece of parchment that was folded. She slowly took it from his hand and opened it. Her eyes studied the sketch of herself with a description and reward for information. She looked at him. "How were you sure this was me?"

He locked eyes with her for a long moment and said, "Ah, at first I doubted myself. However, I asked my friend about the paper I found on his desk." Matthew folded his arms, continuing, "He said he received it from an investigator looking for a lady who had disappeared under unusual circumstances. Apparently from an extremely wealthy family."

He unfolded his arms and raised his eyebrows. "He told me that her name was never mentioned, but she had disappeared nearly three months ago. I assumed her name was not given to keep her identity a secret due to a scandal. Rumor has it that the Bow runners are trying to find her. The sketch and description looked a lot like you."

"How did you know my name?"

"I heard Laura call you Lady Julia on our trip from London. I thought it was odd and it may have been an inside jest." He ran his hand through is hair. "I just never forgot it."

Julia stood up and stepped toward him.

He studied her face, "John and Laura know, don't they?"

Julia nodded her head. "I am so sorry, Matthew."

"I just don't understand why you didn't trust me." Matthew took her hand and held it up to his mouth to kiss it before pulling her closer to him.

She hugged him, and he held her tightly. "It's complicated."

Pulling back from him, she walked back to the chair. Matthew quietly watched her and waited for her to speak.

"My father is an earl, and we came from Boston for my

arranged marriage. My experience in London and in the *ton* was a life I did not know or desire. I was a difficult child to my parents and my betrothed."

Matthew came up beside her and motioned for her to sit with him. She took a chair, and he sat beside her. "Go on. Who was your betrothed?"

"The Duke of Shallot."

Matthew's eyes grew wide. "What? You gave up marrying a duke?" He raised a brow and smiled. "You're unlike any woman I have ever met. What did he do to you?"

Julia shrugged her shoulders. "He was very kind to me and showered me with compliments and gifts. All of society was anticipating our wedding."

Matthew looked at her in amusement. "He sounds awful. I would have left him too." Julia started laughing and felt more at ease.

She turned serious. "He was not awful—he just didn't love me."

"Have you ever been in love? Maybe he did love you and you just didn't realize it."

She looked away, gazing into the darkening sky. "I thought I was in love once. His name was Randolph, and he was a prince that was a cousin of the Prince Regent."

Matthew let out a choked cough and backed his chair away from her. "Are you telling me you had a relationship with a prince and a duke?" He sighed. "And then you fell for a poor stable boy."

She reached out her hand and touched his face. "I wish I could be Rachel for you."

He took her hand and kissed it again. He smiled. "Don't

stop now. Your story has me in suspense. What happened with these two men?"

"Randolph loved me but chose duty first. He had an arranged marriage with another royal and told me we could be *special* friends, but he was unable to marry me. The duke was in love with another noblewoman but was going to marry me because our families had arranged it." She felt tears start to form in her eyes. "It's typical life in nobility, but I chose to escape it all."

He was silent, taking a minute to respond. "You can't run forever, my lady."

She snorted. "Please don't start calling me that. You can call me Julia."

He looked at her. "How are Laura and John involved in this charade?"

She looked down, biting her bottom lip. "John's sister, Mary, was my lady's maid, and they did this as a favor to her. Please don't blame them—they were only trying to protect me. Please, Matthew, keep my secret."

He held her hand. "I will keep your secret. But I must ask about your feelings for me."

Her stomach dropped, knowing that Matthew had strong feelings for her, and she did not want to hurt him. She gently pulled her hand away. "Matthew, if my circumstances were different, I would fall in love with you in a minute. You have become my best friend; however, my heart belongs to another, and I am no good for you."

"Whom does your heart belong to?"

She looked away. "I wasn't even sure if it was true, but I think I am in love with the duke." Covering her face with her hands, she continued. "He loved another, and I could not live that way. I am hoping that one day I can give my heart to someone who will love me back. I just don't think that I am ready yet. I'm sorry... I don't want to hurt your feelings."

"Julia, I just want you to be honest and trust me."

They sat in silence before Matthew said, "I should get you home now." He helped her mount the horse and sat behind her as they rode to the cottage.

As they approached the door, Matthew helped her off the horse and walked her to the door. "One last hug?"

Julia lifted her arms, wrapping them around his neck, and Matthew held her closely. He whispered in her ear, "I will miss you."

She backed away from him. "Please, Matthew, can't we still be friends?"

He took a deep breath. "My heart can't take a friendship right now. It would hurt too much." He began to walk back to the horse.

"Matthew!" He turned around to look at her. She didn't say anything, and he put his hat on. "I need to go, my lady." He mounted his horse and left.

Julia entered the house and ran up the stairs to her room. She sobbed loudly, trying to catch her breath. She'd done it again! Hurting another special man in her life. Knowing she could not stay there any longer, she would make plans the next day to leave.

Chapter 32

THE NEXT MORNING JULIA GOT up early and broke her fast with Laura. They had planned to go to church that morning, then for a picnic.

John came inside. "Eli just came by and said Matthew was not able to join us today."

Laura drew her brows together. "Is he unwell?"

John shrugged, "I am not sure, he was acting odd yesterday after the dinner." They both looked at Julia.

She took a deep breath. "He knows the truth."

They looked at each other, and John cleared his throat. "How did he find out?"

"He had found a missive on his friend's desk that came from London with a description of me. He had other suspicions and asked me to confirm it with him, so I confessed the truth because I didn't want to lie to him any longer."

John sat down, taking a sip of his tea. "I will speak to him later. He just needs time to cool off."

Julia shook her head. "I think it's more than that, John. He feels I am not the person he grew affection for. I feel I must leave now."

Laura gasped. "No, we love you being here. You are like a part of our family now."

Julia smiled at the couple. "You two are very kind, but I have neglected my responsibilities. It's time to face them. I must return to London to get Mary and speak to my parents."

John nodded. "Very well, if you insist. I can take you to London in a few weeks."

Julia shook her head. "Nonsense, I won't let you miss any more work. I will hire a carriage in town and leave tomorrow."

John tried to argue about having a chaperone, but Julia stopped him. "I am a ruined woman now, and a chaperone will not be necessary. I still plan to travel as a maid and go by the name of Rachel."

John shook his head. "I don't like it."

She looked at him. "I know, but I will be fine." They sat in silence after that, and Julia went back upstairs to pack.

John was waiting for Julia when she came down the stairs. He had asked Eli to go with her to town and make sure she had a ticket for the following day. She could stay at the hotel since the town was a few hours away.

Julia insisted on giving Laura and John the money for her boarding that month and for the carriage ride to London. She paid Eli to be her escort and said goodbye to John and Laura. Laura had tears in her eyes, begging Julia to promise to come back soon. They rode to town in one of the estate's carriages instead of the cart. Matthew had insisted that Eli take it for Julia, but he refused to say goodbye. Julia was saddened to part the way they did but respected his wishes. She knew she could not come back there for a long time. She would plan alternative accommodations if her parents did not forgive her.

The carriage ride to the inn went by faster than Julia remembered. Eli insisted on staying at the inn's stable for the night because he didn't want to leave Julia alone in town. Julia told him he could leave, but Eli refused. She thanked Eli and told him that she was grateful for his assistance.

Julia's accommodation was a small room with a single bed and dresser. Eli had carried her trunk upstairs for her and bid her a good night. Julia was happy to be on her way to London but felt reservations regarding her arrival. She was frightened of the harsh words from her parents, and she wasn't sure if her heart could take seeing Lady Janel and Frank together.

Julia gathered her belongings the next morning and broke her fast with an apple that the innkeeper gave her. He helped Julia take her trunk down the stairs. She spotted Eli just outside of the inn's front door. She appeared in front of him, and he smiled at her. "The carriage leaves in an hour, so we should load your belongings now."

"Thank you, Eli, for everything. Please tell Matthew thank you for the carriage." Eli smiled again and tipped his hat. He took her trunk and carried it toward the carriage stop. He waited for her to enter the carriage and waved goodbye as he took off back toward the estate. Julia felt sad watching him leave. She knew Matthew had asked him to stay and offer her protection until she departed. She sighed at her good fortune to have such wonderful people care for her on her journey.

Chapter 33

THE TRIP TO LONDON WAS rough. Passengers were packed in tight in the coach. Julia tried to rest, but the close quarters made it impossible. Her whole body ached when they finally made it to an inn that night. Most of the rooms were taken, so Julia and another passenger shared a room in the servants' quarters. Julia's roommate was an older woman who was a cook for a viscount back in London. She was visiting her mother for a fortnight and had to get back to London quickly. Julia enjoyed her shared recipes and her companionship on the trip. She knew the woman did not have a lot of money because she had not been working. She offered to pay for their accommodation. However, the woman kept refusing until she finally agreed at Julia's persistence.

Julia only slept for a few hours before she woke up thinking about the duke again. She tried to put him out of her mind because she could have no regrets when it came to her decisions. Her plan of what to do after she saw her parents had formed in her mind. She could sell the diamonds from Randolph, and that should give her enough money to survive for a few years. Maybe even buy a small cottage. Her saved pin money was almost gone, but she may be able to get some money from the pearl necklace that was a gift from her grandmother. She hoped it was still in her jewelry box. She just needed to convince Mary to go with her instead of staying with her brother. Julia could no longer stay at the farm because of everything that happened with Matthew.

The second part of the trip was quieter because the passengers were talking less—she thought they might have run out of things to talk about. Julia didn't mind the stillness. She closed her eyes at the rocking of the carriage. She woke to the sound of someone speaking to her. It was the woman she'd shared a room with offering her some bread that she had saved from breakfast. Julia accepted it with a smile while speaking to the lady about the different ways to make cinnamon buns. They shared a room again the second night.

They arrived in London later in the day. Julia could smell the stench of the city. It may not have been Mayfair, but it was a welcome relief to be off the coach. What a difference from being in the quiet country to the hustle and bustle of busy city. Julia and her new friend found a hack for hire to take them to Mayfair. They loaded their trunks, paid the driver, then were on their way.

It was so nice to be in a familiar area as the driver drove them past beautiful townhomes. Julia offered to drop the woman off first, and she thanked Julia, giving her a hug when they arrived at her employer's house. Julia wished her well and slipped a few coins in her hand. The lady tried to decline, but she insisted. Julia gave the driver directions to her parents' new town house next, hoping she could remember which one her parents had bought.

She remembered the etchings on the door and thought she could find the right one.

The driver dropped Julia off a few minutes later, helping her with her trunk. Julia paid and thanked him. She tried to carry the trunk to the side of the house, dragging it part of the way. The heaviness of the trunk took a toll on her, and she took a seat on top of it to catch her breath. After resting a few minutes, she composed herself.

It was time.

She was nervous to see her family. Her first thought was to look through the windows. Most of the house was dark even though the hour was not too late. Julia walked around the large house, looking for any sign of someone that was home. Finally, she found a stream of light from the kitchen window. Peeking in the window, she saw a woman she did not recognize stacking some dishes. Julia was hesitant as she did not know if she was at the wrong house. She watched as another woman came through the door. Trying to see her face, her heart leaped when she recognized Mary. She wanted to get her attention without the other woman knowing, so she waited to see if she could attract her notice. She saw both women talking and laughing. Julia grew anxious as she wondered how long she would have to wait outside.

Mary finally went toward the door to take a bucket of water outside. Julia's stomach fluttered anxiously at the opportunity. She waited until Mary opened the door and stepped out onto the kitchen stoop.

Julia whispered, "Mary!"

Mary jumped, giving a little shout.

Julia covered her mouth with her finger. "Shh!"

Mary dropped the bucket, embracing her with a huge hug. "Oh, my lady!" Mary was crying and would not let go of her.

"I am so happy you are home. I have so much to tell you." Mary would not let go of Julia's hand.

Julia smiled. "Are my parents' home?"

Mary hesitated, looking at Julia with regret. "They went to their estate in Savory soon after you left. They were very broken-hearted and feared for your safety. I was kept on their staff as their kitchen maid. There are only a few of us here to maintain the house. Your parents have not returned since you left."

Julia fretted, twisting her hands. "Do you think any of the staff will recognize me?"

Mary lifted the corner of her mouth. "They hired only a few servants to maintain the residence, and you can share my room. No one should see us."

Mary guided her to the servants' entrance, and they went up to Mary's room undetected. Julia collapsed on her bed and took in a deep breath of relief. "Mary, your brother and sister-in-law treated me like an honored guest, and I am indebted to them and you." She turned to her side and shook her head. "But I am afraid that they may be cross with me. Unintentionally, I think I hurt their good friend."

"I don't understand." The worry lines on Mary's face deepened.

"They introduced me to a man who John works with. We became close friends, and he had affection for me that I did not return. He found out the truth, and I am afraid I may have hurt his feelings. He is a great man, and I am not sure why I let it go that far. I think it was just nice to be with someone ordinary. But I was wrong to hurt his feelings."

"I will write John a letter. Or better yet, I hope to visit soon and will let him know that you meant no harm. I am sure it's not as bad as you think it is."

Mary changed her clothes and sat beside Julia on the bed. "Are you going to ask me about him?"

Julia bit her bottom lip. "I was afraid to. Is he engaged?"

Mary closed her eyes. "Oh, my lady, you broke his heart. He came here shortly after you left and begged me to tell him where you were. I told him that I didn't know, and I know he didn't believe me. Your parents were frantic and looked everywhere for you. Your father even hired an investigator, and the duke hired a Bow runner."

Mary stood again and went over to the chest. "I just felt so guilty, but I kept my promise."

Julia stood up and walked over to Mary, putting her hand on her shoulder. "Forgive me for putting so much pressure on you."

Mary turned around with tears in her eyes. "It's alright, my lady."

Julia shook her head. "No, it's not. I have been selfish. I just want to make things right."

Mary looked at her. "After a few weeks, the visits by His Grace stopped, and your parents never came back to London. Your cousin watched me closely as I think she suspected my involvement, although she never confronted me." She walked away and played with some ribbons on the table. "The wedding was postponed, and the dowager duchess sent out regrets. The story was that you had a family emergency in Boston and postponed the wedding."

Looking down, Mary hesitated to make eye contact.

"The gossip is now that the duke turned you down for Lady Janel and you made a quiet exit."

Julia rolled her eyes and bit her bottom lip. "Are they happy?"

Mary finally looked at her. "I don't know, my lady. I am not privy to such information anymore and only read the scandal sheets now. As far as I know, there is no official announcement, although the sheets talk about them."

She took a brush to Julia's hair. "I saw the look in his eyes. I think we may have been wrong about him, my lady. He was desperate for you when he begged me to tell him where you were." Mary took her hair and started to braid it. "I think the rumors may not be true. Perhaps he did love you."

Julia jerked her head away and looked back at Mary. "Mary, please don't say that. My heart can't take any regrets." Mary hugged her, and she finished Julia's hair. They spoke a while longer and said good night. Julia turned on her shoulder toward the wall. She had tears in her eyes until she finally fell asleep.

When Julia woke, Mary was gone. She sat up and looked through her trunk. She did not know if she still had any dresses in the house and decided to read her new book while she waited for Mary.

Mary appeared soon with some hot chocolate for Julia. Julia smiled and took a drink. "You're not my lady's maid anymore. I can get my own hot chocolate."

Mary laughed. "I enjoy doing this for you."

Julia smirked. "I have been thinking, Mary. We must change plans. I need to go to Savory to see my parents, and then we can go to Bath. I have read a lot about the city, and we may be able to start over there."

Mary agreed to help Julia. They would hire a driver to take them to Savory the next day. Julia asked her to accompany her to buy a few supplies in town. Mary agreed and went to retrieve some of Julia's old dresses. Julia wanted to keep a low profile until she spoke to her parents. The girls sneaked out the servant's entrance and went into town.

Julia and Mary split up and decided they would meet at the bakery as their destination—Julia wanted to get some new slippers while Mary went to the bookstore. Julia walked down the cobblestone sidewalk and glanced up at the buildings. She noticed a broad-chested man with impeccably tailored clothes depart from an office building. A woman with a parasol came up beside him and took his arm. As Julia came closer, she gasped and pulled her hood over her head.

It was the duke and Lady Janel!

Julia's heart sank into her chest. She watched as Lady Janel went into the bonnet store after a brief conversation with the duke. The duke waved, turning on his heel, and was headed right toward her.

Looking down and trying to cover her face, she rounded the corner to hide behind the buildings. She was trapped in the alleyway as he got closer to her. Panicking, she turned her back toward the road as he passed by, and she tried to keep quiet but could not hold it in and yelled out his name.

The duke stopped, looking around. Julia stepped away from the building, removing her hood from her head. The duke's mouth fell open as he stared blankly at her.

Julia gazed at him for several seconds. "Can I speak to you for a moment?"

The duke stepped into the alley without a word. Julia took a deep breath. "Forgive me, I just got into town and wasn't prepared to see you yet." He kept staring at her, and she shifted her feet lowering her eyes. "I wanted to return something to you."

The duke's brow creased with a puzzled expression. Julia removed the bracelet that she had worn every day since the outing with Matthew. She took it off her arm and took a step closer to him. The duke stared at her and held out his hand as she dropped the bracelet and stepped back. He finally cleared his throat and said, "I hope you're well."

Julia smiled. "Yes, I am doing well. Thank you."

"Have you seen your parents?"

Julia looked down, afraid to answer as the shame and consequences of her actions were becoming unbearable. "I tried. But I didn't know they were at their country estate. I went to their new home, and their staff told me they didn't reside there anymore. I will leave to see them in the morning. I don't know if I will be accepted, but I must try to make amends. I stayed at their home last night with Mary, my maid. She let me use her room and will accompany me tomorrow to Savory."

The duke nodded.

Julia bit her bottom lip. "I hope you don't hate me. I was a coward and should have spoken to you first without running away."

The duke stepped toward her. "Julia, I..."

Suddenly, a voice interrupted them. "Frank, is that you over there?" Julia turned and saw Lady Janel coming down the alley. The duke turned to look at Lady Janel, and Julia pulled the hood back over her head.

"Who is that?" she questioned, walking toward them. He turned back to Julia as she frantically shook her head, meeting his eyes as she lowered her head.

The duke's face was torn, seemingly trying to say more, but he turned away from her and walked to Lady Janel. "I don't know… someone just needing some help." He guided her back towards the entrance of the alley away from Julia.

Lady Janel took his arm possessively, telling him about the two bonnets she had just purchased. The duke turned his head back toward the alley to see if he could see her, but she had stepped into the shadows, waiting for them to leave.

Julia ran until she found Mary and grabbed her arm. "We must go at once, Mary."

"What's amiss?"

"I saw Frank! He was with Lady Janel, and we must go now!"

She nodded her head and agreed as they went back to the house to prepare to leave the next day. Julia told Mary she wanted to lie down, and she would pack later. Mary went to the kitchen to prepare dinner. The other kitchen maid had the day off, and the only other staff member in residence was the housekeeper.

The duke rode to Julia's house and waited for the staff to open the door. It took several knocks before the housekeeper finally opened the door. Handing her his card, the duke straightened his coat. "The Duke of Shallot to see Lady Julia."

The housekeeper was confused. "I am sorry, Your Grace. There is no one by that name in residence."

The duke's jaw flexed tightly. "Very well, may I speak to the maid named Mary?"

Suspiciously the housekeeper took in his request before answering, "We do have a maid named Mary. Please come inside, Your Grace. I will show you to the parlor."

The duke followed the housekeeper and waited by the settee. Mary appeared a few minutes later. She opened her mouth and then quickly shut it as she saw him looking back at her. She curtsied. "Your Grace, how can I help you?"

"I am here to see Lady Julia."

Mary closed the parlor doors. She wrung her hands. "Um, she is not receiving, Your Grace."

The duke took a deep breath. Trying to maintain his patience, he crossed his arms before speaking through his teeth. "I am not leaving until I speak to her. Get her now, or I will expose this charade."

"She is sleeping, Your Grace."

The duke took an intimidating step closer. "Wake her up, or I will."

Mary slowly swallowed. "I will be back in a few moments, Your Grace."

Mary woke Julia and tried to quickly make her presentable. Julia was nervous to see him but knew she owed him an explanation. Hurrying to the parlor, she took a deep breath on the other side of the parlor doors before opening them. The duke was standing by the fireplace.

She curtsied. "Your Grace, I must admit that I am surprised to see you."

The duke walked toward the settee and sat down. "I wanted to finish our conversation." Julia nodded and sat beside him.

She had memorized many explanations and practiced what she would say if given a chance. "Do you remember that day in the park when you told me that marriage could be based on mutual affection and friendship?"

The duke looked confused but nodded his head.

Julia continued. "I thought it could be true because my affection for you grew. I had developed a fondness for you."

The duke seemed to be listening intently as she struggled with her words. "You treated me kindly, saving me from that lunatic, and I felt safe and protected by you. I started to look forward to seeing you."

Julia took a breath as the duke's expression changed— he seemed wary as Julia looked away. "I thought that would be enough when I agreed to marry you."

She stood up and started pacing around the room. Turning back around, she looked at him. "My feelings changed, and I knew it could never work."

"I don't understand... what changed?"

She felt his gaze, closing her eyes, "I... I, um... I fell in love with you, and I knew my heart would not be able to handle the consequences."

He looked bewildered. "You couldn't marry me because you fell in love with me?"

Julia nodded her head. "Don't you see? I grew jealous of Lady Janel and knew your heart was hers."

The duke opened his mouth but closed it again looking at Julia. She held back her tears. "I heard you that day in the library, and my feelings were crushed. Don't you understand? I had to leave as I could no longer be part of a marriage just based on friendship. I needed your love. I wanted that or nothing at all." She caught her breath and looked away again. "I know you never told me that you loved me. It was a marriage of only friendship, but that would not work anymore. I had to leave."

The duke put his head in his hands. "Julia, how could you not know?"

He stood and walked to her quickly, pulling her into his arms as he leaned down to brush his lips softly against hers. Julia trembled. He held her closer as he pressed into her lips—his kiss was passionate. Not the chaste kisses she'd expected. He opened her mouth as she lifted her hands to embrace his neck. He played with her tongue, deepening the kiss, pulling her off the ground as he held her close. Finally, putting her down, he cupped her face with his hands. "I love you, Julia."

Her heart skipped a beat, a feeling of warmth filling her body. The beat of his heart vibrated against her. Finally separating, they held hands as they sat on the settee. Julia had tears in her eyes, just wanting to breathe him in.

He rubbed her hands. "Oh Julia, I still want us to get married."

She looked at him. "What about my reputation? I am sure the *ton* has branded me ruined."

The duke shrugged his shoulders. "Perhaps, but I

don't care what they say. They can hang. I don't care about propriety anymore. I love you and want to marry you tomorrow."

Julia tilted her head. "But what about Lady Janel?"

The duke looked at her confused. "I don't love her, Julia, and I never did. That day in the library was a goodbye. I told her she would be okay and that my heart belonged to you. She has tried to be my friend, but I never had any intention of marrying her."

"I heard them say that you were only marrying me because of my father's business deal—that you needed the money."

The duke smirked. "Julia, I am wealthy even without the title. Trust me that we will never want for anything. I don't need your dowry. I only need you."

He walked her to the chair and sat down, pulling her onto his lap. He gave her soft kisses as she laid her head on his shoulder. "Julia, I will take you to your parents, but I need you to give me a day to get a special license, so we can marry right away. Although, you have not answered me... will you be my wife?"

Julia kissed him on the cheek. "Yes, I would like nothing more than to be your wife. We can wait another day to leave. I have a few things to take care of as well."

He held her close and took the ring out of his pocket, placing it on her finger. She looked at her hand, gazing at the ring. They sat in silence for a few more minutes before getting up and going to the front door. He kissed her softly once again before departing. They had made plans to have dinner the next day. The duke insisted that she stay at his house the following night, so she could have a proper room.

He had to also notify his mother. Julia's stomach felt uneasy at the thought of what the dowager duchess would say to her. Saying good night, she leaned against the door after he had departed. She snuck back into Mary's quarters—who was waiting for her on the bed still awake!

Julia showed Mary her hand, and Mary squealed, hugging her. She told Mary she was leaving to go to her parents with the duke the next day but had some errands to run first. She wanted to dress as a maid until her parents knew about her plans.

The next morning, Mary helped Julia dress, and then she went to see her father's solicitor. She was hoping he was in his office today and would receive her.

Julia was surprised when her father's solicitor embraced her.

"Lady Julia! I am so excited to see you. Please tell me about your visit." The solicitor motioned for her to sit down. "Your father has been so worried. I had joined the search efforts, but we couldn't find you. He had feared something bad might have happened to you."

"Thank you, sir. I assure you that I plan to visit my parents tomorrow and will relieve their worry." She sat down, carefully placing her reticule in her lap.

He leaned back in his chair. "Very good, my lady. Your father has had much distress. I trust you are well, and you will explain your absence to their satisfaction. I never believed you went to Boston... your father did eventually confide in me the truth of your departure."

Julia paused, smoothing her dress with her gloved hands. "I actually came to see you regarding a personal request."

The solicitor raised his eyebrow curiously. "What kind of personal request?"

Julia removed the black velvet bag from her reticule and handed it to him. The solicitor shook the diamonds out of the bag, widening his eyes as he reached for his glasses to get a better look.

Julia bit her bottom lip. "How much do you think I can get? I need the money quickly."

The solicitor looked at the diamonds. "Probably around ten thousand pounds if you need it quickly. I know a buyer and can help you secure the sale."

Julia smiled and agreed to the terms. "Once the sale goes through, I need you to put the money into three separate accounts."

"I don't understand... you're giving the money away?"

Julia smiled. "Yes, one account for five thousand pounds for my maid Mary. The other five thousand pounds will be split between my friends John and Matthew to raise their own racehorses."

The solicitor blinked his eyes at her. "You truly surprise me, my lady." He prepared the paperwork and gave it to her, so she could give it to her friends.

Julia took the paperwork. "Thank you. I will give my father your regards tomorrow."

Chapter 34

MARY WAS PACKING JULIA'S CLOTHES when she arrived home. Julia reached for her arm. "Mary, you don't have to pack my clothes. Please, sit down, I must speak to you."

Mary pushed a few pieces of loose hair away from her face. Sitting down, she fiddled with her apron. "What is it, my lady?"

Julia smiled coyly, reaching for her hand. "Mary, you have worked hard for me over the last few years, and I cherish your friendship. I trust you more than anyone else in this world."

Mary blushed. "I feel the same."

Julia continued, "I was given a gift to be able to live a life that I chose. Now, I am giving you the same gift. I put five thousand pounds in an account for you." She handed her the note.

Mary gasped, covering her mouth. "Oh, my lady. I can't take this money."

"It's yours. But there is something else I need your help with." She handed Mary the other two notes for Matthew and John.

"Your family and Matthew treated me with such

kindness." Julia started to get choked up. "I want them to have this gift too."

Mary looked at the papers and back up at Julia. "I am without words."

"I am counting on you to make them take this gift and invest it in their farm. I will also be a future customer and will spread the word about them all around the *ton*. Being a duchess will have some benefit." Mary laughed, hugging Julia.

"Mary, you are no longer my maid. You will always be my best friend. You must go to your brother's tomorrow. Please deliver this news in person and stay with John." Mary held the papers to her chest with tears dropping to her face.

Frank arrived in a white carriage with his crest on the side. Julia did not have any footmen to help her and dragged her trunk through the door. His footman slid off the carriage and helped her with the trunk.

Frank looked at her with admiration. "You have learned to be independent on your journey, my love."

Julia smiled, and her stomach did a flip when he used the term "my love." He took her hand and kissed it, helping her into his carriage. Once inside, he pulled her onto his lap and gave her a hug. "I thought about you all day."

She smiled, kissing him on the cheek. "I thought about you too, and I am anxious to hear what your mother said about our marriage."

He slipped her glove off to hold her hand. "She was surprised at first and was hesitant of my decision."

Julia looked concerned. He let go of her hand to touch her face. "I don't care what anyone says, Julia. I love you and will marry you."

Julia leaned down and softly brushed her lips against his. Their kiss stirred something inside her as he opened his mouth to her. The intensity of their kiss took her breath away. He held her close as she felt the carriage slowing down. Breaking away from him, she realized they were approaching the duke's house, and she had to straighten herself out. She pinched her cheeks and smoothed her dress. The duke put his gloves back on and handed Julia's gloves to her. He got out of the carriage and helped her down. Julia leaned against him and was nervous on making their entrance.

When she approached the doorway, she saw Lord Jacob, the duke's brother. He smiled at her, greeting her with a kiss on the hand.

"Ah! Lady Julia, I missed you and welcome you back."

She smiled turning toward the duke. "I am happy to be back in London."

Then, the dowager duchess approached, giving Julia a cold stare. "Lady Julia, I see that you are well. You had us most worried." The dowager duchess did not smile.

She curtsied. "Yes, Your Grace. I am well. Thank you for your concern. I plan to visit my parents tomorrow."

The dowager duchess nodded with no expression. Julia felt uncomfortable, waiting for the duke to say something more. Lord Jacob looked between them and then addressed Julia, "Lady Julia, would you like some tea?"

Julia smiled at him. "Yes, please, that sounds wonderful." The duke asked the footman to take her trunk to the room that was prepared for her. She would be staying in the duchess's chamber that connected to his.

Julia concentrated on her tea, trying to stuff her mouth with some small cakes. She thought it would be better to eat than to talk. The dowager duchess kept quiet, stealing glances at Julia. Most of the talking came from Jacob, who was talking to the duke about going to the country. They were going to stay at Shallot Manor while Julia visited her parents. He had arranged for three carriages to accompany them as they traveled in the morning.

After a few more minutes of conversation, the dowager duchess finally broke her silence. "I don't see what the rush is to marry. Lady Julia has just returned and will need to be reunited with her parents. I feel that announcing a wedding in the same week could be overwhelming."

She gave Julia a look, lifting the corner of her mouth in a bitter smile. "Perhaps next year, after you two are reacquainted."

Julia's stomach felt ill. She knew the dowager duchess had doubts that she would go through with the wedding, probably assuming Julia was using him and concerned about society's opinions.

The duke reached for her hand. "We don't wish to wait and have already decided to marry within a few days. I am a grown man and can make my own decisions."

The dowager duchess glared at her son and took a sip of tea. Lord Jacob shifted in his seat. "I am happy for you both." Julia smiled at him, and the duke thanked him.

The dowager duchess stood. "Very well then. Far be it from me to interfere if your mind is set. I will retire tonight and accompany you in the morning."

Julia stood, not knowing what to say. "Your Grace, could I escort you to your room? I would like to speak to you privately."

The dowager duchess looked surprised and hesitated as she looked at the duke. "If you wish."

The duke touched Julia's arm, and she turned to him. "I will be okay." He nodded and stood as the women left the room.

Julia touched the dowager duchess's arm as they walked up the stairs in silence. Approaching the upstairs parlor, Julia motioned toward the door. The dowager followed her into the room and stood by the winged chair. "Your Grace, I deserve your skepticism regarding my intentions. I have not proven to you that I am worthy to be a duchess in your home."

"It seems it will be your home soon."

Julia turned toward the window. "I understand my behavior may have been juvenile. I reasoned with myself that I was making the right decision for all that were involved." Julia sighed as tears pooled in her eyes, and she turned to the dowager duchess. "After much time, I realized that I needed to make matters right with my parents. I also wanted to face the consequences of my actions with your son."

She took an uneasy breath. "He was so very kind to me and told me for the first time how he truly felt about me. I had not known as I thought he loved Lady Janel."

The dowager looked puzzled at Julia. "Lady Janel? They are just friends."

Julia smiled matter-of-factly. "He feels she is a friend, but she has other intentions."

The dowager closed her eyes. "Are you telling me that this has been a misunderstanding?"

Defensively, Julia held up her hand. "Part of it was a misunderstanding. I also left because I felt my feelings for him were stronger than his feelings for me."

The dowager shook her head. "You are such a naïve girl."

Julia sighed. "I know I was unreasonable, and I want to make amends. I hope you will forgive me."

The dowager duchess walked over to Julia. "You broke my son's heart. He would never admit it, but a mother knows. I still have my doubts about you, but my son's intentions are clear. You will be his duchess, and I will not stand in his way."

Julia looked down. "I understand, Your Grace."

She looked at Julia with resignation in her eyes. They stood in silence for a few more moments, "I will try to like you, Lady Julia. I think it's important that we get along." Julia went to curtsy to her, but the dowager hugged her instead and left the room.

Julia left the dowager and went to find the duke. He was in his study and smiled apprehensively when she entered the room. "How did it go with my mother?"

She sat down in the chair opposite of the desk. "I think she may accept me in her own time."

He walked around his desk and kissed her on the cheek. She stood up, and they walked to their bedchambers, where he bid her a good night. A few minutes later, she heard a knock on the door that joined their chambers. Nervously, she opened it.

The duke smiled, holding her bracelet in his hand. Julia smiled and took it back. "Thank you, it means a lot to me." She looked down at it as he latched it on her arm. "Did you know that I wore it when I was away?"

The duke stood in the doorway. "You haven't really told me about your time away. You only said that some new friends took care of you on an estate where they raised horses."

Julia hesitated—she didn't want Mary to be in trouble. He took his finger and placed it over her lips, then whispered, "No secrets."

"I will tell you, but you can't hold anyone responsible. I must have your promise. It was my decision and no one else's."

He looked at her, touching her chin. "I promise."

Julia smiled at him and kissed his cheek. She sat in a chair in the sitting area, and he took the chair opposite of her. She told him the story of Mary's brother and wife, explaining to him that everyone was nice to her and made sure that she was protected. The duke was upset that Mary hadn't told him the truth but understood her loyalty to Julia. Julia told him that she sold some jewelry that funded her trip but did not mention that Prince Randolph had given her the gift.

Julia smiled as they sat in silence. "I would like to pay them back someday and make sure that our future horse purchases come from their farm."

The duke nodded his head. "I can also let my friends know where to find their next horses." He scooted his chair closer to Julia. "Will you have to find a new maid soon if Mary stays with her brother?"

Julia gave a sad face. "I don't know how I will replace her, but I must find someone."

He leaned down to brush his lips across hers. They stood up, and he cracked a smile. "If I don't leave soon, I may forget I am a gentleman. We will be married soon enough."

Julia's heart leaped as she walked him toward their adjoining door. "I will see you in the morning."

Julia woke early the next day and dressed for her journey. The dowager duchess's lady's maid offered to help her dress because Mary was on her way to see her brother. Julia was nervous about her parents' reaction and hoped that they would accept her back. She offered to go alone, but the duke insisted on accompanying her. Julia chose a blue dress with a white trim. She put on matching earbobs and the duke's bracelet. She wore her hair partially down and chose her lavender perfume. The lady's maid helped her with her laces and excused herself as Julia gathered her thoughts. She looked around the room, thinking to herself that the next time she entered this room, she would be married woman. She was excited as well as nervous about the expectations of marriage.

The family was waiting for Julia as she went to break her fast. The duke and Lord Jacob stood as she entered the room. She greeted them and helped herself to some toast with jam. The kitchen maid offered her some tea, and Julia graciously accepted.

The duke smiled at her. "I hope you slept well and that the accommodation suited your needs."

Julia smiled at him. "Most definitely." The dowager duchess remained silent as Lord Jacob stuffed his mouth with breakfast cakes. Julia quickly finished and stood up from the table to walk to the drawing room.

The duke ordered the carriages to be brought around

so they could depart early to see her parents. The duke and she would share one carriage, and the dowager and Lord Jacob would share the second one. The servants and luggage would occupy the third one.

The duke helped Julia enter her carriage and sat beside her as they departed. They would have two days of travel and one night at the inn. Julia's mind raced as they took off, and she thought about what her parents would say to her. The duke put his arm around her, and she laid her head on his shoulder.

After a long silence, Julia took a deep breath. "Your Grace, do you think my parents hate me?"

The duke squeezed her next to him. "Please, call me Frank. We are to be married. And of course, your parents don't hate you."

Julia waited a few more minutes. "I am frightened of my father."

"I will protect you. He may be angry, but I won't let him hurt you."

"He has never struck me, but I know he has a bad temper at times."

Frank took his arm away and held both of her hands. "Don't worry, my love. It will all work out. Why don't you try to rest, and I will wake you when we eat lunch?"

Julia lay down on the opposite couch, and the duke put his coat over her. She closed her eyes and tried to concentrate on sleeping but found it difficult to stop thinking about the inevitable reunion.

Chapter 35

JULIA WOKE UP STARTLED AS Frank tried to settle in the carriage next to her. She had missed lunch, and they were already stopping for the night. He told her he'd tried to wake her to eat lunch, but she hadn't wanted to wake up, so he'd let her sleep. Julia was starving. He secured three rooms. She and the dowager duchess had their own rooms, and he shared one with Lord Jacob.

The supper was delicious, and Julia was looking forward to a bath and a nice bed. Her neck hurt from the carriage. She was escorted upstairs by the innkeeper's wife to a beautiful room with brown-and-gold bed coverings. She thought of the irony of her situation with the accommodation she now enjoyed to what she'd slept in a few days ago—in the servants' area of the inn. She thanked God for her good fortune.

The next day was a long day as it took several hours to reach Shallot. They stopped there first to freshen up before she and Frank continued to Savory. Julia didn't remember the estate as she had not visited since she was a child. His estate was larger than her parents' home in Savory. There was a beautiful lake, four stables, and two guesthouses on the property. The home itself had two additional wings and was surrounded by a garden that Julia was looking forward to exploring.

The duke showed Julia to the duchess's chamber, and she dressed quickly. The anticipation of seeing her parents was causing her insides to twist. She needed to see them as soon as possible so she could alleviate any of their worries. When she returned downstairs, the duke was waiting for her in the foyer. He introduced her to part of his staff as his future duchess. Julia blushed as they curtsied towards her.

Savory was only an hour's ride by carriage. Frank kept rubbing her hands, kissing them as they traveled. Julia took deep, calming breaths as they entered the driveway. She thought back to her childhood, trying to remember the estate. It became more familiar as the carriage rode up the hill and they approached the manor.

Julia and Frank neared the door and were welcomed by a footman whom Julia did not recognize.

"Good evening. Are you dinner guests of his lordship?"

Julia's chest pounded, and she turned toward Frank for direction. The duke patted her hand reassuringly. "We are not part of the dining party. We are here to see Lady Savory." He handed the butler his card.

The footman saw the card. "Of course, Your Grace." He turned to leave.

Julia couldn't help herself. "Pardon me, did you say there was a party going on at the estate tonight?"

The footman looked at Julia. "Yes, Lady Savory's sister and family are visiting with some other guests."

Julia thanked him as he walked them to the parlor. After he left, Julia turned to Frank. "I can't do this. Not now... we can come back tomorrow."

He embraced her. "It's going to be fine. I will help you through this." She sat on the settee, fidgeting with her hands.

A few minutes later, Lady Savory came into the parlor and saw Frank standing in the doorway. "Your Grace! What a pleasant surprise. You must join us for dinner."

As Lady Savory stepped into the room, she saw Julia from the corner of her eye. She gasped, placing the back of her hand to her mouth. "Julia, is that you?" She ran the rest of the way, screaming, "Is it really you?"

Julia nodded her head as her mother grabbed her from the settee and embraced her, nearly knocking her off her feet. She put her hands to Julia's face. "Are you okay? Were you hurt?"

Julia tried to control her emotions, smiling at her mother as she hugged her again. Lady Savory's eyes filled with moisture. "I am never letting you out of my sight again."

She looked up at the duke. "You found her, Your Grace."

He smiled shaking his head. "She found me."

Lady Savory looked back at Julia. "I have hundreds of questions." Frank sat on the other side of Julia.

Frank smiled. "We know, and there will be time for all of that later. Our first order of business is to let you know that we are getting married within the week."

Lady Savory's mouth dropped open. "How... what?"

Frank and Julia both laughed, holding hands, and Julia said, "It's a love match."

Lady Savory clutched her chest. "My heart is overflowing with emotions right now." They were smiling and laughing about the good news when they heard the earl approach. "What is going on in here? We have guests in the dining room."

When the earl entered, the duke moved, and he spotted Lady Julia next to him.

The earl squinted his eyes. "Julia? What in the world?"

Julia rose, walking to her father and stopping in front of him. "Yes, Father, it is me."

The earl looked at the duke, his mouth hanging open in surprise. "I don't understand, what has happened?"

Julia looked down biting her lip. "I have come home, Father."

He shook his head and looked at Lady Savory.

Frank stood beside Julia. "She came to see me a few days ago. We worked out our misunderstandings, and we will be married within the week with your blessing."

The earl kept staring at Julia. He looked at the duke, taking a seat on the settee beside Lady Savory. He turned to the butler. "I will need a stiff drink."

The butler nodded. "As you wish."

Julia took a seat in front of her parents, and Frank stood behind her. The earl looked at both. "I don't pretend to understand your actions, Julia. The worry and humiliation that you caused your mother and I was inconceivable. There is no excuse for your behavior."

Lady Savory approached her daughter and took her hand. "I don't care, Charles. She is my only daughter, and I am just happy she is home."

The duke put his hand on Julia's shoulder, reassuring her. "I will take responsibility for her. It was my fault why she left."

The earl looked at him and let out a sigh. "I doubt that."

Julia straightened her shoulders. "I won't let him take blame for me. I chose to go because I was frightened to stay. All I can ask for is your forgiveness."

Lady Savory looked at her daughter. "Of course, my dear. I forgive you."

A footman approached with the drink, and the earl gulped it down, asking for another. He stood up, looking at his daughter. "We have guests and can't keep them waiting."

Julia faced her mother dejectedly. "We will go back to the duke's manor."

The earl smoothed his jacked. "You most certainly will not. You are not married yet and will do what I say."

Julia looked at her mother as she cracked a smile. Lady Savory nodded at her husband. "Very well, Charles. I will ask the footman to add two place settings."

The earl patted Julia on the shoulder, then turned to leave. Seemingly changing his mind about something, he turned around. "Your Grace, may we have a minute in the study?"

The duke looked at Julia, and she nodded. She left her with her mother. "Oh, my sweet girl. Come with me up the stairs. I had your old room prepared in case you ever returned. I will give you a moment to freshen up."

"Thank you, Mother." She took her arm, and they walked up the stairs.

Mrs. Savory held her arm tightly. "I will let your father prepare the family. They will be anxious to see you. Sara especially."

They reached her room, and Julia hugged her mother, who smoothed her hair as she held her. She let Julia take a few minutes in her room while she went to inform her sister of the wonderful news.

Julia washed her face with water in the basin beside the bed. She looked around the room, taking in her surroundings. This was home or at least close to it. It had been a long journey, and for the first time in months, she could breathe again. She missed Mary but knew Mary would be better off choosing her own life not dictated by her circumstances. She lay back on the bed, staring at the ceiling...

Julia must have fallen asleep because she was startled by a knock on the door. She rose to answer it and saw Frank. He escorted her to the dining room as the guests had been prepared for her appearance and were most anxiously looking forward to seeing her.

As she entered the dining room, Sara ran toward her. She was hugging Julia when Lord Jason came up behind her. Julia smiled at them as Sara showed her the wedding ring. They had been married a few weeks ago, and Julia congratulated them with such happiness.

Julia's father sat at the head of the table. He asked her to sit to the side of him followed by her mother on the other side. The duke took the seat beside Julia, sitting across from Lord Jason. The family welcomed Julia home, and her father made a toast to the happy couple. During the dinner, the earl made a point to pat his daughter's arm. He did not look at her as he took a sip of his soup. His small sign of affection touched Julia. At that moment, she knew everything would be okay.

After supper, they went into the drawing room as the men drank port in the study. Julia's aunt and mother took turns asking Julia questions about the journey she had been on.

She tried to appease them as they chatted at once. "I met Mary's brother on an outing. I knew he was leaving out of town and paid him to let me rent a room from him and his wife." Julia was careful not to mention Mary's help. Although she was no longer working for the family, there was still a chance they would blame her.

"I had no contact with Mary. Her brother hesitantly agreed to my request." It was not a lie—that part was true.

Her mother shook her head. "It matters not. You are home now, and that is all that matters."

The men joined the women, and Frank took the seat beside Julia. Holding her hand tightly, he cleared his throat. "Julia and I will plan to marry in a few days. There will be no London extravagance, just a quaint family affair. I wish you all to attend."

"Only a small affair?" Lady Savory blurted out. "Nonsense, this is my only daughter."

Julia looked down. "I can't face the London gossips. I just wanted to be married without the fanfare. It's too much."

The duke nodded his head. "I agree. It will be a small village wedding."

"Very well." Lady Savor sighed. "At least let me insist on a new gown. We could do a little shopping in the village. The villagers will appreciate the business and probably want to attend."

Julia looked at Frank and then back to her Mother. "I will agree to that."

"I must go back to Shallot and prepare my mother."

He looked at Julia. "Please walk me outside." He knew she would be staying with her parents until the wedding. At which time, he wanted to take a wedding trip to the coast and stay at one of his estates. They would reside in Shallot as their main living quarters.

Julia stepped onto the porch, and she turned toward him. "I can't believe this is real. I hope I don't wake up if it is a dream."

He pulled her close. "It's real, my love." He kissed her softly and told her he would see her the next day. She waved goodbye, watching him enter the carriage pulling away. She had an ache in her heart as she missed him already. He was her rock, and she didn't want to be without him. As soon as he was out of sight, she came back into the house and said good night to her family. She was emotionally exhausted.

Her mother woke her up early the next day. "Julia, get ready for some shopping. We have so much to do. I can't believe you gave me less than a week to plan a wedding."

Julia rolled her eyes. "It is only going to be a few guests, and we do not need any elaborate planning."

"You are the Earl of Savory's daughter, and you are getting married in Savory. Of course, people will expect an elegant affair. Now, up with you. I will have a lady's maid here in a few moments." Lady Savory was running around the house, barking orders at everyone, as they had a wedding to plan in four days.

Sara entered Julia's room as she was dressing with a new maid named Catherine, whom her mother had hired. She was starving as Sara handed her an apple tart. "I thought you may be hungry. Your mother has already ordered the carriage, and we will have no time to eat."

Julia sighed exhaustedly but secretly enjoyed the madness of her home. She'd missed them. Taking a bite of the tart, she looked up at Sara. "Thank you, cousin. It will be a long day."

They soon met their mothers' downstairs and headed to the carriage for a day of shopping.

Julia was fatigued from the outing and wanted nothing more than to take a nap. When she arrived back to her parent's home, she saw the duke's carriage. She knew then that she would not get any more rest for the day. When they arrived in the drawing room, she saw Lord Jason entertaining the dowager duchess and Lord Jacob. They stood when the women entered the room. The earl was out on business, visiting his tenants with the duke. Julia curtsied to the dowager duchess and welcomed her to their home.

She nodded at the ladies. The tea was brought in shortly afterward. They spoke about the guest list. Julia did not want a lot of guests, but the family insisted that at least the local gentry should be invited.

It was decided that they were to be married at the chapel in Savory. The dowager duchess insisted on having the wedding breakfast at their estate in Shallot. The estates were an hour apart, but the group wanted an open carriage ride and celebrations in each village. Julia took a deep breath, and drained of energy, she asked to be excused. They barely noticed as she left and continued with the planning. She escaped upstairs to go lie on her bed.

A few minutes later, as Julia was trying to fall asleep, she was interrupted by a knock on the door. She rose from her bed to open it, surprised to see her father. "Did I wake you?"

Julia yawned, shaking her head. "It's okay, Father. Did you need something?"

Julia's father hesitated at the door. "I... well... I..."

Confused by her father's demeanor, she opened the door a little wider. "Please come in." He accepted the invitation, and he sat in the chair by the bed.

Julia sat on her bed and looked at him. He had a box in his hand and handed it to her without speaking any words. She slowly took the box from his outstretched hand and opened it, seeing a gold broach inside. It was small but beautiful.

She looked up at her father as he smiled at her. "It belonged to your grandmother. It's the only piece that she gave me directly. I inherited the rest when she died."

Julia smiled at her father as she traced the broach with her finger. "Thank you, Father. I will cherish it always." Julia's chest tightened as her father had never given her a gift before. He had bought her many presents, but her mother had always given them to her and told her they were from him.

Her father had a tough time expressing his feelings about his only child. He had not been raised in a household where the word "love" was used. He had never told Julia how much she meant to him, and when she had disappeared for so long, he had feared the worse fate; his heart had ached to see her again. His anger would not allow him to express his relief when he saw her in the drawing room the day before, but he knew he wanted to make things right with her before she left him and married the duke.

The earl looked at her. "Julia, I am happy you are home. Please don't ever leave like that again."

Julia nodded at her father, her eyes filling with tears. The earl looked down, embarrassed by his tears, and stood up from the chair, walking toward the door. He turned around and hesitated. "Julia, I... I... I love you."

Julia ran to her father, embracing him. He held her in his arms for a few minutes, laying a kiss on top of her head. He left the room without looking back or saying anything more. Julia cried on her bed, overwhelmed with the emotion of it all.

The wedding day finally came, and the house was a flurry of activity. Her father ordered a white open carriage to take them from the Savory estate to the chapel. The same carriage would take her and the duke from the chapel to his estate in Shallot.

The family went ahead of Julia, leaving her father and her to meet them at the chapel. Julia's father waited for her in the foyer as she came down the stairs in her wedding dress. He swallowed hard with tears in his eyes. "You're beautiful."

Her light-blue dress had lace embroidered all through the skirt, and it hung down her waist and fanned out with an attached train. She wore a veil and a tiara covered in sparkling precious stones. Her hair was pulled up in the front and hung down to her waist with small white flowers draped in the back of her hair.

"I love you, Father," she said, kissing him on the cheek as he proudly offered her his arm and escorted her to the waiting carriage.

Julia was stunned seeing the citizens of Savory lining the streets to the chapel. *So much for a small wedding!* She waved to them as they called out well-wishes and cheers. She'd had no idea that they were so eager for her wedding to the duke. She received flowers from villagers as they all celebrated.

Arriving at the church and ready to walk down the aisle, the music started to play, and she spotted Frank standing next to the vicar. The church was packed full of people whom Julia did not recognize, but she was so focused on the duke as she walked down the aisle that she hardly paid them any notice. He smiled at her when her father placed her hand in his, and he kept her steady throughout the ceremony. Julia and the duke exchanged vows, and he kissed the bride with cheers coming from the inside and outside of the church. Julia smiled as he escorted her down the aisle.

The cheers did not stop from Savory to Shallot, the residents of Shallot also lining the streets to Frank's estate. They waved to everyone. Julia was feeling slightly overwhelmed by all the people and the attention. She was looking forward to the wedding breakfast and celebrating with her family. Frank held her hand throughout and snuck in kisses when he could on the ride to the celebrations.

When they arrived at his residence, the duke picked up Julia in his arms and carried her through the open front door and over the entrance. Their family cheered as he put her down and gave her another quick kiss on the mouth.

She smiled at him and embraced the family around her as they gave her their congratulations.

Julia's eyes widened as she noticed Mary sitting near the parlor with John, Laura, and Matthew. She squealed in delight and raced to them to hug them. She did not care about propriety and was so happy to see that they were here to share in her special day. They were dressed in their finest with huge smiles on their faces.

Julia introduced Frank to her friends as her new husband. John looked at her. "We've already met, Lady Julia... I mean, Your Grace."

Julia looked confused. "How?"

Mary smiled. "He sent for us and paid our fares to come right away. He wrote to the lord of the estate where they work and secured a few days off, so we could be here for you."

Julia was overwhelmed, glancing up at the duke. She kissed him on the cheek, "Thank you, my husband."

He smiled back. Julia was relieved that her mother made no fuss about propriety and allowed Mary to be a guest. John and Laura escorted Mary to the refreshment table as the duke spoke to his brother. Julia was left to stand by Matthew alone and smiled up at him.

She whispered, "You clean up nice."

He laughed out loud. "Seems I am now able to afford some nicer clothes these days."

Julia smiled as she bit her bottom lip. "You deserve it. You have worked very hard, and I wish you all the happiness."

He tipped his hat. "Lady Julia... Your Grace, you are one classy chit, and your duke is a fine gentleman. I want to thank you for everything."

She shook her head. "No, I want to thank you. May God bless and prosper you."

He gave her a quick bow and then tipped his hat as he turned to leave. She watched him as he offered his arm to Mary and they went to take their seats. She sighed and felt joy for her friends. They were truly her friends, and she was lucky to have them.

Julia enjoyed her family and the wedding celebrations. Frank and Julia thanked their guests for coming at such short notice. Julia was excited for the future and knew she had made the right choice. She'd escaped kidnapping and found her true love match, and she reveled in how much life had surprised her.

Chapter 36

PRINCESS MALLORY APPROACHED HER BROTHER'S house after a long journey. She was exhausted but wanted to see him at once. His staff welcomed her as she visited with her new sister-in-law, Princess Reba, for a few minutes before asking for her brother. They told her he was working in his study, so she walked to the door, opening it to surprise him. His face lit up when he saw her, and he stood up to embrace her.

"Good to see you, Randolph." She went to sit on the other side of his desk. He offered her a drink and poured himself one.

He smiled at his sister. "What news from France?"

She smiled and shook her head. "Not much from France, but I did come across a London society paper." She removed a folded-up paper from her reticule and handed it to him. She got up and told him that she would see him later at dinner.

He nodded to her as she closed the study doors. He unfolded the paper to read "The Duke of Shallot Marries Lady Julia of Savory After a Broken Engagement." The article said that hundreds of well-wishers had showed up to give their cheers to the happy couple.

Randolph took the paper and burned it in the fireplace. He watched as the ashes quickly consumed it. He walked to the window as he took a drink. He had told himself he would have no regrets, but the paper tugged at his heart as he thought about her and what he had given up for duty.

The End

About the Author

GG Shalton has been writing short stories most of her life. Often entertaining friends and family. At their encouragement she wrote her first novel in 2016 for publication. Although, she received her Bachelor's degree in Business Management, her real passion is history. Her fascination with different time periods is the inspiration for most her stories. GG is an avid reader and can often be found in various hiding places around her home enjoying a good book. She loves happy endings and most of her free time is spent developing story lines and writing. She is married to a wonderful husband who inspires her to pursue her passion. They met while both of them served in the US Navy. Her heart belongs to her two sons who both promise that one day they may read one of her books. She thanks Jesus for her multiple blessings each day, especially the gift of storytelling.

Authorggshalton@gmail.com.
https://www.facebook.com/gigi.shalton.7

Made in United States
North Haven, CT
15 February 2025

65817568R00169